Praise for 7

G000144222

"*The elegance of Joan Za*
makes this story so memo
right through me and led me into a story so full of life, nature and
relationships. I never wanted it to end."

Ashley Merril, Front Street Review

"*The Scent of Oranges by Joan Zawatzky is the first book I've read*
by this author but hope to read more. Right away I was transported
to South Africa. I could picture everything that Linda saw as if I
was her. Joan captures the essence of South Africa with the mystery
and intrigue of murder."

Cheryl's Book Nook

"*I think this novel will really appeal to people who like to sit and*
savour the writing and …a mystery unfolding."

Peeking Between the Pages

Praise for *The Elephant's Footprint*

"*Joan Zawatzky has a very smooth writing style. I enjoy reading*
her books as they take you through the story with just the right
amount of detail. The romance is an added bonus for the romantics
out there. This was a very enjoyable read."

Ashley Denis, Front Street Review

The Third Generation

Joan Zawatzky

First published in Australia in 2012 by: Veritax. Victoria, Australia

Website: www.placeofbooks.com

Cover design: Brennen Lukav: Rank One
Printing and typeset by BookPOD

ISBN: 978-0-9871340-7-3 (pbk)
       978-0-9871340-8-0 (ebook)

About the Author

Joan Zawatzky was born in South Africa. After completing her studies, first in art and then in psychology, she moved to Australia, where she worked for many years as a counselling psychologist. Though painting remained a hobby, she decided to try her hand at writing. She wrote *There's a Light at the End of the Tunnel*, to help her clients overcome depression. *The Scent of Oranges*, her first novel, is set in South Africa and was shortlisted for the Australian Books Alive Programme in 2007. In 2011 she added *The Elephant's Footprint* to her South African series. *The Third Generation* is her latest novel. Joan lives in Melbourne with her husband.

Other books by the author

There's a Light at the End of the Tunnel:
Self-Help and Hope for Suffers of Depression. Stories, Solutions
and Strategies.
Publisher: Hybrid 2002

The Scent of Oranges
Publisher Australia: JoJo publishing 2006
Publisher UK and USA: Garev Publishing International 2008

The Elephant's Footprint
Publisher: Veritax 2011

Acknowledgements

I would like to thank my sister-in-law Estelle for all her help. My thanks also go to Gitta Stanger for her patient final proof reading and to Chris Callanan and Pinuccia Hopkins for their assistance. My writers' group, the Blackburn Writers' Collective is always a source of inspiration.

For my husband, Hymie.

One

The day I boarded the plane for Australia was one of the worst days I can remember. I was leaving Vienna, the city of my birth and was about to embark on a new life. I reminded myself to think positively, to look at it as an adventure, but my attempt at optimism was a waste of time. I loathed the thought of hurtling into the unknown.

Leaving for a country so far from Europe was the last thing I wanted but how could I hold Richard back? As one of his company's top engineers, he was offered a promotion to head up the Australian division, a crucial step in his career. How many times does an opportunity like that fall into one's lap? Our eighteen year old son Anton, was thrilled about the move, and could hardly wait to enrol in an Australian university, unlike his elder brother Gabe, who happily remained in Vienna.

At least the interminable packing was over and all our possessions were in boxes, ready to follow us across the sea. Crazily, I bought things that I imagined were unavailable in the backwaters of Australia – Richard's cotton underwear and my perfectly fitting bras, fine bed linen, easy wash table cloths, our medicines and much more. From countless pamphlets I'd read, I expected to arrive in a hot country with endless surfing beaches, where people ate barbecued food and sport dominated their lives.

In the packed plane with its narrow seats, the sleep I craved came in short bursts. Towards the end of the long journey, I dreamed we were back at the airport, our friends clustered around us, saying their final goodbyes. Somehow I smiled and managed to appear animated. Flowers and chocolates were pressed into my hands, kind words uttered. 'Leaving Vienna won't be that bad. You'll be back soon, you'll see.'

Ernst Weingarten, an elderly friend of my dead mother, handed me a small package. 'It belonged to my father. I have no family and I want you to have it.'

I kissed his cheek and slipped the gift into my handbag. I scanned the group. Where was he? Then I spotted Luke running towards us. When Richard joined his business colleagues, Luke took my hand. With an eye on Richard, his kiss brushed my lips.

'*Auf Wiedersehen Liebchen.*'

'*Auf Wiedersehen*' I whispered.

The captain's voice crackling on the microphone woke me. 'This is your captain speaking. We're about thirty minutes from Melbourne. '

'Look, look… now you can see the land clearly,' Anton said excitedly.

From the tiny window the flatness was endless, unlike the cultivated green I was used to when flying over Europe. Richard leaned across me to peer out.

'Acres of land out there, with that beautiful crystal sky. Isn't it marvellous?'

During the journey, whenever I opened my eyes, he was glued to his laptop, oblivious of everyone on the plane. If he talked at all, it was to enthuse about the revolutionary new engineering plant and its huge staff he was due to head up. We eased back into our seats. The *fasten seatbelts* sign flickered and the captain announced that we were about to land in Melbourne.

'Where are all the kangaroos?' Anton asked flippantly.

'They're not running around everywhere,' his father grunted.

I groped for my handbag under the seat. Lipstick and a comb through my hair would help to at least create a good impression. Apart from receiving a stamp on my passport with a welcoming smile, my memory of our arrival and our passage through the customs and immigration was hazy. During the drive from the airport with Martin Keene, one of the company executives, Richard sat in the front discussing business, while Anton and I were in the back. My head spun. Concrete, glass, blobs of green and the silhouette of the city zoomed past. Only occasionally, Anton glanced up from his Iphone to check his surroundings.

The car jerked and we pulled up in front of the company owned house. The white two-storey with its circular façade, was one of the ugliest I had ever seen. We followed Martin down the steps and through the front door. Our suitcases were deposited, the workings of the major appliances explained and we were handed a folder of instructions. An unusual jingle at the front door startled me. Two men stood there. One had car keys in his hand.

'They've brought your company car, Richard. It's outside,' Martin said. 'Let's have a look at it.'

Richard was grinning when he returned. After Martin pushed a bunch of brochures into Richard's hand, together with numbers to phone in emergency, he left. At last we were alone in the house.

A musty smell enveloped the house and I battled with stiff windows to let in fresh air. The kitchen was shiny and white. The appliances were still in their boxes and most of the crockery had not been unpacked. The surfaces would need a good scrub to remove the film of dust. I tried to stop thinking of my cosy, wooden kitchen in Vienna and moved on to view the rest of the house. In the sitting room, I noticed a sparkling cobalt glass vase. I lifted it, felt its ridges and turned it upside down. Made in China, the label said. It was identical to the one I had bought in Vienna for the first Spring daffodils only months earlier.

The pale blandness, the white walls, cream furniture, cushions, curtains and uncarpeted floors dismayed me. The house contained all we needed, but nothing familiar, none of the wooden beams, Persian rugs or paintings I was accustomed to and liked. I reminded myself of our luck at being offered a furnished home during our settling in period, and at such a low rental.

From the sitting room I could see the garden. As I slid the glass doors open, unusual but pleasant fragrances enveloped me. A rambling blaze of colour hugged the walls, tall trees and foreign shrubs flanked the fence. Immediately I loved the garden. As I walked across the lawn, tears that I had held back until then, wet my face. Sobs overcame me and I sat, on the lawn, in front of the rosebushes. I picked a dusty pink rose in full bloom and buried my face in its fragrant, velvety petals.

Once I had unpacked my clothes and hung them in the closet, I opened Ernst's gift, a prayer book. I ran my hand over the worn, leather cover and faded Hebrew letters. It was the first time I had held a Jewish prayer book. Opposite each page of the Hebrew writing was a translation in old German script. I read the first lines of the Morning Prayer for the Sabbath slowly and then closed it. The words spoke of a belief that was mine, but one I knew nothing about. I placed the book on the table next to my bed. In hotels bibles were kept in drawers near the bed.

Vienna dominated my thoughts, while the days formed a cycle of eating and sleeping. I floated through the house and garden, no longer combed my hair or cooked and cleaned. As crumbs and papers fell to the floor, I left them there. I did not turn on the television or the radio, ignored the ringing phone and the strange voices leaving messages on the answering machine.

My piano, the one thing that would've connected me to this new place, was swathed in plastic bubble wrap, bolted into a crate and on the water to Australia. Though the movers had given me an approximate date of five to eight weeks for the arrival of our possessions at the Melbourne docks, they made no commitment on how long clearance by customs and delivery might take. The wait felt endless.

While I waited, I played classical CD's over and over on the portable player I had brought along with me, and the familiar music reverberated throughout the large, empty house.

Anton remained in his room and came downstairs only to raid the fridge or snoop in the pantry for snacks. Occasionally he hovered around me wordlessly, sipping coffee, but any attempt of mine at conversation and he was gone. His dull eyes and tight mouth told me that his earlier enthusiasm about the move had disappeared. I guessed that it was not just the different environment bothering him, but that he was missing his brother. Anton was due to start his university course in a few weeks and I hoped that the university environment would bring him friends and a means of adjusting.

My boys were close friends but as different as any brothers could be. They shared most interests, celebrated each other's joys and unstintingly defended each other in down times. Though they had not been separated before, this time they made the decision to part, for a while. It was a difficult but practical decision. Gabe was almost twenty-one and in his second year of post graduate study. In order to complete his thesis, he had to stay on at the university in Vienna. I hated leaving him behind. Though he was an adult and independent, I was certain he still needed his family's support.

If I had been given the opportunity to think more clearly before we left, I would've refused to accompany Richard to Australia and stayed in Vienna with Anton and his brother. We would've been together, and Gabe wouldn't have been left alone. But Richard's enthusiasm about his promotion in Australia carried me along and I fell in with him.

Two

I solated and confused, I found myself in an ugly house, in a city I had only glimpsed through a car window. Memories came in snatches and plummeted me into the past. At least, with all its imperfections, the past was known.

I was back in my childhood in Leopoldstadt, Vienna's once Jewish ghetto. I was born in Leopoldstadt in 1963 and spent my early years there but I had no sense of belonging to the mainly Jewish community. Inside our double storey with its solid walls and shingle roof, I was content playing my piano and singing at the top of my voice. One of the things I remember Mama telling me was that I was a natural on the piano, like my grandmother and that I had an unusually good voice for my age. She told me this when I was very young but I remember it clearly. After all, she did not compliment me often.

Even by today's standards, my parents were older than most. Mama had turned forty when I was born and Papa was fifty-three. I grew tired of being called a miracle child or an afterthought. I realised early, that Mama had suffered considerably during her youth. Not that she told me this directly; I pieced it together from fragments of our conversations. She could sit in a room with me for ages without saying a word and when she did speak, it was in a Viennese German dialect with a lilting Hungarian accent. Accustomed to the quiet, I daydreamed and created my own space. Occasionally she crocheted during her silences, making the same lacy motifs from fine ecru cotton. When she had made several, she sewed them together into runners and tray cloths that she gave to friends as gifts. One magnificent tablecloth she made adorned our table on special occasions. She told me that her mother and grandmother had crocheted the identical motifs. Working as they had, she felt that she was carrying on the family tradition. Several times she tried to teach me the stitches, but I was impatient and threw the hook down in frustration. At least I still have her tablecloth.

Mama gave me only occasional hugs and kisses. My birthday kiss was placed formally on my forehead. Each morning I looked forward to the routine of her combing my long, unruly hair with a tortoiseshell comb and taming it into plaits. Her scent of lily of the valley and the touch of her silken, shoulder length hair on my face as she bent over me are still with me. This was the only time of day that I was certain of her full attention.

Her red hair was eye-catching and by far her best feature. When she developed grey hairs she plucked them out. Later she coloured it vibrant henna. Her strong chin prevented her from being pretty but men's stares of appreciation told me she was attractive. I doubted that Mama's friends really knew her. When she was with them she talked fast, laughed and smiled a lot, and was nothing like the mother I knew.

She protected me from all sorts of known and unknown dangers. During both winter and summer I was dressed too warmly for the outdoors, with heavy shoes in case the weather changed for the worse. I was forbidden to play with the neighbourhood children, whom she considered rough and could hurt me. There were streets she warned me not to enter, where she had heard alcoholics and anti-Semites lived.

I longed to know about my father, who had been ill for many years after the war and had died two years after I was born. Though she fed me morsels of information about him at different times, it did not satisfy me. If I pressed her for details, her eyes filled with tears, she placed a finger to her lips and turned away. There was only one photograph of him in the house, in a gold frame on the dressing table in Mama's bedroom. When I ached to know more about him, I stole in to look at it. If I sat there long enough, I was sure he smiled at me. I always smiled back.

Late one evening, I was sitting on the couch drinking cocoa with Mama, when she looked at me directly, something she rarely did. Speaking softly she told me that my father had been an exceptionally gifted man, and that I ought to be proud to be his daughter. He had started off as a singer and later became a well-known comedian in Jewish theatre, following in my grandparents' footsteps. I don't remember my reply, but I know I was both surprised and delighted.

I recall her sipping more of the warm drink before continuing. 'There was more to his talents. A little before you were born, he turned to painting and he was a good artist but unfortunately I don't have any of his pictures to show you.'

As questions formed on my lips, she tapped her watch and shook her head. It was time for bed.

❧

Turning six, was an important year for me. On my birthday, Mama told me two essential things. The first was to remember that I was Jewish, and that being Jewish was special. It made me different from other children. The second, was that my father was not only an artist and entertainer, but a very brave man who had helped others during the war. She promised to tell me more about his bravery when I was old enough.

Knowing that my father was both talented and brave made me feel warm inside. It brought me both wonder and sadness. I had a father who was exceptional but he had died when I was too young to know him. From that one photograph in Mama's bedroom, I imagined I was with him, sitting on his lap while he stroked my head and told me he loved me or accompanying him on the piano while he sang, so that together we made beautiful music. He was never in a hurry like Mama and he listened to me if I was sad and offered advice when I needed it. In those early years, he was constantly with me in my imagination.

Though I nagged Mama to tell me more, she put a finger to her lips. 'As I promised, I'll tell you all about him when you're older.'

That I was Jewish meant nothing to me. I had no Jewish friends. Mama did not encourage me to make any, nor did she take me to the synagogue or suggest I go there on my own. She made a point of distancing herself and me from the small Jewish community in Leopoldstadt.

'We're not going to live like them,' she would say, pointing to a black clad man or a woman in a dress to her ankles. 'They're still in the sixteenth century. It's far safer not to have too much to do with them. Rather blend in with the general community and don't make yourself obvious. There are still many anti-Semites here in Austria who would be happier if we had all burnt in the ovens.'

Memories of the sights and smells of my childhood drew me back home. The mix of languages - Yiddish and a variety of Eastern European tongues; smells of clean washing drying in the breeze; chicken soup wafting from doorways and aromas of fresh bread baking are still with me.

Friday was a special day. It marked the end of the school week and it was the day I ought to have looked forward to. Instead it threw me into confusion. The narrow lanes of Leopoldstadt were alive with Jewish wives rushing to be first in line at the sprinkling of kosher shops that sold food for the Sabbath. Mama complained that the prices were ridiculously high and besides she refused to abide by the rigors of a kosher kitchen.

At sundown, the start of the Sabbath, I perched on the tip of my toes and peered over the railing on the edge of the narrow tiled balcony on the upper floor of the house. From there I watched the procession of black hatted men and their elegant wives on their way to the main synagogue on *Seitenstettengasse.* Sunday morning was the important time for the gentiles living amongst us. Their families congregated at the corner and then walked together to the church with its fine, tall spires. I didn't belong with the gentiles either.

Candles flickered in Jewish windows but we did not light any and we rarely had chicken soup. We ate our schnitzels at non-Kosher restaurants and regularly bought sliced ham for sandwiches. All our Jewish neighbours went to *shul* (synagogue) on Friday night or to the Saturday morning service, or to both. No one worked or drove their car until Saturday night after sundown.

I asked Mama the same question again and again, 'Why don't we go to pray? Everyone else in Leopoldstadt prays.'

Her answer was unsatisfying. 'I don't believe in a God and neither did your poor late father. The Holocaust has shown us clearly that there can't possibly be a God.'

I argued that there were many survivors of the concentration camps who still believed. Mama shrugged and told me that I didn't have to follow her ideas, I could make up my own mind later.

The only Jewish person I knew well was Mama's friend Ernst, not that he admitted to being Jewish unless prodded. To my young eyes his grey hair and arthritic gait stamped him as very old. During the day, he spent more time at our house than at his own and I grew accustomed to seeing him. He had a knack of telling gripping, old-time stories that were so exciting that I begged him not to stop.

When I was older, I realised that Ernst was more to Mama than a friend. He rarely spent the night in our house but on the occasions he did, he moved into the front bedroom with Mama. Good luck to them, I thought, when I heard slow, muffled sounds through the wall.

I was curious about Jewish customs and one afternoon I was alone in the bakery with Devorah, who was one class ahead of me at school. She helped her parents in the bakery.

'The women talk about making *cholent*. What is it?' I asked.

'But you're Jewish aren't you?"

'Ye…s, but we don't follow …'

She pursed her lips in disapproval. '*Cholent* is a stew that is meant to last over the Sabbath, so that women don't have to cook. Any work over the Sabbath is forbidden. I don't know exactly what my mother puts in it ... cut up beef, beans and barley.'

None of the children at school would've guessed the extent to which the topic of religion perplexed me. As Mama encouraged me to guard against revealing personal or family information, I learnt to be secretive.

Three

Three days after we had arrived in Melbourne, we made our first telephone call to Gabe in Vienna. His tired voice told us that we that woken him. Richard clicked on the speaker phone so we could all hear the conversation.

'How are you son? How are things?' Richard asked.

'Just fine. No problems.'

'Are you still okay for money?'

'Yes, thanks Papa fine... but I'm missing you all already.'

'I wish you were here with us... but you insisted on staying.'

'I had no choice Papa. I couldn't transfer my course to an Australian university, you know that.'

'Yes, yes.'

Then Gabe wanted to know our impressions of Melbourne and he was curious about the house, the suburb and street.

'It's far too early, son... we've just arrived... but we'll send you pictures as soon as we can, I promise.'

Richard looked at his watch. 'If I'm calculating correctly you're going to be late for university this morning.'

'No, Papa, I have a late tutorial today.'

Richard handed me the telephone. 'Hello darling, I'm missing you already.'

'*Mutti*, please! '

'Okay. Okay.'

'Have you settled in? It must be a big change,' he said, sounding concerned.

'It's too soon. It will take time.'

'Yes I suppose... 'his voice faded

'Tell me, are you eating well… looking after yourself?'

'Of course, Mutti. Everything is just fine, please don't worry.'

'Glad to hear it.'

Anton tapped me on the arm.

'Come on, it's my turn. I want to talk to Gabe now?'

I handed the phone to Anton. 'Let the two of them talk,' I said to Richard. From the sitting room we heard guffaws and giggles. We phoned Gabe again two days later. I could tell that he was enjoying testing his wings. After that we phoned less often. Images of wild parties in his flat flitted into my thoughts but I did my best to ignore them.

Before leaving Vienna, Anton spent hours researching the courses available at Melbourne universities. He wanted to study business law and decided on Monash University. He sent his application to the university along with all the details of his schooling and was accepted. Richard and I were under such pressure before we left Vienna that neither of us spent sufficient time discussing his choice of subjects. Over the weekend we drove to the campus with him. I don't know what we expected, but seeing the modern economics law building with its excellent facilities was a relief.

My bed did not feel or smell familiar and as I left the haze of sleep, I didn't know where I was. Rather than face my strange surroundings, I pulled the doona over my head and went back to sleep. Through most of the day I remained in the bedroom. My few possessions from home, my alarm clock, hairbrush, comb and my cosmetics lay scattered on the bedside table next to me. There was comfort in having the familiar objects near.

Late in the afternoon I showered and dressed. Avoiding the kitchen, I wandered into the sitting room, where I sat on the hard, leather couch in front of the television. Foreign images flashed before me but made hardly any impact.

One night, Richard stopped for fast food on the way home. He carried his beers to the armchair and ate his meal. He talked optimistically about the company and his place in it, boasting about the way the executive staff treated him like a messiah. A welcoming luncheon had been held for him, followed by speeches lauding the expertise he had gained at the Vienna head office. He wriggled in the chair and took a swig of beer before mentioning Jake O'Connor, the plant manager, who had been with the company for twenty years or more. If not for Jake, Richard would have felt more secure. When Dave Rider retired, Jake was convinced he was next in line but then Richard came along and snapped up the top job. Richard feared that Jake could become a problem in the future.

'This type of thing is not unusual. It's happened in the Vienna office too. Every man is a team player with an eye out for himself,' he said, in an attempt to console himself.

'Watch your back,' I warned. He laughed off my advice but nevertheless I repeated it.

Conversations like this came easily to us. We cared about each other's welfare and about our children. But care was not passion and I had not felt stirrings of passion for Richard for years. I had no idea how he felt about me as we did not discuss emotions, least of all how we felt about sex. How could I say we made love? What we did about once a month, was have marital sex. It was not loving or stimulating and afterwards I was tense and unsatisfied. When we first met, Richard's regular features, tall, slim build and his smiling confidence appealed to me. Now he was developing a paunch that was far from attractive.

Our lack of intimacy was the issue. We had not approached the move to Australia as a joint adventure, or a novel family experience. We ran through our daily news each night, but avoided sharing our innermost thoughts. We were not a true family, a couple with one of our children in a new country, finding our way together. We were two individuals out there battling on our own with Anton tagging behind us. And for me, Luke was always there, a shadowy figure in the background.

Four

I first met Luke Krause when his parents and his older brother, Guenther, moved into the house across the road from ours, that was owned by their grandmother. It was a dark, brick house spread across the block and with almost no garden. The Krause family were German Catholics who had moved to Vienna from Frankfurt when Luke was a baby. They were one of the three Catholic families in the winding street. Even in the late 1930's before Hitler's SS marched into Vienna, the area had been part of the original ghetto and mainly poor Jews lived there. Mr Krause, a skilled pastry chef, had intended to open a business in the city that adored cakes and pastries with their coffee. When his business failed, the family had nowhere to go and had no choice but to move in with his mother.

Mama refused to send me to kindergarten, insisting that she could teach me all I needed to know at home. She taught me well and by the time I went to school, I could read and write. I knew the names of the streets in our area and all the important buildings. Used to the freedom of learning at home, I disliked the discipline of school. The days were so boring that I counted the hours until the final bell rang. At least the late afternoons were mine to sing and play my piano.

One afternoon when I was almost five, I spent longer than usual on the piano and as I sat near the window to rest, I looked down on to the garden and noticed a blond boy standing at our gate. I ran out and was in time to catch up with him.

'Was that you playing the piano?' he asked.

I nodded, shyly.

'It was beautiful,' he beamed at me. We formed an instant friendship. As Luke was two years older and taller, I felt safe with him. Most days after school we were together. Leopoldstadt became our world and through the laneways we ran together, climbed trees and scaled walls or jumped on a pile of rubble that had been a building or a temple before the war. We discovered the parks with the softest grass, the most shade in summer and the best hiding places. If we had the money we bought chocolates, liquorice balls and delicious ice creams. We shared everything.

Luke was smarter than me, or to be kind to myself, I could say we each had a different form of intelligence. Even when he was young, his ability to plan and organise was masterful. I was the imaginative one who frequently came up with unusual solutions to problems. He was a confident boy who stood tall and looked at one in a forthright manner.

It surprised me that he chose to play with me. We spent hours together in our concrete and grass backyard, strewn with bits of brick. Flowers and weeds sprung up between the ancient concrete crevices. When I was a little, this was my fairyland, and the only part of the property that I refused to share with Luke. The tiny creatures I saw amongst the flowers remained my secret.

Our mothers avoided each other in the street and at the shops but neither of us knew the reason. That was another thing I asked Mama about, but received nothing more than a shrug for an answer. Luke's family detested noise or mess, discouraged visitors and refused to allow us to play in their garden. They tried to prevent him from having anything to do with us, though he was too polite to admit it. It was just as well that Mama liked him and welcomed him into our home.

Luke's old grandmother was a dedicated tidier. From my window, I watched her brushing odd leaves from the path, snipping away at stray blades of grass or shining the brass doorhandle. Towards twilight on most days, a storm raged in the house across the road. The blinds were pulled down but the old woman's screamed obscenities were broadcast for the street to hear. As with most things that happened in Luke's family, he did not talk about it.

I smiled when I thought of the Krause family walking to church each Sunday in identical formation. Mr Krause walked ahead with long paces, behind him was his wife taking smaller, frantic steps to catch up, followed by Luke and his brother Guenther side by side but about a metre apart.

What a naughty boy Luke was; in scrapes with other boys and up to any number of pranks, constantly in hot water at school and at home. But to me he was gentle and considerate. He didn't pull faces at me or call me nasty names like the other boys did. When he held my hand and told me I was his special friend, I knew he meant it.

After school, I had no girlfriends to talk girlie talk with. Mama did not encourage strangers in the house and there was no one to help me to decide on the length of a dress or reassure me about my first period. Mama was there but she considered my questions "nonsense chatter that wasted her time." There was no one except Luke and I talked to him about almost everything. He did get fed up with my chatter after a while though. If something bothered me for too long he'd insist I stop talking and do something about it. He was never short of suggestions. Luke was the one who initiated most things we did. I relied on him and later I wished I hadn't.

We had played our fun games and had been close friends for so long, that when I sprouted breasts and he grew fuzz on his face, it came as a surprise. Our usual banter became more sexual and an awkward steaminess developed between us. We attempted to maintain a distance from each other but that did not work. We kissed with each greeting and parting and lay together close, caressing and stroking each other. Our experiments in pleasuring did not last long. Our kisses turned to passion and lust took over. The first time we made love, I was fourteen and he was almost sixteen. On an afternoon in the middle of summer, we rode our bicycles into the forest and leaned them against a shady tree. No words were spoken but we nodded to each other in agreement. We could not wait any longer. Following his lead, I pulled off my dress and lay on the soft grass. The sensation of him entering me that first time was at once painful and exquisite.

It was our summer. I thought of nothing but Luke, the smell, look and feel of him and how much he excited me. It wasn't only his fine nose and the curve of his chin, his large brown eyes fringed with eyelashes, far too long for a male, but his proud stance that made him handsome, the only word I could find that adequately described him. Of course I knew about sex and contraception, but it was book learning. I could tell that Luke was sexually experienced but I did not want to know who had taught him. It was just as well that he always carried condoms in his wallet. I did not think of the consequences of our pleasure and left the responsibility to him.

When the winds blew in the cold and the leaves fell, it became too uncomfortable to make love outdoors. Our need drove us to take risks. We waited in the house until Mama went out, which was not frequently, or when she was busy enough in the kitchen not to notice we were in my bedroom.

Before descending into sleep each night I'd picture our wedding day. My dress was full and lacy, nipped in the waist with just a decorous amount of breast showing. Luke wore a silver grey morning suit and looked striking. My image didn't include a church or synagogue for the ceremony.

Perhaps it was just as well that towards the end of winter, Luke's family moved to the neighbouring suburb of *Dobling*. I remember the chill of the day and the snow inches deep, when Luke's father loaded a borrowed truck with their possessions and drove to the community housing known as *Gemeindebauten*. Though Luke did not tell me why his parents decided to leave, from his few muttered words about his grandmother, I surmised that they could no longer stand her yelling and were forced to find their own place. A year or two later, I heard that she had been hospitalised with dementia.

Once, when Mama visited an old friend living in *Dobling*, I accompanied her and saw the area for the first time. To get there, we travelled along the Danube canal in the direction of the woods. At first all the greenery and the old buildings with character delighted me, and I imagined Luke happy there. That was until we passed the ugly and exceptionally long apartment block, a fortress of a building, where Luke and his family now lived. Mama explained that the apartments were built before World War II by the Social Democrats in Austria to improve appalling living conditions of working class people. The flats were small and basic amenities were shared but they had parks where children could play safely.

All Luke said about his new home was that he had a magnificent view from his window, even though the room was a cat box. He had changed schools and that put an end to our afternoons together, but it did not stop us meeting. We travelled to the city by train and met at a café frequented by students and arty types. The inexpensive food and coffee was not the best in Vienna but the people sitting near us hugging and kissing freely, did not notice our hands held under the table or our kisses.

I longed for weekends and school holidays, when we met in the baroque *Augarten* Park, one of my favourite parks in Vienna. It was only a bus ride away for us both and we were able to store our bikes in the rack under the bus. Once there, we rode furiously to our leafy, safe spots. Hungry for each other, we made love like rabbits in the meadows. We caught up on news of the week as we pushed our bikes back through the avenues of blossoming chestnut trees.

Our parents treated us like big children and not hot blooded teenagers. It was unlikely, that they even imagined we were involved in a lusty relationship. They lectured us on the dangers we might face in the park and we were each given sufficient money for the bus and a ride on the big wheel. We used our own savings for a ride on the miniature railway and a bratwurst and sauerkraut roll. The rolls were treats and we ate them on the grass under the magnificent chestnut trees.

Luke had started school two years before me. I was completing my studies at senior school, while he was at university studying physics and science. By the time I was half-way through studying to become a librarian, he was a qualified geologist.

My head was continually crammed with fantasies about our future together, our marriage, home and children as we lived happily ever after. None of this I shared with him until one Sunday in Spring during one of our walks under the blossoming chestnuts.

'Do you ever think of us being together in the future?'

'Yes…sometimes but we're so close I expect it to continue that way.'

'I mean later…what do you think will happen?' Of course, I was fishing.

'We're so young, too young to think of the future. You have your studies to finish…and there are my further studies.'

He hadn't talked about further studies since completing his four year degree. Wasn't four years enough study, I asked myself.

'Come on, you're lagging behind,' he said with a laugh. 'The future will take care of itself.'

One afternoon, after we had made love, he lit a cigarette. It was the first time I had seen him smoke. He looked up at the sky, at the clouds shifting in the breeze.

'A change of weather coming,' he said, taking a long draw of his cigarette and rolling blades of grass in his fingers.

'First time I've seen you with a cigarette?' I said, touching his arm. As a sportsman, he had scoffed at smokers. There had to be reason for him smoking.

He shrugged.

'Something worrying you?' I asked.

He grunted and then looked away. At last, in a hoarse voice, he blurted out a halting account of the many inquiries he had made to universities in Vienna about a post graduate course in geoscience, and that none of them provided courses that interested him. When he found a Canadian University offering postgraduate study in earth sciences, he sent in an application.

He had been accepted and was due to leave for Canada in a month.

He extended his hand in a reassuring gesture and then withdrew it. I closed my eyes, bent forward and grabbed my knees, aching as if I had been kicked. My eyes refused to open. I was rocking to and fro until he helped me to stand. As he stroked my hair, his breath came in short sobs as he assured me he didn't want to leave me. We clung to each other before walking on through the avenue of trees.

Later, when I recovered from the shock, I told him how angry I was that he had been so secretive, and that at least he should've warned me that he was seeking a course overseas. The signs were there, but I had not taken him seriously enough or listened carefully. He had become increasingly involved in his studies, spending late afternoons and evenings at the university and joining his professor on some weekends. We were spending less time together. I ought to have realised that his studies in geology were of prime importance to him, even more important than me. It wasn't as if he hadn't complained about inadequate facilities for further study in geophysics. If I'm honest with myself, I recall him mentioning the possibility of having to study elsewhere. I thought only of being together, of him in relation to me. When I searched his face it was for the love he felt for me and not for his happiness. It was impossible to imagine him going away. Over that month I begged him not to leave countless times but I knew he had a career in geology to follow. He had to go. All I could do was to treasure my last moments with him, hold them in my memory.

The weekend before he left, I lied to Mama. I told her that Luke's friends had organised a going away party for him and that I intended to sleep at a friend's home that evening. Surprisingly she agreed. Luke and I had our own party at a city hotel. We ordered a meal in the room and spent the night in each other's arms. I pretended I was happy and tried hard not to cry. It was our last shared time and I knew then that the passion of my youth had ended. I would not feel that intensity of love again.

The day he left, I did not see him off at the airport. As the days without him passed, I felt as if part of me had been severed. My body throbbed, I hardly ate and I cried myself to sleep for weeks. Mama was not much help. She told me to forget him and churned out the "there are many other fish in the sea" story. What hurt most was her saying that she had never believed anything would come of our relationship. All the while, I held on to my picture of him at our last meeting at the hotel. He wore one of his bright jumpers. This time it was crimson.

Since we were little, I had relied on him and let him take the lead with most things. I was not used to making decisions alone. Luke or Mama had their say in most things I did. Without him, I had to learn to stand alone and my feet felt wobbly.

As in lonesome and sad times during my childhood, I turned to my piano. Initially, I refused to go out but invitations to parties became too hard to refuse. I decided to change my appearance. With my hair cut, new clothes and a little make up, I faced the world without Luke. The first few young men who showed interest in me I rejected. They did not have a hope of measuring up to him. Months later when Luke's letters petered out to a dribble, I gave in and began to date more seriously. That was when I met Richard.

He liked the opera and concerts, and was the first of the young men I had met who understood and appreciated classical music. He sat misty eyed while I played and clapped afterwards. Richard was the perfect boyfriend, sending me flowers, bringing me the dark nut chocolates I loved, always attentive and charming. He was good looking in a smooth urban way, tall and lean with straight dark hair and dark eyes. But he lacked Luke's fine features and dynamism. I did not love him but I liked him a lot. I had dated one man after the other and most only once, but Richard was the only one who had me thinking and made me laugh.

He nagged to show me his apartment. I expected the usual bachelor flat but was surprised to find walls of shelves. One group of shelves contained his trophies won at athletics at school and university. The rest were filled with books and well over a hundred ornamental elephants.

He laughed at my surprise. 'Don't I look like an athlete with an obsession about elephants?'

I laughed with him.

He had been collecting elephants since he was in his teens and added to them during trips overseas. I was mesmerised and couldn't be dragged from the ornaments until I had picked up each one and inspected it. On the only remaining wall his framed certificates stating his degrees in engineering and his attendance at courses formed a wallpaper collage. When my astonishment abated, I noticed how clean and neat he was. He had dusted often and polished all the trophies.

We had been going out for a year when he asked me to marry him. My idea of marriage had always involved Luke and our declaration of undying love for each other. Mama convinced me that with four years study ahead of him, away from me in Canada with only his tutoring to live on, my love for Luke was only a dream. She thought Richard was a perfect match for me. To add to it he was Jewish, and that she said, made a difference.

When I wrote to Luke with the news that I was engaged to Richard, he replied immediately. I printed his email and kept it.

I love you Ellie and I always will. Distance and lack of money have ruined things for us. You are the one I've always wanted to marry and have children with. There has never been anyone else. Remember that always. Please think carefully about your decision as the rest of your life will depend on it.

I chose an elegant, flattering dress and Richard and I were married in the Park by a celebrant. I was disappointed that for this one special occasion, we had not chosen a synagogue but Richard was adamant about his rejection of Judaism. On our honeymoon, each time we made love, I was with Luke.

When we returned, it was just as well that my job as a librarian at a girls' school occupied my time and thoughts. We settled into an unromantic routine. Richard needed his sleep to concentrate on his job and I hardly saw him. His ambition drove him to spend part of the weekend in the office and come home late.

When I think back on how difficult those first years of marriage were, I could easily have left Richard, if not for meeting up with Luke again. One morning Richard and I were out walking the *Ringstrasse*, when we came across Luke and his wife Hilde. We talked, and before moving on, Luke slipped his business card into my pocket.

I phoned him months later when I was going through an especially dull patch with Richard. The next bit slipped into place naturally. We met at the café, where we had met as students all those years earlier. I knew that we would continue to see each other.

Five

I tied the sash of my dressing gown and went into the kitchen. The familiar act of pouring boiling water over coffee granules and adding milk was satisfying. I took my cup onto the patio with its view of the garden, cool fragrances, treetops swaying in the street and the cobalt sky. In the house next door, a car rumbled and children shrieked. I waved to a tall skinny woman across the fence, whom I had not yet met.

My logical inner voice told me that it was time to venture beyond the gate, to investigate the world outside the house. My walk took me along the unfamiliar street, past faceless houses that looked the same and empty driveways that led to closed doors. Letterboxes were jammed with mail, not even dogs barked. I realised that children were at school and most parents were at work. An energetic walker nodded and I nodded back. After a few blocks I turned back, afraid to lose my way.

With another cup of coffee in my hand I returned to the patio, pacing restlessly and wishing I was back in Vienna. I was unable to concentrate on reading and the television still made no sense to me. If only I had taken the time to familiarise myself with Australian history and politics.

Logic told me that what I needed was something other than myself to think about. Later, I went to the computer to search for advertised activities in my neighbourhood. A book club in the area looked interesting. I phoned the contact number and a woman answered. She had trouble understanding me at first but I explained slowly that I had recently arrived from Austria. She said that a group of women met every second week to discuss books and I was welcome to join them. When she inquired if I liked reading, I told her that I had worked as a librarian in Vienna and loved to read. She was silent for a few seconds and then asked for my address. When she offered to give me a lift to the meeting, I accepted gratefully.

Two days later a blonde woman in a sundress and sandals knocked on my door. She smiled and introduced herself as Ida Larson. As the meeting in a church hall was only a few streets away, there was hardly time to talk during the drive. Ida introduced me to the group of ten. Though they discussed a book I had read recently, I said nothing as my insights were different to theirs. During the tea break, the women were polite but soon I was forgotten, an outsider amongst women who had known each other for years. After the meeting, I thanked Ida for her kindness and made my excuses. I was grateful and relieved when she dropped me off at home.

I made another attempt to meet new people by enquiring about a music appreciation group. Keen for new members, Jean Gregory, one of the convenors, agreed to give me a lift. She talked all the way there, assuming that I would appreciate her chatter, but I could barely understand her broad accent. A scatter of older women occupied the four rows of chairs in the room. I was introduced to them and asked to take a seat. Their choice of music was pleasing and I listened with closed eyes. I spoke a few words to some of the women during the tea break but I sensed that they were being polite, pretending to be interested in what a new foreigner had to say. In the car, Jean asked whether I had enjoyed the afternoon. I said that 'I'd had a wonderful time and what lovely ladies they were.' Back home in the white house, I sat on the hard leather couch and cried. I would not return to the group. It was easier to turn on my music and listen alone instead of feeling isolated in company.

That evening I checked my emails, hoping for news from Luke. A message from him appeared on the screen. As I read it my cheeks felt warm.

I miss you so much, Ellie. You've always been part of my life and I've relied on you being there. The day you phoned me at the university to tell me you were leaving for Australia was one of the days I won't forget easily. The shock made me realise how much I love you and how important you've always been to me. Though we are married to other partners, we have a special connection and we both know it. And now you've gone from my life like a puff of smoke.

I remember watching you, a tiny thing with a halo of blond hair like a fairy on top of a Christmas tree. It was a windy day, your mother's skirt was puffed out like a balloon and you were battling to hold on to her. Such a lovely memory.

I thought of Luke alone in the flat he had rented at the university and imagined him hunched over his computer, a lock of grey hair over his forehead, beer and cigarettes beside him. I could almost hear the click of the minute hand of his old clock and the rustle of dry ivy stalks on the window outside.

He'd spoken often of his *practical arrangement* of staying on campus during the week and returning to his home and his wife Hilde over the weekend. He told me that he had married her because he could not have me, and that now he stayed with her for financial reasons. Recently they had both lost too much on the stock exchange to consider shifting. And then there were his two adult daughters, whom he adored.

I would have to accept that longing to be with Luke would always with be with me. I thought of my heartbreak when Luke left for Canada. His leaving resulted in two broken relationships. That was how I saw it. When I married Richard, Luke remained in the shadows. My hope that he would return, ensured doom for our marriage. How could Richard live up to my image of Luke?

Six

Mama visited soon after Richard and I returned from our honeymoon. We had rented a small apartment in the inner city suburb of *Josefstadt*. She gave the small sitting room her practised eye and went about repositioning ornaments. I liked the few we owned placed haphazardly but she organised them rigidly. She straightened the pictures and photographs too. I was upset, even angry, that she felt free to correct the way I had set up my home. Later I realised that she did this without malice and that it was part of her orderly nature.

'Nice. Very nice,' she said feeling the weight of the curtains. She stroked the velvet couch before sitting, seemed satisfied and added, 'I hope you'll both be very happy here.'

We sipped our coffee and I told her about our honeymoon in Paris. She smiled wistfully as I described the places we had visited. Once she had drained her cup her expression became more earnest. 'Have you thought about starting a family?' she asked.

'Of course we've discussed it but I want to wait.'

'Well, don't wait too long. You'll settle down and then soon you won't want to disrupt your work.'

I knew she was speaking from experience. I was born ages after my parents first met. I had often wondered if Mama had been a reluctant mother. She had explained my birth late in their relationship was due to my father's instability and an alcohol problem, but I doubted it was the reason.

I did not want children. After four years of marriage, I had avoided having a family. I told myself that a child would tie me down but my real fear was that a child would demand something of me that that I could not give. Though I loved animals and other people's children, held and played with them, cooing over them was not for me. Perhaps, I thought, I was not maternal. But my dolls were once my children and I held and kissed each one of them.

In those early days of marriage, I made certain that Richard wore a condom. He did as I asked but he longed for children and nagged incessantly. When by our fifth year of marriage, my attitude to childbearing had not changed, he insisted I see a psychologist. To please him I made an appointment.

I had read that psychologists were meant to be non-judgemental and empathic. Well, this psychologist was not.

'It is definitely unusual not to want a family,' Mrs Altman said, in her soft but monotonous voice.

In the days between my appointments, I slept less than three hours a night and in my dreams I recreated my mother's stories of her past, melding them with my own. In the mornings, I woke wrung out. She probed endlessly about my relationship with my mother. I told her that Mama kept her distance, and that there was a cold, closed part of her that sometimes felt like an icy rock. I explained that Mama's moods were as unpredictable as the Viennese weather and this made me wary of her. I explained how hard I had tried to please her but no matter what I did, she was not satisfied. This was disheartening and I gave up trying after a while.

Forty was old for childbearing in those days. Mama ran and played with me energetically when I was little, which makes me think that her age had little to do with her feelings about me. By the time I was in my teens and she was heading for sixty, she tired more easily and she was irritated by my chatter about school and friends.

Mama had difficulty explaining why being Jewish was special or why it was different to being Christian. It took me a long time to figure it all out. I could tell by her darting eyes that she was fearful when she warned me against showing my Jewishness to others. 'Keep to yourself, or you'll be singled out,' she'd say, 'and then you'll be looking for big trouble.'

As she would not tell me who would single me out and what sort of trouble I could expect, I was constantly afraid. From the talk on the street, I learned of the terrible suffering of Jews during the war and some of the torments people were continuing to face. The stories made me more anxious.

In her most solemn voice, Mrs Altman said that by discouraging me from attending shul and mixing with groups of other Jews, Mama had prevented me from feeling Jewish. She shook her head with displeasure.

'I expect you can't blame your mother, she went through such a lot. But no wonder you learned to be afraid.'

I tried to explain to Mrs Altman that there were days when I wondered if the woman who called herself my mother had found or adopted me.

'You have an identity issue,' she said. 'It's common with children of survivors of the war.'

I looked at her and said nothing. There was nothing I could do about my so-called identity problem and she did not offer any suggestions. After her pronouncement, I decided not to see her again.

Several months after my last appointment, my negativity about having a family shifted enough for me to fall pregnant. The early nausea and discomfort cancelled out all emotions. Richard was so thrilled with the thought of the child to come, that he busied himself painting the spare bedroom. I was indifferent. Towards the end of my pregnancy I was huge and uncomfortable but healthy. Giving birth was not easy. It was a protracted and painful labour and when the midwife placed the tiny creature on my chest I felt nothing but relief that it was over.

Richard thought the baby looked like an angel and chose the name Gabriel for him. I made a determined effort, from the time he was very little, not to be a mother who was anything like Mama. I tried to be consistent and loving but this was asking a lot of myself. I slipped up more often than I acknowledged. It was as if I had no control. I was sponge that had absorbed my mother's pain and angst and without realising it, I poured it out on Gabe. Nevertheless he was healthy, strong and appeared happy enough.

Seven

Once more cooking and cleaning became part of my daily routine. As I threw myself into boring household chores, I worried whether our possessions would arrive intact and if our property in Vienna would be well looked after.

I ached for our home near the Vienna Woods. It was nothing like the typical wooden chalet style houses in our street, but it was far from modern. The old red couches covered with throw rugs we had owned for years, were the sort one sank into. We had slept on them and made love there too. The front room was far from perfect. Walls were scratched from the boys' bikes and cats' claws had left their mark on the wood, but it was ours.

In addition, we owned Mama's old home in Leopoldstadt. Before we left Vienna, I had the time consuming task of finding tenants for both homes. Luckily Richard's cousin Charlie agreed to stay in our current house while we were away. It was a relief to have a person we knew and trusted in our home. If we returned soon, which I believed was likely, at least the house would be available to us. Charlie, a middle aged bachelor, who was unsociable and tended towards perfectionism, was an ideal choice. Finding a suitable tenant for the house in Leopoldstadt was more difficult. The elderly couple, who had lived there for years left months earlier to stay with their children and I hadn't bothered to look for new tenants.

Before letting the old house, I had to check that it was in good condition. This was an excellent excuse to visit my old home again and I welcomed reviving my memories. From a distance, the turn of the century house appeared unchanged - a cream, solid, double storey, flanked by tall trees and flowering shrubs. As I walked up the driveway, I noticed that the walls were filthy and the curved pillars of the front portico were spattered with mud. Plants no longer filled the garden beds and only a few shrubs and trees remained. The fairies I once saw peeping through the daisies had no home now.

The house was clean inside. The couple had cared about their living space while they obviously ignored all beyond it. Now that it was empty, it held fewer memories than I expected. I left quickly, satisfied that I could employ a handyman to clean and paint the outdoors and that the garden could be easy replenished.

Two weeks later, the exterior of the house was patched, painted and looked inviting. I visited the nursery and planted flowers, bulbs and shrubs. Rents were cheaper in Leopoldstadt than in some of the more upmarket suburbs and I expected the house to attract scores of young people with a family. From the long list of applicants, I chose a newly graduated doctor, Franz Brauer, his young wife Alex and their two children. The Brauers were a delightful couple who appeared to be responsible.

When I left the house for the last time, I stared hard at the columns and portico trying to commit them to memory. It was an irrational feeling but I sensed that it would be the last time I would see them.

When they were little, the boys were drawn to the old house with its ambling garden and old trees. When we visited, they were in the garden in minutes, climbing the same trees Luke and I had climbed as children. In the tallest chestnut they found the remains of the tree house that Luke had built and made their new house in the same spot. When it came to her grandchildren Mama gave them all the affection she had denied me. I assumed that by not being her own children, they were removed from her and she could love them. The children revelled in the attention she gave them, and of course they looked forward to receiving her presents.

By the time they went to school both boys were less keen on visiting their grandmother. Her effusive hugs and kisses became an irritant and the garden no longer held mysteries. Though she listened attentively to what they had to say, as always, she avoided answering personal questions. The boys looked forward to Christmas as I had. Each year Mama made it a grand occasion with a glittering tree, gifts, a turkey and all the trimmings. We ate in the front room, facing the snow-decked garden, where I believed Santa's reindeers stopped for a rest.

When I was little, I didn't understand why other Jews did not celebrate Christmas and Easter. Mama said there was no harm in enjoying the holiday because we were Jewish. She confused me, and later I confused my children by allowing her to continue the family tradition with her grandchildren. Richard didn't care, though he should've and stopped it. He was the one who understood Judaism, though he didn't follow it.

Eight

One night when taking out the garbage, Richard met our neighbour Karl Weber. Karl and Magda had lived in Melbourne for the past sixteen years but were originally from Stuttgart in Germany. Karl was a man's man, tall, tanned and muscular. When I met him for the first time, he was wearing shorts and a torn polo splattered with paint and dirt. He wiped his hand on his shorts and stuck it out towards me in greeting.

I admired Magda, a slim, diminutive blonde in her late forties who smiled almost all the time. There wasn't an ounce of excess fat on her streamlined body. She was outgoing and generous, nothing like the wives of Richard's colleagues, who kindly invited us for dinner and a company barbeque, but after that first invitation we did not hear from them again. When I was with Magda, we spoke German. She talked a lot and filled me in with details about our neighbours. She had visited Vienna often and said she loved it. I felt comfortable with her and we found an instant connection.

The Webers' house stood close to the street with no greenery other than a low well-snipped hedge. The inside was stylish, decorated with slim couches on dark floorboards, the windows free of curtains and only a lamp relieved the starkness. They owned a piano. It was open and I ran my fingers over the keys, longing to play a melody.

'Do either of you play?' I asked.

'Karl used to play once, but not now. Our grandchildren are learning and we keep the piano for them. They entertain us when they visit.'

Over coffee and cake we found that we read the same books and both enjoyed classical music. I listened intrigued to Magda's account of how she had built a business from home, by selling boxed chocolates on the internet. All her chocolates were imported from Germany and she packaged them attractively. She boasted how well her small enterprise was doing. 'I can manage to spoil myself now, life is good here and there are marvellous opportunities. You'll find that out.'

'Yes, perhaps I will in time.'

'You'll have to start doing something… eventually, you know.'

I sank deeper into the couch. Magda's attempt at encouragement frightened me. Her words were beyond my grasp. Keen to change the subject, I enquired about a group of photographs on the side table. They were pictures of Magda at different ages and of her relatives. She had been a stunning blonde bride and Karl, handsome in his morning suit.

The following Sunday, Karl offered to drive us to the nearby Dandenong Mountains for afternoon tea. I had read about the mountains and was keen to see them. We set off early in Karl's taxi. He explained that in Stuttgart he and his father had owned a fleet of taxis. When he arrived in Australia he bought a taxi. Now, he owned eighteen cabs and had several drivers working for him.

As we drove, the endless flat suburban blocks were replaced by gentle hills and large, well-tended plots of land. I watched the scenery intently. The trees and farm animals reminded me of the Austrian countryside. Though the mountains were low compared the ones I was used to, I was a mountain lover and looked forward to seeing this range.

We climbed slowly at first, and then so rapidly that all I could see were the banks of emerald ferns and incredibly tall eucalyptus trees with ribbons of bark dangling from their trunks. The ferns were exquisite and the silvery green trees had a softness and charm. I sniffed the powerful, clean smell of eucalyptus.

It was nothing like the picture postcard of the Alps with wild flowers, granite peaks and sombre black pines below the snowline. I thought of Luke and wished he was sitting beside me instead of Richard. Luke loved mountains too and would've been fascinated. As we reached the peak, Richard continued talking sport to Karl.

Magda pointed her finger. 'Port Philip Bay is down there.' I looked down at the view of the sea stretching out before me.

'And what is… that wide, dark band of land?' I asked.

'It's one of the areas that burned during the fires on Black Saturday.' Karl gave me details about the tinder dry bush, the terrible fires that swept through the area and how many of them were purposely lit.

Magda spotted a sign advertising Devonshire Tea and urged Karl to slow down. I had no idea what Devonshire Tea was. After we parked, I took a deeper breath of clear, sweet air and surveyed the cluster of Victorian buildings against the mountain backdrop - the lawns, pink and white flowers and pebbled pathways. The sight spoke to the romantic in me and I liked it.

The tea was served in white porcelain with a platter of homemade scones, raspberry jam and heaps of thick cream. I spread the red jam and cream on my scone and licked my fingers. The jam tasted like forest berries and for that luscious moment I was back home.

During the drive home I pretended to be asleep but I was combing through all that I had seen that afternoon and delighting in the images. Little details like coils of bark on the roadside and a kangaroo hopping across a path replayed in my thoughts. They would sustain me for days.

I stepped into the garden, breathing the fragrances that heightened at twilight and listened to the buzz of the advancing night. I picked gardenia for my hair. The scent reminded me of the first bouquet Richard had sent me. If the camellias, roses and gardenias with a huge box of chocolates hadn't arrived, perhaps I wouldn't have accepted his invitation to a concert.

Before leaving Vienna, we celebrated our thirtieth or "pearl" wedding anniversary. Richard gave me a string of pearls and my gift to him was pearl cuff links. Neither particularly inventive nor exciting presents. We spent the night at a magnificent hotel, danced and drank champagne. Later, my jollity and sweet phrases were tested. Sex on the satin sheets left me with tears of sadness instead of pleasure, but I wiped them away and went on pretending.

Since our arrival in Australia we had hardly talked. Most of it was my fault. In my first weeks of misery, I sealed myself off from him. He watched me, shook his head in despair or was it disgust, and did not try to break through my wall of gloom. Though he boasted of a warm reception, adapting to the Australian arm of the company was challenging. Some empathy from me might have made it easier.

We had each other but we might as well have been strangers. Karl and Magda were our only friends but we hardly knew them. Anton was passing through the late teen self-involvement phase and had his own battles.

Nine

I opened the plastic folder of family photographs I kept in my handbag and found Gabe's photo. I smiled, remembering what a beautiful baby he was on the day he was born. His golden curls and grey-green eyes like mine and Richard's olive skin tone made him a stunner. Everyone commented on his looks and they still do.

I was twenty-seven then, and like many new mothers, when I took Gabe home I feared I might drop him, scratch his fine skin with my nails or bruise his tiny body with a knock against the bath tub. Fortunately my confidence grew within days of handling him. Initially I was grateful that I had sufficient milk for him but when it dried up in two months, I was relieved that he stopped suckling. Fortunately he took to the bottle without difficulty and gained weight.

Long before he could talk, it was clear that he knew what he wanted. If he did not get his way, he wailed and kicked. In this sense, I thought he took after Richard. After checking that he wasn't wet or uncomfortable, I ignored his tantrums until he calmed down. In a similar way, I ignored Richard when he became too demanding. I wasn't like other mothers who doted on their babies, nuzzling, tickling and kissing them. I kissed him only when I put him down to sleep. Rearing him was a duty and I cared for him well.

When the childcare nurse visited, she was satisfied with his development but concerned about me. Over a cup of coffee, she suggested that I might be depressed. It was common she said, for new mothers to have post natal depression. I knew she was incorrect. There was nothing wrong with me. When Richard took over caring for Gabe for a few hours and I was free to go out, I was happy.

Gabe walked and talked early and played with his toys. By the time he was one and a half, I could barely wait to be freed from the house and caring for him. Childcare was my way out. I found a reliable crèche and went back to work for three days a week. It did not bother me that I was working to pay for his care and he thrived on the new environment.

When I discovered I that was pregnant again, I did not welcome the idea of a second child but I kept it to myself and pretended, even to Richard, that I was thrilled. Anton came early and spent his first few weeks in a humidicrib. He was tiny but he grew fast. He was a beautiful baby too, but in a sweeter way than Gabe, with shiny hazel eyes, reddish brown hair and pale skin like Mama's. At a few months, he giggled and smiled a lot and unlike his brother was easily pleased. When he cried it was because he was wet, tired or hungry.

From the day I brought Anton home, Gabe played the role of older, protective brother. When Anton was just over a year, I sent both children to the crèche. To afford the care, I worked an extra day, but it was worth it. They were happy playing with each other as well as the other children.

I had intended to give each boy time alone with me, but with my job and household chores, it did not work out that way. I doubt that Gabe suffered but Anton probably did. He was the more sensitive one who needed more attention. While Gabe happily kicked a ball or tore things apart and then tried to fix them, Anton liked to sit near me and play his imaginative games. He could read by the age of four and write his name. He played the piano soon after. As much as I didn't want him to be like me, he was.

Ten

From the Big Wheel at the *Prater* Amusement Park, I looked down on the green avenues and Baroque splendour of the inner city. Suddenly the wheel spun uncontrollably and I clung to the rail of the open gondola in terror. I woke from a dream with my heart pounding and my nightgown sweaty. I fell back against the cushions waiting for calm. Why was I dreaming about the Ferris wheel? After discounting inconsequential issues, I decided that my anxiety about the move was the likely reason. Was I so insecure? In Vienna with Luke as my support, I had floated through life, whiling away hours in coffee shops, my family substitute. But now my hold was tentative and I had no idea where to begin.

The house was still. I tiptoed down the stairs and looked out on to the garden, rosy in the flush of dawn. When I turned on my computer there was one message from Dr Franz Brauer, the young doctor who had rented the house in Leopoldstadt. As I read the email, I wished I had left the computer to later in the day. He wrote of an early blizzard and the heavy snow that had fallen in Vienna a week ago. The attic was flooded and water had seeped through the ceiling and down some of the walls of the upstairs bedrooms. He went into infinite detail, describing methods he had already employed to pump out the water and prevent further damage. He promised to let me know whether his efforts were successful and if the attic and ceiling had dried out. It was a long email that included an approximate estimate of the cost of the damage totalling thousands of dollars. Over past years of blizzards and heavy rain the house had remained solid and water proof. This damage was unusual.

The bowl of fruit on the table was tempting. I stretched for a perfect green pear and as I bit into the sweetness, I thought it just as well that Mama was not there to know about the damage to the house. As I sucked the pear core, I wondered what Mama would have thought of Melbourne. I doubted she would've liked it. It was too different from Vienna. I turned my gaze to the garden and watched shy flowers turn towards the sun.

Stretching lazily, I stood and went upstairs. The bathroom was the one room in the house I liked. It was white and tiled with a wide frieze of cornflowers. I threw my nightdress into the corner of the room and stepped into the shower. One of my going away gifts was pine scented shower gel. I applied it lavishly and luxuriated in the hot water. Once the radio was turned on to a music station, I hummed to the tune playing.

As I adjusted the hot water, I looked up. Above the shower head, dangling in the corner of the room was an enormous, plump spider, larger than a golf ball. In my moment of panic, I thought it was a tarantula, though I had never seen one. Swallowing my scream, I turned the taps off frantically and grabbed a towel. Still dripping, I shut the bathroom door behind me and ran to the bedroom.

As soon as I was dressed, I checked the bathroom door once more. It was incredibly stupid of me, and I can laugh about it now, but I blocked the space under the door with newspaper to stop the "thing" from escaping. More secure, I went downstairs to make a strong cup of coffee. One of the men would have to attend to it.

The front door banged. I collared Anton. He shuddered when I told him about the "thing" in the bathroom.

'I'm not going near it, ask Papa to get rid of it when he comes home.'

I reminded him that he had caught and killed a mouse that had jumped out of a packet of corn flakes when we moved into our Vienna apartment.

He laughed. 'That was ages ago and it was a tiny fieldmouse … I didn't kill it, I took it by its tail and threw it over the fence into the neighbour's house.'

'That was awful, you shouldn't have.' I covered my mouth with my hand. 'That unfriendly French couple?' I couldn't suppress my giggles.

He gave me one of his testing looks. 'Something to eat first, I'm starving. Then I'll see to it, I promise.'

'But what if it has crept back into the ceiling by then?'

'Mutti, don't be ridiculous!'

His eyes shining, he smiled one of his sardonic smiles. 'Oh, all right then, I'll go up now,' he muttered, heading for the stairs.

I followed him and watched him disappear into the bathroom. Within seconds I heard a loud gasp and he rushed out.

'Close the door,' I yelled.

'Whew! It's huge… the biggest I've ever seen. Get me an empty jar.'

Quickly I emptied the coffee granules from its container and hurried back upstairs. I held it out to him. 'Just get rid of it,' I said as coolly as I could.

'I'm taking it to university tomorrow to find out if it's poisonous.'

The following day, I showered in the narrower shower downstairs. The once lovely white bathroom was off limits. I was not taking chances.

That afternoon, Anton found me in the kitchen.

'Mutti, about that spider… It's called a Huntsman and it's almost harmless but common here in Melbourne. Scary though,' he said with a laugh.

Eleven

Mama avoided talking about my father but she told me about her youth many times. She was at her most relaxed in the kitchen and while helping her prepare the evening meal, I listened to her stories.

She was fifteen years old in March 1938, when the German tanks rolled into Vienna. They were welcomed by most of the Austrian population. My grandparents had left it too late to escape but their concern was to protect Mama.

My grandmother packed Mama's suitcase and together they took a train to the wealthiest part of the city, to Jana Mueller's imposing home. Jana was an old school friend of my grandmother's, who had married well. Once Jana's family had lived near my grandma in Leopoldstadt, the only section of the city they could afford then. Though Jana's family was Catholic and my grandmother's Jewish, they attended the same school and played together most afternoons.

Mama repeated the next part of story so often that I could anticipate each word. When they arrived at Jana's home carrying the suitcase, Jana welcomed them and offered them food and drink. My grandmother explained that she had not come on a social visit but that she was there to seek protection from the Nazis for her daughter.

'We've spent most of our lives together and we are like sisters," Jana said kindly. 'Of course I will make sure your child is safe.' She paced the elegant sitting room until she spoke again. 'I've thought of a plan and I'm sure it will work. Ella is old enough to work for me as a maid. In that way she will be able to move about freely in the house and no one will ask questions. She'll be perfectly safe.'

'Are you sure…she won't be too much of an imposition?' my grandmother asked.

'Not at all. I know you would do the same for me.'

'It's settled then,' Grandmama said in her sternest voice. 'You'll stay here and work for Jana. If you do whatever she says, you'll be safe.'

Mama wept and clung to grandmama.

'Let her go,' Jana said taking my grandmother's hand. 'I will see to it that your daughter is well cared for. When the danger is over, come back and she will be waiting for you.' Jana bustled my grandmother out of the door and closed it before she could change her mind.

Mama stayed with the Muellers throughout the war and with her light colouring, her Jewishness was never challenged. It was understandable and even predictable that gradually she became part of the Mueller family.

I met Jana once, a few years before she died. Mama and I travelled to Jana's house by train, taking the same route that she and my grandmother had taken fifty years earlier. We walked along the cobbled street flanking the Danube, where the houses of sixteenth century patricians had been remodelled for the modern day wealthy Viennese. Mama hurried me along the stone path to the ornate front door, giving me barely enough time to admire the Meuller's three level dwelling. She stood at the door uncertainly before pulling the bell. A butler opened the door and when he saw Mama, he hugged her.

We were ushered into a lavish parlour. Mama had not seen Jana since her visit five years earlier. In spite of her raptures about Jana's beauty within and without, I wasn't sure what to expect. While we waited, I admired the marble topped tables, velvet curtains, satin couches and exquisite porcelain ornaments.

When the door opened, a nurse wheeled in an old lady with an almost unlined face and hair dyed blonde. Mama greeted Jana warmly and introduced me, but the woman's glazed blue eyes looked past us. Mama addressed her again, this time giving Jana a kiss on her cheek but the old lady was unresponsive.

'You should have come back earlier,' the nurse said, stroking Jana's arm. 'She doesn't know you or anyone, now.'

During the train journey home, Mama was in a reflective mood and talked about the *Anschluss*. She could recall the day clearly, the 12th March 1938. She and her parents were gathered around the radio when they heard that Hitler had marched into Linz and announced the annexation of Austria to the German Reich. The radio captured the jubilation of the crowd. Two days later, Mama stood on the upstairs balcony watching the crowd beneath grow as they waited for Hitler to arrive. Men, women and children lined the streets to welcome him and his troops. Some threw flowers at the soldiers, others held out their arms in the Nazi salute. By then she was old enough to understand the implications of Hitler's arrival.

'The days after the *Anschluss* I would rather forget. The Nazis took pleasure in humiliating Jews. They forced us to clean toilets and scrub the streets.' She wiped a tear from her eyes. 'Jews were attacked in the street and humiliated, many of their shops were destroyed and homes plundered. Those who thought they could hide their religion by converting to Christianity wasted their time. They were rounded up and eventually sent to concentration camps.'

Mama sighed and was silent. I listened to the chug of the train and recalled film footage I had seen of Hitler amongst rapturous crowds. We were half-way home when Mama spoke again. 'Do you understand now why your grandmama took me to her friend Jana?'

'It was a clever thing to do. If only grandmama could've found her own place to hide.'

Mama grimaced. 'By the time she made up her mind to leave…it was too late.'

'You were with Jana and her family for a very long time,' I said.

'She treated me well and her husband was polite, even if he didn't warm to me. I was comfortable enough in my own small room with a bed and washstand.'

'But it must've been difficult.'

'I made sure not to complain or express a personal opinion. She was kind to me and treated me well. I was a servant, sitting with the family like a member of the family at some meals, and served them at others. On Sundays I joined them at church and celebrated all their festivals. Judaism was a vague memory. After the first year of attending mass and observing all the Catholic rituals in the household, I forgot the Hebrew I had learned and almost all the songs. Christ's gentle face appealed to me and I understood his pain. I forgot that Jews did not pray to him. If I had not returned to Leopoldstadt after the war and then met your father, I probably would've remained a Catholic.'

'And did Jana's children accept you?'

'They were nasty to me in the beginning and refused to talk to me. In time they became used to me.'

That must've been very hard…'

She held up her hand to stop me.

'I didn't mind. I was lucky to be safe, have a place to sleep and food. No one in the house except Jana's husband knew who I was. She told the children and the servants that I was the daughter of a poor cousin from the country, that she felt sorry for and that she was training me to become a house servant. They never found out who I really was.'

As the train sped on, I thought of Mama, a fifteen year old in a stranger's home, afraid to speak out. How confusing it must've been for her to be at once a servant and a token family member. At least she had a room where she could be alone. I thought of the tears she would have shed longing for her home and her family.

For days the sick old woman in the wheelchair who had kept my mother safe during the war was in my thoughts. She could never know my gratitude.

When the psychologist asked about my mother's background, I ought to have told her about Jana. But Jana was a family secret and I said nothing about her. I was just like Mama.

Twelve

We did not need persuading when the Webers invited us to join them on a camping holiday. We were eager to see the Australian bush and the unusual animals we had heard about. Anton surprised us by agreeing to come along. It might have been Beverley, the Weber's attractive daughter who'd enticed him. I was thrilled, we would be a family again, as we once were when the boys were younger and we went hiking in Tyrol or skiing in Salzburg.

Magda promised that the caravan park would provide all the facilities we needed. Best of all, we would sleep under tall gum trees that were home to koalas. If we were lucky, she said, we might even catch a glimpse of kangaroos. Magda wouldn't hear of me bringing food, but I contributed beer and cool drinks. All we had to do was to pack a small suitcase with our casual clothing.

Soon after arriving, the men set up the tents, while we organised a makeshift kitchen. Magda unpacked meat for the barbeque and fresh vegetables for salad.

Karl had brought a camp fridge and a hotplate. It astounded me that we had almost every convenience. Fortunately there was running water close by. The young ones headed off and the four of us took a stroll through the forest. The smell of the wet earth, the pungent eucalyptus and the sounds of the birds were all new and interesting. I was thrilled to recognise birds that visited our garden. Karl told us that we would have to go much deeper into the forest if we hoped to see kangaroos.

After our first outdoor meal, we were in bed early. Richard fell asleep immediately but I lay in the tight bed listening out for koalas in the gum trees. Soon I drifted off to the hum of the forest.

Hammering noise woke us in fright. Richard sat up. 'A gun's firing,' he yelled as he pulled on his track suit. He ran out and I followed. There were sounds of running but it was too dark to see a thing. Karl arrived with a high beamed torch and shone it over the ground, trees and bushes. All was quiet apart from a rustle in the bushes and the screech of an owl.

The next morning, a young couple camping close by told us that the ranger and three policemen had arrived at dawn. Two koalas had been killed and they were searching for the culprits. Apparently, over the past few weeks possums and cockatoos had been shot. Two young men carrying rifles were spotted. Richard, Karl and Anton joined in the search and returned hours later, filthy and tired. Other than footprints and bullet casings, there was no sign of the offenders.

After a warm drink, Anton disappeared into the caravan. Karel stretched out in his chair and relaxed but Richard held his face in his hands and rocked to and fro.

'We saw the dead koalas lying there. What sort of people would do something like that... purposely kill defenceless animals... for the fun of it?'

'Who knows what goes on in their heads and why they did it,' Karl said, flexing his shoulders.

'Have something to eat and drink. You'll feel better,' Magda said, placing a plate of food in front of Richard.

Richard left his food and strode into the bushes. I followed him and found him propped up against a tree breathing heavily. When I touched his shoulder and asked what was troubling him, he dropped his head. 'I have to get out of this place as soon as possible.'

He answered none of my questions and turned away.

I made our apologies and we packed our few possessions. Anton decided to stay on with the Webers and Karl drove the two of us to the nearest town. From there, we took a taxi.

Richard was silent all the way home. Though I didn't comment, I was pleased to leave after the harrowing incident.

Richard retreated to his study. A day later, he sat next to me on the couch and explained. 'When I was a child in Poland, after the war, food was so scarce that there were times when we had nothing to eat and we were on the verge of starving. It was winter and my mother had no choice but to send me into the forest to hunt for food. I could barely hold a rifle let alone fire one.'

I'd had no idea it was that bad. By the time I growing up food was plentiful.

'Men with guns and even women and children hunted for anything they could find to feed their families - rats, ferrets, birds. I heard the shots, saw the dead animals in their hands but I couldn't shoot a thing for my mother's pot. I'll never forget the animals, the blood and the smells.'

He turned his head aside as if to wipe his memories away. After a few minutes of silence, he stood slowly and without speaking, returned to his study.

Later Karl and Magda returned from their holiday and told us that the police had charged two teenage boys who were on drugs. Karl talked about the increase in drug use amongst young people and went on to describe the rest of their holiday. 'You two will have to come along another time and see all the places you missed out on,' he said, slapping Richard on the back.

Richard gave Karl one of his false smiles. 'Sure, sure... another time.'

Within a few days, Richard appeared to have put the episode aside.

In moments of sleeplessness, my encounter with the spider, followed by the visit to the campsite fused and turned Melbourne into a frightening, wild place. My mood slumped and right then I could've packed and booked a seat on the plane back to Vienna.

Thirteen

I picked up the prayer book on the table next to my bed and ran my fingers over the faded leather as I thought of Mama's friend, Ernst Weingarten. I remembered an afternoon in the school holidays when I was practicing Bach's piano concerto in D minor.

I was twelve years old, and learning piano at school. It was my first attempt at Bach and I was proud that I had mastered the piece.

Ernst's clapping halted my playing. 'Sorry I disturbed you. You play like an angel.'

My cheeks warmed with pleasure.

'If you don't mind, I'll sit and listen while I wait for your mother.'

I continued playing for a little longer and then offered him coffee and what was left of the apple strudel and cream. He licked the last of the cream off his fork and sat back in his chair.

'Performing is in your blood, my dear. And if you practice, you never know, you might be famous.' He smiled his kind smile.

I closed the piano and stroked the walnut lid with my hand.

Ernst looked at his watch. 'I wonder where that mother of yours is.'

'She should be home soon.'

'She played the piano when she was younger.'

'I know she loves to sing but I didn't know that she played.'

'Not classical music like you play…popular melodies. Friends gathered around her and sang as she played. Those were the good old days!'

'Please, tell me what you can remember about her, then.'

He smoothed a crease in his trousers. 'My dear, I'm not sure if you know what a beauty your mother was?'

Before a serious comment, he addressed me as "my dear".

'It was soon after your father died, that I met your mother through a group of friends. I wasn't the only man to fancy her but I consider myself lucky. She wasn't at all interested in marrying me …' He hesitated. 'But she wanted a friend…an older man she could rely on, like me.'

I asked again. 'Please, tell me everything you can remember about her.'

'You must know she worked in the city?'

'Yes, but she hasn't told me much about that.'

'Well, when your father became too ill to work, money was short. She had to find a job and she didn't have much experience. She worked in a bakery and a few factories. It was pure luck that a couple who lived in your street and owned a small dress shop in the city were looking for an assistant. Your mother impressed them with her manner and style and offered her the job. Why wouldn't they?'

'When I was little, she wore the same skirt and jacket but added a blouse, scarf or a necklace and looked elegant. I remember that.'

'Your mother has always been clever that way. She didn't have much money to spend on clothes but she looked good.'

'Tell me more about the shop,' I nagged.

'It was in a good location close to the big, expensive hotels but the owners were getting on and didn't keep up with the trends. Within a year your mother turned it into a thriving, fashionable boutique. The owners made her the manageress and she was earning well.'

'That's amazing!'

'Yes, my dear, that mother of yours is smart. I don't know how she did it, and with no business experience.'

I remembered the rush to get ready in the morning so that Mama would be in time for work.

Ernst had stopped talking and idly stroked his silk tie. He always wore pure silk ties.

He was in a talkative mood and I took advantage of it. 'Please, tell me about your life in Vienna before the war.'

He had told me about his privileged childhood before but I enjoyed listening to his stories about the past. His embellishments that altered each time he told the story did not seem to matter.

'Alright then, my dear. I might have told you that we lived in what today would be called a mansion, in the best part of Vienna, close to the *Ringstrasse* and near the park. We had servants, in the kitchen, house and garden. Five if I remember correctly. And we children were spoiled, our clothes made to measure and our food...' He closed his eyes to savour the memory. 'Hannalore was the best cook I've come across. Her dumplings and roast duck...' He smacked his lips.

He continued, impressing me with his detailed descriptions of the vast garden and the interior of the house, the brocade curtains, fine ornaments, velvet couches and crystal chandeliers. Once he started talking about his childhood spent in luxury, he could not stop.

The best part was his description of the summer garden, where the adults had their tea and strudel, while the children sipped fresh lemonade with chocolate cake. To me, the gazebo on a square of lawn surrounded by flowering shrubs and shady trees sounded like a fairyland. I tried to imagine the blocks of ice covered with straw, he said were stored to the side of the garden, in the cellar, to keep the butter, milk, cheese and meat fresh.

He smiled as he spoke of the square of lawn, frozen in winter. 'It turned into a skating rink. *Wunderbar!*' He rubbed his hands 'But I did fall on the ice a few times.' We both laughed. 'On Saturdays lots of visitors came.' He closed his eyes remembering. 'Aaah, the men spinning on the ice to show off, the women in their long dresses like a moving picture and the children squealing with joy.'

'How beautiful!'

'In winter, when I was a child, I sat around the fire with my two sisters. They took turns in playing with me and telling stories. We roasted chestnuts and I had my first taste of wine. Both my sisters played the piano but not as well as you do. When they'd had enough playing, they called the maid to crank up the gramophone player. There was always music in our house.'

He laughed about his domineering governess who terrified him but made him study hard. He said he had her to thank for his grounding in mathematics and science. As always, he did not mention his parents, or say much about his sisters.

Suddenly he stopped talking, his mouth sagged and his gaze was distant as he fingered his tie.

'Tell me more, please.' I sensed he needed to finish his story.

He sighed again. 'Of course, none of it lasted. It was a dream. After the *Anschluss* was announced, Jewish newspapers published their final editions. In the months that followed, all Jews in Vienna were prevented from following their professions and their businesses were closed down by those Nazi pigs.'

'Yes…it's awful.'

'It gets worse. Are you sure you want to hear the next part? It isn't pretty.'

'I think so.' I took a deep breath and waited.

'I knew that Papa was planning our escape from Vienna by ship, but he had trouble getting the papers in time. The Germans were everywhere by then, but he had been told that there was a chance of sending us children to England. English volunteers organised a rescue mission for children in danger of being sent to the concentration camps, called *Kindertransport*. One morning, all three of us were dressed in our best clothes and taken to a small office in the city. I remember climbing lots of steps with my sisters and being told to hurry. The interview is a blur now, but I recall that it was decided that I was the one who would leave first and my sisters would follow. I still don't know why this decision was made. I think that my father favoured me, being his only son and I was brighter than my sisters at school. Perhaps he thought I had a chance of a future. Later that week,

I was woken early and taken to the station. I didn't want to go and I tried to run away but my father caught me in his arms. He hugged me and whispered a prayer. The rest of the family were there and everyone tried not to cry as I was placed inside the carriage with other children.'

Ernst wiped his eyes. 'When we get out we'll write to you, tell you where to join us,' Papa said. We both knew they wouldn't be able to leave. Mama cried and kissed me and my sisters tried to joke saying they were pleased to be rid of me. Of course my sisters didn't follow me, and I didn't see my parents again. I was the only one to survive. They were all killed in Auschwitz. I can't bear picturing what they looked like.'

He wiped his eyes again.

I didn't know what to do or say to comfort him.

'I'm sure Mama will be along soon. She's very late. In the meanwhile would you like some more coffee?'

He shook his head. 'No thank you, my dear. I suppose you'd better hear the rest of my story.'

'Yes, please. Did you actually go to England?'

'Yes, my dear, I did. The train took us to Antwerp and from there we travelled by ship to Harwich on the East Coast of England. It was a rough journey and horribly cramped but we knew how lucky we all were. I made friends on the ship I still have today.'

He swallowed hard and continued. 'Either we were sponsored by families or our passage and expenses paid for by kind English citizens - Quakers and members of Christian churches. I met my foster parents, Barney and Tina Rosenberg, in London. They had asked for a young boy. My English was poor and I struggled to understand them but the look in their eyes was kind. We all took the train to Kent. We were met at the station and then driven to their house. They had a large home but not a mansion like the one I once knew.

'Later I found out that they didn't have children. I was fond of them but I couldn't regard them as parents. Naturally, I appreciated all they were doing for me and tried hard to show them warmth, to reciprocate their growing feelings for me, but

I couldn't. When I found out that my whole family had died in the camp, it froze me inside.'

I sighed.

'The Rosenbergs sent me to school and selected my friends. At first I hated the constant rain and cold in England but I grew accustomed to it. I loved the long coastline, the beaches and the dramatic white cliffs of Dover that were only a bicycle ride away. When I was older, I found I could travel around England by rail and I enjoyed that. I spoke English without an accent and did well at school.'

'They must've been proud of you.' He nodded.

'They thought I'd stay with them after the war. But they were too clingy…too possessive of me. They were religious Jews and I became tired of attending synagogue so often. We were not religious at home.'

He looked at me and slapped his thigh. 'And so, my dear, I left for Vienna, promising to return to England, but in spite of my gratitude, I never saw them again. I did write to them though. I learnt a lot from Barney who was a solicitor.   I learned the value of a profession.   Later, when I had saved up enough money, I studied at night to become an accountant. The profession served me well. My father would have been proud. I guess Barney would've been proud too. He and Tina, his wife are both dead now.'

We talked for few minutes longer and then Mama arrived.

Fourteen

From the warmth of the café, I watched the stream of lunch-hour passers-by. Magda was late. A man walked past my table who looked familiar. Surely not, Bernie? I asked myself. He worked at the magazine kiosk outside the metro station in Vienna? The man noticed my stare. It was not Bernie, but someone who looked a lot like him. I was so homesick that every few days I saw someone I thought I knew amongst the strangers in Melbourne. Houses and shops I had never seen before looked slightly familiar too. I missed Luke terribly. When I felt low, Luke brightened my mood. When I was uncertain, he chased out the negatives. I sipped my coffee and imagined being with him again.

It was spring in *Augarten* Park. I was holding Luke's hand as we walked under the blossoming chestnut trees, and along the decorative flowerbeds. But I was unaware of the burst of blooming finery. My thoughts were of Mama, angry with me for coming home late after spending longer than usual with Luke. I had managed to convince her that my lateness was due to traffic problems - another lie I told her that she believed.

Luke drew me closer and kissed me. Arm in arm we walked across the wide expanse of grass. I heard giggles behind us. I turned about. Four of the girls in my class, carrying baskets and blankets were searching for a picnic spot. They passed us and we waved to each other.

Edna, one of the girls who had just walked past, had flirted openly with Luke at a school party, even though she knew we were a couple. It was clear that she fancied him. He didn't budge from my side all evening but I could tell from his throaty laugh and the flicker in his eyes that he revelled in the attention. I pretended I hadn't noticed but the episode made me feel vulnerable. More than ever, I needed Luke's reassurance. We were admiring the garden, when he took my hand and kissed it.

'When you're older men will fight over you,' he said. 'I love you enough for both of us.' He spoke with authority and had a way of making me believe him unquestioningly.

⁂

Apart from household chores, walks in the neighbourhood and reading, my days were empty. Meetings with Magda for coffee on Fridays at the same suburban café had become a ritual. The order we placed did not vary–cappuccino, toasted cheese and tomato for Magda, a long black and cake for me. The owners of the café were friendly and had created a warm atmosphere. In small ways, the café reminded me of a *kaffeehaus* I once visited in Vienna.

Magda bounded in tossing her head to show off her new blonde hairdo. She placed her expensive, red leather bag on the table and set about asking her customary questions about my family's health. 'So, tell me, are you settling in... feeling better?'

I lowered my head and shook it vigorously.

'I can understand that you feel homesick. I felt the same way when we first arrived. It's fourteen years that we've been here and I doubt we'll ever be true Aussies like our kids.'

'A long time for you to still feel that way.'

She plucked at her fringe. 'I do try to make the best of things but it doesn't always help. Small things can make me dissatisfied and cranky. Since we went camping, I've been dreaming of our old home in Stuttgart with a view of the mountains. Aaah, all those wonderful old birches, alders and almonds. There's nothing I've seen here to equal that view.'

69

'The forests in Europe are beautiful but I must say that I found the forests here fascinating. I love the fresh smell of eucalyptus and the magnificent ferns.'

She laughed. 'It'll take some time but one of these days you'll turn into a real Aussie.'

She took another sip of her coffee and stared at the hazy view of the mountains. 'We live for our visits back to Stuttgart. We save like crazy and then in a year or two we go back home. It's something to look forward to.'

'Mm.'

Magda smiled mischievously. 'Let's be devils and have some pavlova, enjoy its Aussie sweetness.'

We spooned up the last bit of the passionfruit and cream and in minutes our plates were empty. Magda nudged me. 'I've told you all there is to tell about myself but you haven't said much about your life in Vienna.'

I took off my cardigan and draped it over the back of my chair before answering. Here goes, I said to myself, as I explained that Mama lived with her family in Leopoldstadt for many years until war broke out. In 1946 she returned to her family home in *Weintraubengasse*. It was still standing and empty but in an awful mess, strewn with boxes of bullets, a German soldier's cap, old boots and dried rotten food. My mother's entire family who had lived there were dead. They all perished in the Dachau Concentration Camp.

'Oh dear! I'm sorry about your family.' Her fingers tightened around the strap of her handbag. So, you're Jewish?'

I took a deep breath before replying, 'Oh yes.'

'I'd never have guessed it. Richard maybe, but not you.'

In the silence between us, I thought how blunt Magda's last comments were. She hadn't meant to upset me but then I was thin skinned. Her hand covered her mouth and I detected a slight sigh.

'My uncle Jonas, my mother's brother, was a political objector.' She paused. 'And early one morning in '39 the gestapo marched in, shot him like a dog outside his house and in front of his family.'

I stretched across the table to touch her hand. 'Oh, no!'

'My aunt survived the war but she never spoke again... the shock got to her and she lived in a shadow land until she died.'

There was nothing more to say. We hugged.

Joan Zawatzky

Fifteen

Franz Brauer's failure to contact me was on my mind all week. It was about time he revealed the real reason for the damage to the house. I checked the time. If I phoned Vienna right then, he and Alex would be up and about. After all, they had young children.

Sounding sleepy, Franz answered the phone. I apologized for disturbing him and went directly to the point of my call, the reason for the damage. He hesitated, coughed and then the truth emerged. It had been a warm day, Alex had been drying the children's jumpers in the attic and had opened all the windows. She'd had a lot on her mind, he said, and had forgotten about the windows. A day later, the weather changed dramatically and heavy snow fell. He was silent then, and all I heard was a buzz on the line. He said nothing further regarding the damage and offered no apology. I was furious and thought it best to end the conversation before I said something I regretted.

Watching the local television news became a way of familiarising myself with all that was new and strange. When I discovered SBS, a channel with an international slant, I felt more in touch with the rest of the world. What shocked and upset me most were the asylum seekers, mainly from Afghanistan, Sri Lanka, Iran and Iraq arriving in Australian waters aboard their flimsy boats. Several thousand had escaped from countries of persecution and were now held in Australian detention centres surrounded by razor wire, while they waited for their refugee claims to be assessed. I listened appalled to stories of psychiatric problems amongst the detainees.

Here I was complaining about having to resettle in a country not of my choosing, when there were all those refugees desperate to be accepted. When I heard that the government had begun to release some detainees on temporary visas to live with family and friends, I was relieved. About 100 of these bridging visas would be issued each month.

I had to be fair, there was another side to this. Terrorists could be hiding amongst the genuine asylum seekers. It was necessary for the government to assess any new entrants to the country, but I found it confusing.

One evening after work, a colleague of Richard's followed him home in a small blue car resembling many I had seen in Vienna.

'I chose this especially for you,' he smiled his happiest smile. 'You have an international driver's licence… it'll help you to get around.'

The car's stylish shape and pretty blue lured me inside. It was a second hand car that had been sprayed with a new leather scent. The following morning, I adjusted the seats, fiddled with the mirror and in seconds the motor was humming. It was an easy car to drive and I was off without knowing where I was going. Soon I was lost. Sweat poured down my shirt. In the jungle of houses, all looked the same and the streets had strange names. When I noticed a man in his garden mowing the grass, I stopped. After fumbling in my bag for the book where I'd written my address, I approached him. He was patient and gave me clear directions home. My confidence was dented, but I knew that I would be tempted out again soon.

The hot weather persuaded me to search for a swimming pool in my area. I found an outdoor pool through the internet, only a ten minute drive away. The whiff of chlorine greeted me as I paid to enter. A quick scan revealed two dedicated lanes for children, a few for older swimmers and one for the disabled. The middle lane was free and I slipped into the warm water. I swam for at least an hour, ignoring the fun loving teens in my path, the straying and the confused. The showers were disappointingly grubby but I washed off the chlorine and left.

I tried not to compare the neighbourhood pool to the scrupulously clean local indoor pool in Vienna. There the water was heated to body temperature in winter and less in summer. Fluffy white towels and a gown were included in the entrance fee.

֍

When I logged on to my computer the next morning, an email from Dr Brauer greeted me. He explained that the ceiling and walls of the house were dry but ugly water marks remained. The carpet in both of the smaller bedrooms had to be replaced, but fortunately the wooden flooring beneath was untouched and in good condition. He included a cost of painting to cover the water marks as well as new carpeting. I looked at the high price he quoted and muttered, 'no way'.

I had experienced many snow storms but couldn't recall ever having seen melted snow seep into the house. I replied saying that I would pay for the paint if he covered the stains on the ceilings and walls himself but that I would not consider replacing the carpets.

The wives of Richard's colleagues kept phoning and reluctantly I invited them to visit. Four women arrived carrying platters of cakes and biscuits. Though nothing they prepared tasted familiar, I was polite and commented on their delicious baking. I found it tiresome that they all asked the same question. "What do you think of Australia?"

Of course I smiled and said 'I love it. I'm so lucky to have come here. It's absolutely wonderful.'

One of the women called Dianne played tennis. Two of the others, whose names I've forgotten, spoke at length about their charitable work. The fourth, Jeanette, belonged to an amateur theatre company and I found her most interesting. She had played main and small parts and helped out with the lighting when she was not on stage. After telling me about the variety of parts she had played, she invited me to attend the theatre group one evening.

While we were seated around the table drinking tea, the tennis player, Dianne, asked me whether I played tennis. When I told her I had played in Vienna, she questioned me on the strength of my game, took my contact details and promised to arrange a friendly match.

The next morning, the phone rang while I was in the garden feeding the birds. It was Dianne, inviting me join her and her group of friends for a game of tennis. I had brought a tennis dress along and my racket was stacked away with Richard's golf clubs.

Anton was home early and gave a long whistle when he saw me dressed for tennis.

'You look really cool. You should wear short skirts more often.'

It was the nicest thing he'd said to me since we had arrived.

'Feeling better?' he asked.

I pulled myself upright, surprised by the question. 'Oh yes, I'm fine.'

'I didn't think you'd make it... thought you were cracking up.' he added.

'I'm tougher than you think,' I replied a little sharply.

'It hasn't exactly been fun around here.' He scratched his arm and looked down.

'You haven't said a thing about your new friend or university. Is everything okay?'

'Everything's fine and I like it here,' he said a little too quickly.

'And what do you like best about Melbourne?' I asked intrigued.

'It's more relaxed, not some many small stupid rules and the people are great. They know how to enjoy themselves, live for the day. And they're not as boring.'

When I asked how the rest of the holiday spent with the Webers went, he shrugged. 'It wasn't that good. I should've come back with you and dad. That old bloke Weber's a bit of a dictator... had each minute of the day mapped out for us.'

'I've noticed, he's very organised.'

He took a few steps in the direction of the staircase.

'Everything going okay with settling in?' I asked.

'I've met a few people,' he said, walking towards the staircase. 'Enjoy the tennis,' he called out, as he took the first steps up the stairs.

Dianne's directions were simple to follow and I found the courts easily. I was nervous about playing with strangers at first, but after introductions were made, I ran onto the court to face my opponent. My nerves had settled and my first serve was in, hard and fast. Though I enjoyed the game, my play was uneven and I lost by a wide margin. I was surprised when I was invited to play again the following week.

Later that week, I followed up Jeanette's invitation to the acting group. It was in a church hall in the next suburb. I had only performed on stage as a piano soloist. Though my father was an actor and his parents had been actors in Yiddish theatre, I doubted that I had inherited their talent. It did not concern me, producing a play required many helpers and I'd find a spot. I was greeted with words of welcome by the eighteen members. Jeanette introduced to me each one, from the older women dressed as hippies in long skirts and beads, to the three conservative men in flannels and cardigans. The rest fitted somewhere between. I immediately felt at ease.

At the first meeting, my reservations about my lack of acting talent proved correct. I had hoped that the brilliance in my genes would flow through me and animate me, but I was wooden and awkward. It was not the sort of thing one could practice or learn. One either had the ability or one didn't. But they were delighted that I could paint and asked if I would help with the scenery. I had not held a paint brush for many years, yet I was confident that I would be able to call on my talent in that area.

Over a weekend, five of us painted the scenery for the rural drama set around the turn of the nineteenth century. We took more time over reaching agreement on the design than in paining the cottage, trees and mountain backdrop. Once we began to paint, we worked as a team and enjoyed ourselves, laughing and joking at our efforts. The countryside we painted looked rough and too gaudy for my taste but I doubted it mattered. The players were thrilled with it.

By the final rehearsal, my task was complete. I sat in the audience and watched the entire play for the first time. Though I enjoyed the acting, the pace was too slow to engage me. In the anonymity of the near dark, I sank into the velvet seat and imagined that the men dressed in costumes of the period were my uncles, cousins or even my grandfather. Though Mama had told me that my paternal grandparents were actors in Vienna's early days of Yiddish theatre, it was Ernst who had filled in the details.

I thought of Gabe, the more outgoing of my boys. He liked to perform, played the guitar well and sang. Though his voice was not exceptional, he could draw a crowd at university. Like me, Anton avoided being in the public eye and appeared to have no misgivings about his lack of dramatic talent.

Sixteen

Once I had discovered that Ernst was an abundant source of information about my family's past and that he enjoyed talking about it, I waited for opportunities when we were alone to question him. One evening, Mama invited Ernst for dinner but dashed to the shops for a last minute purchase. Though I offered to do the shopping for her, Mama suggested I stay with Ernst instead. I offered him coffee while we waited.

He winked at me. 'You've found that good coffee helps me to remember. Not so, my dear?'

I nodded and smiled.

'Your mother prefers not to think about the past but I'm older than her and I find myself thinking of it all the time. What is it you want to know this time?'

'Did you meet my father's parents? I don't know anything about them.'

'Your Opi Maurice and Omi Dora?'

I nodded again.

He laughed. 'Everyone knew them. They were amongst the first actors in Viennese Yiddish theatre, celebrities when I met them. Elderly of course, but people treated them like the film stars we know today.' He sipped his coffee and slowly placed the cup on its saucer. 'It was fortunate for them that they died before the *Anschluss.*'

'Were they very old when they died?'

'Your Opi collapsed and died just after a performance in the theatre in the *Nestroyhof, Praterstrasse*. He was about seventy. After that Dora refused to go on the stage or be seen socially and she died a year later.'

'That's sad, poor Omi died of a broken heart.'

'You could say that, my dear.'

I looked at the clock, hoping Mama would not burst in while Ernest was talking. There was so much I wanted to know.

'Your Omi told me that her parents were born in a small town in Romania but moved to Vienna in the early 1890's.' He ran his hand through his curly grey hair. 'Strange how I remember all these little details about the past but I don't know where I left my hat or my glasses.'

I nodded encouragingly, hoping to hear more.

'You know, your Omi's father and brother were players, travelling from town to town singing and performing bible tales and sad stories about the lot of Jews at the time. Women weren't seen on the stage in those days and female parts were played by young men. This changed of course, and by the time she had married Maurice, your Opi, she had had a stage career. Your Opi didn't start off as an actor but he learned fast. By the time he joined the family on stage, he had developed his own style and had a big following.'

'So, my papa was born into a real theatrical family?'

'Oh yes, my dear…and your Opi and your father had more natural talent than the rest of them.'

I laughed.

'By 1930 when your grandparents were stars, theatre was a vital part of our cultural life here in Leopoldstadt. We had brilliant dramas, cabaret and operettas in both German and Yiddish. That's when your grandparents were stars.'

'Why didn't Mama tell me?'

He shrugged. 'A lot of the Viennese Jews people didn't like Romanians…thought of them as *zigeuner*…gypsies, acting and playing gypsy violin music.'

'That's not right…not fair.'

'Well, people considered them as uneducated. Even then, here in Vienna as in Germany, education was very important. In Romania many talented Jews formed troupes of players and roamed the country travelling from town to town playing.'

'Did my papa go to school?'

'No, he couldn't with the constant travelling, but he had tutors amongst the group who taught him the basics. When he was about sixteen he stayed in Vienna for a few years and went to the Polytechnic.'

Just then, Mama burst in carrying parcels. 'What have I interrupted, you both look serious?'

'I'm telling Ellie about Maurice and Dora. She asked about them.'

Mama put her parcels down slowly and busied herself opening them. 'I'm glad that you're telling her about them. I know I should've told her but somehow…'

'It's alright Mama,' I said softly.

Seventeen

Before work, I checked my computer for emails. A message from Luke was waiting and I opened it quickly.

> *I've met a few people who have been to Australia recently and loved it. Right now I'd like nothing more than to get out of the cold. If not for my commitments, I'd join you tomorrow. I've been thinking of taking a holiday in Australia, if I can arrange it.*

After reading the email I deleted it and condemned the file to the recycle bin. As far as I could tell, Richard was not snooping by logging onto my emails but I did not take chances with any of my correspondence.

What had swung Luke around? Only months earlier, "Vienna was the greatest city in Europe" with so much to offer that he could spend the rest of his life there without a holiday.

His mother had died recently, only a year after his father. He had placed her in an aged facility but had not visited her. I doubted whether her death would've accounted for his sudden desire to leave Vienna. Something more dramatic must have happened to alter his views.

Luke talked freely about most things but clammed up about his early home life and I had learned not to question him.

I knew his mother was the stricter parent. I could tell that she had beaten him by the welts on his legs but he refused to talk about it. There was a wide gap in ages between himself and his parents. His father was in his early fifties and his mother was thirty- nine when they had their first son Gunther, who had left home early and rarely visited. Luke came along two years later.

As much as I longed to see Luke, I would not allow myself to bank on his visit to Australia. Being negative was easier than being disappointed.

The day was unseasonably chilly and the wind gusty. Trees swayed and flowers shook. The *pfutt pfutt* sounds of a motorcycle in the street grew louder as it approached the house. A man clothed in a waterproof yellow coat, pants and helmet pulled up and waved to me, 'Post for you!'

I raced towards him hoping for a package from home. It was a letter. I tore it open. Rabbi Rabinovitz from the North Eastern synagogue in Melbourne, our closest shul, had written to us. It was a formal welcome to Melbourne on behalf of himself, the committee of the synagogue and the Jewish community in the area. Attached to the letter was a brochure outlining prayer times and some of the social activities organised by the committee. My initial impulse was to tear it up but I stopped myself. Richard had a right to see it. Mystified as to how the Rabbi could have discovered that we had arrived in Melbourne and that we were a Jewish family, I left the letter open on Richard's desk. I felt certain that he had something to do with it.

After dinner Richard went to his study. Later he gave a loud guffaw and walked towards me with the letter in his hand. 'The letter from the Rabbi is open ... so you've seen it, eh?'

'There's only one way he could've found out about us. You must've made some inquiries.'

'Quite right. I wrote to the Jewish Board of Deputies here before we left Vienna, to ask what they had to offer us. I knew where the house was.... what suburb it was in. So they've done the right thing and answered my query.'

'But you've never shown interest in Judaism, not since I've known you.'

'Call it an insurance policy. One never knows when we might need them.'

'You mean if one of us dies and we need them for burial?'

He shrugged. 'One never knows what can happen in a strange land.'

'Well I'm not contacting the Rabbi. You can if you want to.'

❧

I met Magda at our usual spot. That day she was dressed in white jeans and a slim fitting top that suited her blonde hair and cut years off her age. She told me how thrilled she was that orders for her chocolates were pouring in from all over the country and that her business was booming.

She took my hand. 'Work keeps me busy and I love the money. If you start working you won't look back. I can't sit around all day doing nothing. I don't know how you can.'

'But...'

'With your qualifications it should be easy.'

'I'm not so sure.'

'Libraries must be the same all over the world and you speak good English. You'll see, you won't have difficulty finding a job.' Magda tapped the table with her painted nails.

'I don't know.'

Magda was a practical woman but she could be pushy. She tossed her head as she explained that she had taken a job two weeks after arriving in Melbourne and not a glamorous job either. Her work on a factory assembly line was a start, but from there she moved on.

'I don't want to take the wrong position in a hurry.'

Magda continued talking but I had stopped listening. My hand gravitated to my unstyled hair. I was a mess. It couldn't have happened in Vienna, where I'd made a point of not leaving the house unless I was well turned out. Perhaps Magda was right, work would do the trick. I'd have to be well groomed at work.

Magda stopped talking when she noticed the shift in my attention.

'Sorry, have I said the wrong thing... upset you?

'No, not at all,' I replied softly and smiled as she went on talking.

Two days later I sat at my desk with the light streaming in behind me. I read as much as I could find on the internet about public libraries in Melbourne, their location and the state's policy. At first I was confused by the bureaucratic language that highlighted differences between overseas and Australian public libraries, but as I continued reading a commonality became clearer. All the libraries were non-profit collections of books of many types for distribution to the general public. I consulted a city map and found a group of suburban library branches. There were two within a short drive from the house. I steeled myself and made an introductory phone call. The first library near home that I approached, asked me to come in for an interview.

I dressed in my only suit, the one I had worn when I left Vienna. Just a hint of lipstick and my hair tied back and I looked vaguely academic. I found the library housed in a rectangular building, tucked behind a clump of trees at the tail end of a shopping centre. Though it was a regional library with a larger range of books than some of the other branches, it seemed small. Inside, the library was modern and airy with a layout that was familiar. The senior librarian introduced herself as Deidre Falconer and looked about twenty-eight. She ushered me into her partitioned space, filled with piles of new books for approval. I didn't wait for her to ask for my credentials and handed her my resume and two references from past employers.

She flicked her cascading hair from her face, placed her elbows on the desk and read about me. While she read, I looked at the titles of the new books in the pile closest to me. Some were tempting and I would have liked to take them home to read.

She looked up at last. 'Very impressive indeed.'

Her questions that followed were direct but asked in a friendly manner. After about twenty minutes, she held up her hand and laughed.

'Enough! You're more qualified than me.' She made a dismissive gesture. 'But, you've only been in Melbourne a short while and at this stage I can only offer you work here on a casual basis.' She glanced at a roster on her desk. 'If you decide to stay in Australia permanently, we can talk and go into the paperwork.'

I tried not to show my disappointment.

'Things can change,' she said kindly.

The duties she listed were simple and the routine was similar to the one I had followed as a junior.

I nodded. 'That will be fine.'

She introduced me to the staff members and I left. It felt strange knowing that I had made a commitment, that I had a job in the new country.

Along the route home I had discovered parkland dissected by a narrow ribbon of water. I parked the car and walked toward the narrow ribbon of water. I held down the grass, tall rushes and avoided the prickly weeds as I made my way to a grassy spot. I sighed with pleasure as I watched leaves stand and fall and clumps of wild flowers quivering in a gust of wind. As I inhaled the scent of the flowers I closed my eyes. Within seconds I was back in the garden of the old house in Leopoldstadt.

Mama was trimming the flowering mauve wisteria that crept along the tall stone wall. Its scent permeated the garden. It was a splendid garden with lilies, lilacs and roses as well as a small vegetable garden along the side of the house. She spent all her free time in the garden and disliked being disturbed with any of my offers of assistance or requests to pick flowers. I watched her from a distance. After completing her work, she sat in front of the tallest of the cypresses, surrounded by an inner row of anemones and a border of pink roses. She said that sitting there made her feel at peace and reminded her of my father. When I was older I realised that she had created the floral shrine for him.

The trees in the garden were huge with old chestnuts and lindens along the stone wall and further in, almonds and fruit trees. I picked all the almonds I could hold, stuffed them into my pockets and then smashed them open with a rock. Mama had a nutcracker inside but I preferred to nibble the broken nuts in the garden. From an early age, I learned to climb the trees and hide amongst their branches. Though I would have liked a real tree house like the ones in other gardens in the street, one summer

Luke and I built a make-shift tree house. We found cardboard, wood and nails in old uninhabited houses, unclaimed since the end of the war. The delicate structure balanced in the crook of branches and was relatively stable. We sat up there reading or eating sweets and cake we had saved. The tree house lasted that one summer until the rains came.

It was my first intense and enthralling period alone with Luke. I was only eight years old but I loved him more than any other person I knew, even more than Mama. I couldn't imagine a day passing without him. He was smarter than all the children I'd met. He knew the names of just about every plant and tree, all about the mountains as well as practical information about survival in the outdoors in different climates and environments. We made up games and spoke in our own language. Our double-talk, as we called it, developed then. He would start a sentence and I finished it. Each time he swore that the words I used were those in his head.

Eighteen

The staff at the library were genuinely friendly and helpful. They organised a welcoming tea for me with a home – baked, celebratory cake. I appreciated the way they included me in their conversations and invited me to join them whenever they went out for lunch. I could not believe my luck and I planned to reciprocate by inviting them home for a typical Austrian dinner.

Of all the staff, Ruth Horvath, a diminutive woman with a slight European accent was the friendliest. She said that she understood what emigration was about. She had left Hungary with her parents twenty-nine years earlier and arrived in Australia as a refugee. She did not expand on her experiences but left me with the impression that she would share the details with me in the future.

The library was a comfortable oasis of familiarity that surrounded me with books, cataloguing systems and readers. One of my tasks was to assist borrowers in locating books on the shelves. In the open plan office, I had access to a computer and phone. I helped many of the local women. It was hard to draw any conclusions from the small sample but the group I met were friendly. I wondered how they perceived me and whether they noticed that I was still uncertain of myself.

Most of the books in the Vienna library were in German or English with a small proportion in other European languages. This was the first time I had come across a large number of books on a variety of topics written by Australians. Each week I took home a pile to read, beginning with classics by Miles

Franklin and Henry Lawson. I hoped to learn about the country through its authors.

I found shopping at the suburban supermarket bewildering and time consuming. Apart from international brands like Nescafe and Sara Lee, food buying was trial and error. I read the labels of locally produced biscuits or cereal carefully but when I tasted them, the flavour or the consistency was nothing like those I knew and liked. It was too soon to acquire a taste for Australian food and I hunted for a delicatessen that sold European delicacies. A narrow, slightly grubby shop in an alley behind the hairdresser sold a few of the foods I missed like bratwurst, leberkase and my favourite cake in a tin, *Linzer torte*. After spending as much at the delicatessen as at the supermarket, I carried home several heavy packages.

The drive home continued to confuse me. I passed a few blocks of tree lined streets with well cared for homes and only a kilometre or two further, the scene changed markedly to overgrown gardens, grass overtaking the pavements and houses with paint peeling from timber walls. What a jolt! I had assumed that like the Viennese, Melburnians had strict rules about keeping homes and common areas like sidewalks and pavements neat.

One afternoon, I was working at the back of the library checking a delivery of new books with Ruth. It was a simple task that allowed us to talk as we worked. Ruth glanced at her watch. She told me that she was leaving early as it was a Jewish holiday and she had to prepare for visitors.

'What are you preparing?' I enquired.

She smiled and described the menu.

I nodded. 'Delicious... I remember.'

I knew some of the names of the delicacies that Mama occasionally bought from the kosher shop owned by Mr Kappelovitz.

She stared at me. 'Oh, so you're Jewish? I wouldn't have known it with that hair of yours and your green eyes.'

'I am, but I don't practice my religion.'

Ruth did not comment and we carried on with our task. At 4.30 she stopped work and retrieved her handbag from her desk.

'I'm off home now.' She leaned forward, kissed my cheek and whispered, '*Chag Sameach*'.

I had no idea what the salutation meant. I had heard it before but I couldn't recall where or when.

She stopped before walking off, 'How about you, Richard and your son joining us for a Sabbath meal...next Friday night?'

'Thank you, I'd love to come but I'll have to check with Richard. And I don't know about Anton but I'll ask.'

Ruth was small and plump but pretty and her light brown hair formed a curly halo around her oval face. Her dark eyes were her most arresting feature. How different Ruth and Magda were and how fortunate I was to have them both as new friends.

Later that evening when I told Richard about the invitation, he initially mumbled excuses. When I explained that Ruth's husband Paul was a solicitor, his attitude changed.

'Perhaps we should go. We know so few Australians and it would be a good idea to make some new friends.'

I was right about Anton not being interested in joining us. He curled his lip and mumbled, 'No thanks'.

The phrase *Chag Sameach* echoed within me and I repeated it again and again. The following day I accepted Ruth's invitation but worried how I would cope with a meal at a religious home, when I did not have a clue about the Jewish Sabbath? I knew about not eating pork and guiltily I thought about how much ham I had eaten on sandwiches.

Joan Zawatzky

Nineteen

One morning while I was hanging out the washing, the breeze was up and I thought of Mama.

Her basket was empty and the sheets and towels billowed in the wind. She sang to herself softly: '_Roshinkes mit mandeln, shlof zhe Yidele, shlof_'

When I asked her what she was singing, she smiled wistfully. 'It's part of a Yiddish lullaby my father sang to me..._raisins and almonds, sleep little one sleep_...but I don't remember the rest.'

'Please tell me about your father...my Grandpapa,' I asked.

'I don't know much, only the little he told me.'

'Please, Mama.'

She picked up the basket and I followed her into the kitchen. While she poured the remains of the morning's coffee into cups, she hummed the same tune. Since Ernst had told me a little about my family I thirsted for more information.

'Your grandfather Avram was born in a _shtetl_, a small village in Hungary in the late eighteen hundreds. For centuries Jews weren't allowed to own a business or have a profession and the only work open to his family was peddling and money lending.'

'Oh, Mama!'

'Sad, but that's how it was.' She sighed and was silent.

'The Emperor Joseph the Second was more tolerant towards Jews. Life moved slowly in the _shtetl_, your grandfather knew only the family peddling trade and with his father's old cart and horse he went from house to house buying and selling rags and second hand clothes.'

'Please Mama, tell me anything else you know.' I said impatiently.

'People were starving and news filtered through that life was easier in Vienna, and so your grandpapa and the rest of the family packed and left Hungary with hope of a better life. By then it was too late for him to choose a new occupation.'

'Poor Grandpapa!'

'You don't need to feel sorry for him. He had no education but he was shrewd and saved his money. Later, when the trade routes opened to Bohemia and Germany, he travelled and bought rolls of silk and ribbons, which he sold at high prices. In a few years he no longer peddled rags but traded in the best fabrics from all over Europe. Today people would call him a good businessman.'

Mama stared out of the window and said wistfully, 'I loved him when I was little…before he was wealthy. During the week he travelled between *shtetls* selling his goods but every Friday afternoon he drove his cart home. He wouldn't say a word to us until grandmama had boiled some water for his bath. Then he'd put on clean clothes and look all pink and smiley. He'd open his arms to my brother and me. We ran to him and he'd hug and kiss us. I don't like to think of my little brother, only five when he died of the flu… and poor little Jennie gone three weeks after she was born.'

'That's very sad, Mama,' I said.

Mama sighed deeply.

I pressed on with my questions. 'How did my grandparents meet?'

She sipped the last of her coffee before replying. 'They met during grandpapa's travels. He stopped at a wealthy man's home to sell his wares and met a pretty girl called Dorit. They fell in love and after some time wanted to marry. Her parents were not at all pleased that their educated, pretty daughter was in love with a rag man. After their attempt to stop the two from meeting failed, they caved in but they made their objections clear. They refused to give the couple money and a small wedding was arranged. She had plenty love but lived in poverty for the first years of her marriage. Then it all changed.'

'What happened?'

'I told you that your grandpapa was shrewd,' she smiled one of her rare smiles. 'Through his smart buying he saved a lot of money. Friends suggested he invest on the stock exchange and so he experimented. His investments paid off and his wealth grew.'

Mama explained that she was ten by then. He could afford to buy her pretty dresses and send her to school. He bought the double storey house in *Weintraubengasse*. The old house looked different in those days, Mama said. She described its marble banisters and serving areas in the kitchen, a lavish sitting room large enough for a piano for grandmama. By then Grandpapa had opened his shop in Leopoldstadt selling fine materials, cottons and braids. The shop was a success and Grandpapa became rich but the family did not join the wealthy Jews who moved to the inner city. They remained in their house but redecorated the interior in the popular Art Nouveau style with the help of artists and craftsmen from the *Wiener Werkstatte*. They owned fine paintings, silverware and furniture.

'Poor Papa. When he was a young man he thought of himself as a German first and then a Jew. They must have known about Hitler's growing popularity and the rise of anti-Semitism but they ignored it in the beginning. They left it too late to escape. By November 1938, on Kristallnacht, the Nazis marched in destroying all Jewish property they came across. They smashed Papa's shop and took what they fancied from the house as well - china, cutlery and fine Bohemian glassware. From what was left, your grandmother took a carved chair and a silver tea set and a few porcelain cups. She wrapped them in sheets and hid them in the attic.'

'Your special chair and the antique tea set that is so tiresome to polish?

'Yes, and I'm lucky to have them now... but your poor Grandmama was so distressed by the upheaval that a month later she died of a heart attack. She was only in her forties, you know. Very young to die.'

'What happened later as Hitler rose in power?' I asked tentatively.

'By 1941 Papa was seized and sent to Dachau Concentration Camp. He perished in his second month at the camp.'

I could tell that Mama would've preferred to stop talking and prepare the meal but I sat there, waiting for her to continue. She explained that the family was not very religious. She remembered going to synagogue with her parents twice a year for the main festivals – *Rosh Hashanah*, the New Year and *Yom Kippur,* the Day of Atonement.

Her expression was sad again as she looked down. 'Each New Year festival I was given a new dress to wear to shul. The last of my special dresses I wore on the day I was taken to Jana's home. I remember it clearly because it was two days after New Year, the last time I went into a synagogue. It was my prettiest dress, white cotton lace with a blue sash. My gold necklace with the single pearl, that Papa had given me for my birthday was clasped around my neck. When Mama told me she had packed a small suitcase for me, and that she was taking me to her friend Jana, I cried at first and refused to leave. But when she explained the reason I understood and went with her.'

Twenty

With only a vague memory of a Sabbath meal at my mother's friend Katia when I was eight or nine, I had no idea how to behave or dress for our visit to Ruth and Paul. My guess was that it would be etiquette to bring flowers or chocolates. The chocolates were easier to find and I purchased a large expensive box. I dressed early in my black dress and jacket. Nervously I added different pieces of jewellery. A shiny necklace was too much and pearls were too formal. Finally I settled for tiny earrings and a silver bracelet. While I fixed my hair, Richard changed his shirt.

Using a map to guide us, we headed towards the inner suburbs. The homes were well maintained on neat tree lined streets. Ruth greeted us warmly and introduced us to Paul, her three children and to her cousin Myra. Their home was a simple brick rectangle on the outside but inside it was adorned with paintings, unusual ornaments and Persian carpets - nothing like the bland house we were living in.

We all gravitated towards the table. On the white lace tablecloth, lit candles stood in carved, silver candlesticks. The crockery was gold trimmed and food was placed on silver platters. I took my cue from the others and stood as everyone sang a lovely melody with a refrain. Later I discovered it was a hymn called *Shalom Aleichem* about two angels, one good and one evil, who accompanied Jews on their way home from synagogue. Paul made a blessing over the wine, and then poured small amounts from his large silver cup into tiny cups so that we could all share in the blessing. We all went to wash our hands, pouring water out of a silver beaker that had handles on either side, and then remained silent until our host was ready to bless the *Challahs* or plaited breads. He held the two *Challahs* together, and said the blessing in Hebrew. He then broke the bread into pieces, placed them in a basket, sprinkled salt on the portions and handed it around the table. Like the others, I ate the sweet bread that tasted like cake. I glanced at Richard, wishing he could explain the meaning of the ritual. Though he chose not to practice his religion, he had studied for his barmitzvah all those years earlier and understood it all. I nudged him. With a hand on my shoulder, he whispered, 'Later. We'll discuss it later.'

The ball of boiled fish, Ruth called *gefilte* fish, tasted foreign and sweetish. I ate mine as the others did, with a dab of pungent horseradish. The rest of the meal was conventional. Soup, roast chicken and vegetables and a light dessert with fruit. At the end of the meal we *benched* which is the grace said after a meal and then we lingered at the table. The children had gone to bed and while we talked we nibbled nuts and chocolates. I discovered that Myra was a musician who played the violin in the Melbourne Symphony Orchestra. She had been to Vienna and to concerts at the famous Golden Hall. She went into raptures about the experience. When I told her that each year I booked ahead to ensure I had a seat to at least one concert at the Hall, she looked surprised.

'I don't meet up with classical music lovers very often in Melbourne and certainly not ones who've attended a concert by the Vienna Philharmonic in that amazing hall.' She rummaged in her handbag. 'I have free tickets for our next concert here in Melbourne, a Beethoven night. I'll be playing so you're welcome to come.'

'Melbourne has a symphony orchestra?' Richard looked up surprised.

'Oh yes, and a world standard one at that,' Ruth replied. 'Come to the concert, I'm sure you'll both enjoy it.'

During the drive home, Richard and I talked more than we had since arriving in Melbourne. Once we had discussed the house, the meal, Ruth, Paul, Myra and the children, I reminded

Richard that he had promised to explain the meaning of the Sabbath ritual.

He scratched his head. 'It's been a long time since I've thought about any of it but I can remember the basics of what I learned and saw in our home. You know how religious my parents were.' He placed his hand on mine, the first touch in months. 'The Sabbath is meant to be a day of rest, away from the stresses of the week to a more spiritual time.'

'Mmmm.'

'I'm sure you noticed the wine, challah and candles on the table. Each is symbolic. The candles are lit by the woman of the house to welcome the Sabbath. The blessing over the wine and bread… well, that's about making the Sabbath holy.'

'You were brought up in a religious home, unlike me and you've discarded it all. I've never understood.'

'I don't want to talk about it… about them. Too much of anything can turn one away.'

We were almost home when I sat up with a start. 'We'll have to reciprocate. Even on a week night it will be a problem. They're religious people.'

'It will be fine. We'll run through a menu together. Don't worry about it.'

Twenty-One

Preparations for Passover were being made in most of the houses in our street and throughout Leopoldstadt, but not in our house. Girls and young women helped their mothers prepare for the *seder*. In Rifka Friedman's home, the dining table had been moved to the front room and was extended by adding on a small table to accommodate the twenty-eight people expected for the meal. It was Rifka's job to dress the table with their best white damask tablecloth and lay places with fine china and glassware, kept especially for this occasion. I helped her give the silver knives and forks an extra rub and place the glasses correctly. She liked the fancy way I folded the napkins to make the table look more festive.

I tried to cover up my ignorance about the relevance of the holiday but it did not take long for her to realise it. Rifka placed her hands on her hips and shook her head in disgust when I questioned the effort she, her sister and mother had gone to, cleansing the house of all bread, pasta, rye, barley and wheat - products called *chametz*, prohibited over the week long Passover festival

'We are remembering the bible story about the time when the Israelites were freed from slavery in Egypt. They were in such a hurry to leave there was no time to bake bread and so they ate unleavened bread like our *matzo*,' she said as she placed the *matzo* at the head of the table. She was about to continue explaining, when Mrs Friedman called us from the kitchen.

Mrs Friedman was frying fish for the meal and gave us small bits as it came off the pan. It was moist and tasty and I longed for more. Rifka and her mother knew that Mama didn't celebrate Passover and I recognised pity in their faces. Mrs Friedman invited me to join them for the *seder*. I thanked her but refused the invitation. I would've been out of place with her family, the only one who had not attended synagogue prior to the meal. Mama had not been invited. How could I leave her at home alone?

During the following morning when most of the residents of Leopoldstadt were at shul, Luke and I decided to have our own celebration. I packed a small basket with fruit, bottled water, sandwiches and a few chocolates that I took from Mama's hiding place in the cupboard. We chose the grandest place we knew, the *Schonbrunn* Palace garden.

It was spring and the best time to visit the gardens. Each visit to the huge baroque palace dominating the gardens was a thrill. We rediscovered the symmetrically arranged flowerbeds, statues, fountains and monuments laid out in the eighteenth century during Marie-Theresa's reign. The formal hedges formed passageways that had hidden enclosures. Luke found a secret spot and we ate when the sun was overhead. Later, with the palace in the background we made love in the soft grass. When we returned to Leopoldstadt the aroma of chicken soup and lit windows in the Jewish homes welcomed us. Dining rooms were crowded and the sounds of prayer emanated from some, while laughter came from others. Luke hurried indoors but I lingered in the street, picturing the people around the Friedman's table.

Twenty-Two

Richard looked tense and tired and no longer spoke enthusiastically about his work. 'At least in Vienna I knew where I was, understood the politics and could plan my strategy. Here I never know when to expect a move against me. I can't seem to do a thing right. '

'But they were so welcoming when you first arrived,' I said

'It's not an easy situation. Before I came, mistakes were covered up and forgotten. I've been unearthing things and asking questions and it's not making me the most popular person.'

Richard talked often of Vienna and hankered for his cousins. He wouldn't admit that he wished he had turned down the option to move to Melbourne, but I gained the impression that he felt that way.

The Sunday before we left Vienna, we visited Richard's cousin Willie and his wife Edna who lived in *Grinzing*, a village in the Woods. Richard and his cousins did not always see things in the same perspective, but they were family and that's what mattered. I found many of Willie and Edna's views strange and authoritarian but when I visited their home, I said little. Though Willie was only two years older than Richard, he behaved like Richard's uncle. Both Richard and Willie had the family's olive skin, dark hair and eyes but there the resemblance ended.

The day was cool and Willie had lit a fire. Once the children and grandchildren had arrived for lunch, we were twenty around the table. Willie thumped the table with his fist to announce that he intended tell *the* family story. Everyone had heard it so often that it had lost its poignancy. The sighs and moans did not deter him.

Every family I knew appeared to have a story connected to one of the two world wars. Willie began by telling us that on a warm spring morning in 1938, his grandfather Max and Richard's grandfather, Rubin, left their home in Vienna at first light and took a short cut through the woods. Hiking and climbing was their passion and this early walk was meant to mark the start of another climbing season. They intended to take the path up the hill, which was a relatively easy walk, descend through the vineyards and then pass the house where Beethoven once stayed. If they hurried they could be back home to eat breakfast and ride their bicycles to school.

When they reached the ancient church of St Josef near the hill's peak, Max stopped to appreciate the view. As he shielded his eyes from the early sunlight, he noticed movement in the distance. He focussed his attention and saw a huge army moving forward. The brothers' fears were realised, the Germans were advancing.

They descended hastily, planning to run home to warn their parents and neighbours but the army was closing in. All they could do was hide. As children, they had often played in the forest and knew of a large hollow tree, where if they squeezed in they thought they wouldn't be noticed. They remained there for three days while the Germans combed the forest for Jews and dissenters.

'How could they have stayed in that tree for three days?' Richard interrupted loudly. 'Dad showed me the tree once. The hole is much too small…it just isn't possible.'

Willie glared at Richard. 'I can only tell everyone the story my father told me.'

He took a sip of wine. 'This is the most unpleasant part of the story, so let's get it over with. I hope we won't have any more interruptions,'

'Once the Germans left, the brothers returned to the house at night, careful not to be spotted by their gentile neighbours, who they feared might have handed them over to the German authorities. The house was empty. Cupboards were bare and all clothing gone, but the food their mother had hidden for *those times when they had nothing*, was untouched. The boys took the food, some old, torn blankets, clothing that had been left by the looters and fled to the forest. They didn't dare think of what might have happened to their parents.'

I watched Richard wriggle uncomfortably as his cousin reached the part of the story where Max became ill during the winter and died, and Rubin had no choice but to bury his brother under a tree.

'This is where things improve,' Willie said, as he told us how Rubin spent the rest of the winter in a friendly farmer's loft and in the spring returned to the forests. He explained that Rubin was attuned to the sounds of the forest at night. When he heard footsteps, he reacted instantly and hid under leafy branches. He listened hard to whispered words and waited for the newcomers to settle for the night. In the morning, he found three children aged nine or ten lying huddled together. He approached them slowly and found that they were alone, having run from their village when the Germans arrived.'

'Why were they alone in the forest?' one of Willie's grandchildren called out.

'Because their parents had been captured or killed by the Nazis and they were left to fend for themselves.'

'Shush, or he'll never finish the story,' Edna whispered.

Willie took another sip of his wine. 'Rubin didn't have the heart to leave the children and suggested they join him. Together they lived in the forest until the war was over. And I'm proud to tell you that two of the children are still alive and members of our community. Unfortunately, the third died.'

Family members clapped loudly.

'Now, you tell the end of the story,' Willie said, turning to Richard. 'He's your grandfather.'

'Ah, come on, Richard,' one of the younger cousins called out.

I put my hand on Richard's arm but he nudged me away.

'Well, here goes then. When the war was over, my grandfather returned to the house where he grew up. Neighbours told him that his parents were seized by the soldiers and sent to Treblinka Concentration camp where they died. I did some research and discovered that both my great grandparents had perished in the gas chambers.'

Then Willie spoke. 'Thank you Richard. That's awful but at least we know.'

There was a silence and then Edna came from the kitchen carrying a huge soup tureen.

'Life must go on. Let's eat,' Edna said, as she placed the tureen on the table.

The rest of the afternoon passed agreeably. Richard made an effort not to argue with Willie or make controversial comments. Finally we kissed the relatives goodbye and left.

In the car Richard exploded. 'I can't see how they all believe that story about the forest. My father didn't believe it either.'

'I believe it,' Anton said.

'My case rests then,' Richard said with a shrug.

Richard's parents had died before we married. All I knew about them was through Richard. He described his father as a frightened man who coped by rigidly following his religion and living by rules. He expected Richard to do the same but by eighteen Richard had completed his schooling and instead of becoming the Rabbi his father had hoped for, he chose to study engineering. He caused a family upheaval when he refused to study in Vienna and moved to Salzburg. The day he left his home and his father, he made a decision to turn his back on religion.

Twenty-Three

A registered letter arrived early one morning addressed to me in German. I opened it at the breakfast table. Richard peered over my shoulder and we read it together. The largest real estate company in Vienna, acting on behalf of their clients, a group of developers, were interested in buying the old house in *Weintraubengasse.* They asked me to let them know if I was interested in selling. They indicated that the property could fetch a substantial amount.

We were both running late for work and there wasn't time to discuss it then. The letter remained on my mind all day. I was certain that the developers would tear the house down and either put up a hideous modern apartment block or several small dwellings on the land. My recent experience with the Brauers had been unpleasant and I couldn't possibly look after the house from a distance. Selling it would be the most sensible approach. Later when we discussed the developers' offer, Richard was in favour of selling. He had advised me to sell the house for years.

The following day, Richard surprised me with a reminder about the concert tickets Myra had given us.

'Yes, let's go,' I replied instantly.

'Saturday night then,' he said, taking a bite of a Danish pastry with his coffee.

'Ummm... where did you find these... just delicious, like home.' he said, rubbing his hands from the sticky pastry.

I told him about the delicatessen near the library but he was no longer listening.

We were early for the concert and followed the throng into the hall. Once seated, I admired the unusual timber-like quality of the concert hall. The buzz of an auditorium with its atmosphere of polite anticipation prior to a concert had been a thrill since childhood. Once the orchestra began to play my surroundings became misty and my mind took flight. I was back in Vienna in the magnificent Golden Hall, enraptured by the Vienna Philharmonic Orchestra.

As the conductor lowered his baton, Richard stroked my arm. I sat up with a start, aware again of the comfortable seat and my feet on the floor of the Melbourne Concert Hall. I tried to disguise my disappointed sigh.

During the brief interval we stood to stretch our legs.

'And where have you been?' Richard said with a smile.

'Oh ... enjoying the music,' I decided not try to explain my daydream.

During the next half, I laced my hands, squeezing my fingers tightly to force myself to concentrate on the Bach Violin concerto. Myra was easy to spot as First Violin and her playing was masterful. We clapped enthusiastically. After a brief encore, we shuffled out of the packed auditorium and headed for the coffee shop. It was noisy and modern inside and the young waiter was rude. It was nothing like my favourite, plush *kaffeehaus* in Vienna. No chandeliers, embossed mirrors or private booths and no *sachertorte* with whipped cream and milky coffee. We had Cappuccinos with muffins instead.

'Isn't the music wonderful? I admit I'm surprised.'

'Oh yes. An excellent orchestra, just as Ruth promised. And did you notice Myra?' I said.

'She's excellent.'

As I sat in the stiff chair, spooning up the dregs of my coffee froth, Richard's voice faded. My imagination was in flight again.

Luke was beside me in the kaffeehaus, after we attended a concert matinee together at the Golden Hall. We went to concerts regularly but this festive concert in the magnificent Baroque hall was a special treat.

I looked at him intently, drinking in his image. Soon I would be leaving for Australia. Would I see him again? Though his hair was greyer than brown now, in every other respect he had not changed much from the tall blue eyed young boy I had fancied.

'I'm going to miss you,' he said as his hand travelled over the white tablecloth in my direction.

As I looked away, he withdrew it. Quickly, I returned to the safer subject of the concert and the particular talent of a young flautist. I watched his forehead crease in a frown.

'You're sure Richard hasn't said anything about us going to the concerts together all this time?'

'No of course not, Richard knows we're old friends.'

Richard's sharp tap on the table brought me back to the modern café with him sitting next to me. He looked peeved. 'Where did you drift off to this time? It's the second time tonight.' He didn't wait for a reply. 'If you've finished your coffee, we'd better get going. Another early meeting tomorrow. I'm worn out.' In the car he didn't say much. He was planning his week at work.

At the library next morning, my mood was flat. I went about my duties with barely a comment.

Ruth noticed the change in me. 'Anything bothering you?'

'Just coming down to earth after the concert. We enjoyed it so much and Myra played like an angel.'

'I'll tell her.'

School children were frequent visitors at the library. I talked to them often but I had to ask them to repeat words. As hard as I tried, I had trouble grasping the Australian accent, especially the slang. At the time, I didn't realise that though I spoke what was termed "a good English" some of the children probably had as much trouble understanding me. Months later I could laugh about accents.

Twenty-Four

I watched the hours tick past slowly, longing to leave. When at last my work day was over, I walked past the busy suburban street towards the car park. No inviting shops to browse through or cafés to lose myself in. I drove to the white house that was not my home.

Not a single light greeted me as I turned into the driveway. Richard's car wasn't in the garage and there was no sign of Anton either. There was a casserole in the fridge and I heated a portion, the flavour intense after standing for a day. As the kettle boiled for coffee, I checked the clock. Still no sign of Richard or Anton. I hadn't known Anton to be as late as this before. I ran through our brief conversation that morning. He had not mentioned a late lecture.

The empty house felt cold, and with a shiver I turned on the kitchen heating. The kitchen became the warmest room in the house. When I switched on the small television, figures on the screen bobbed and talked but I wasn't watching.

I thought of Ruth, the way her customary earnest expression shifted and her eyes shone when she was interested or amused. She appeared to be settled and content, but all she had revealed to me was an idealised postcard picture of her life. Though I had visited Ruth a few times and spent many hours with her at work, I knew no more about her. She knew even less about me. I wondered if she realised that I had no idea of what being Jewish meant.

When Anton called my name, I was back with a jolt. He gave me a perfunctory kiss on the cheek and edged away, avoiding questions. When I offered him food, he held his stomach and said he was too full to eat another thing. He glanced about looking for his father, and noticing he was not home, made his way up the stairs. I called out "good night" and heard a mumble in response.

Richard arrived half an hour later.

'I've given every ounce to this job and it's never enough,' he complained, as he collapsed into his chair.

I placed his microwave heated dinner in front of him as well as three bottles of beer, his usual quota. He nodded his thanks and increased the volume of the television. After his meal, he opened the top button of his trousers and his bulging gut protruded. He was putting on weight rapidly. If his lack of exercise and high calorie intake continued, I dreaded what he might turn into.

Like most evenings since we had arrived, he answered my questions in monosyllables and showed no interest in my day. I tried hard to forgive him, put his self-involvement down to his demanding work and exhaustion, but my empathy was wearing thin. It would be another night without as much as a good night kiss. I had memories of passionate nights when we were newly married. Now I battled to reconcile them with the person I was living with. Had his libido shrunk with his corresponding weight gain or was he being satisfied elsewhere? I did not spend long pondering the question. If he hadn't been so self-absorbed, Richard would've realised that I longed to be with Luke. I wasn't proud of myself but all that was unappealing about Richard made finding excuses for loving Luke easier. I had stopped suggesting he join a gym or offering to make him healthy food to take with him to work.

I left him snoring in front of the television and passed the sitting room on my way to the porch. The night was dark with only a slither of a moon and a few stars. The house was on a rise and the lights of Melbourne flickered in the distance. On the path a lone street light glimmered. At night in Vienna, I could distinguish the sinuous path of the Danube in the old Baroque section of the city and the streets I had once walked. I ached for my way of life in Vienna and the smell of coffee at every other corner of the city.

On evenings like this one, when Richard worked late or went straight to bed after work, I slipped out to the local *kaffeehaus*, only two blocks away. The local with its faux, tawdry décor of gold patterned wallpaper, cheap chandeliers and velveteen curtains, could not match the famous Café Sperl, but it was a friendly port at whatever time I arrived. Thanks to the cafés near my home and work I did not feel lonely. There was almost always someone to share a table with, to talk to and laugh with as we sipped our coffee. Many of us were there to escape boredom or loneliness by turning to the comfort of passing friendships. We were virtual strangers but we greeted each other warmly, talked about our families and then left to re enter our unconnected lives.

That night in my down mood, I was certain that Richard and I had made a dreadful mistake by coming to Melbourne. Richard would not admit that his job was sapping his health and I worried about the new friend my son spent his free time with. Anton resented my questions. All I knew was that this friend drove a fast car and hooted for Anton outside the house in the morning. Richard had not made the effort to find out more about him, though I felt he should have. It was irrational but I could not help my apprehension that something dreadful might happen to my son.

I lay awake throbbing with insistent longing to be back home and fearful of our future. Would I have left Vienna if I had known how tough it would be to live in another country? Australia was not *any* other country. It was vastly different from my own.

I asked myself if others knew, could tell how unsettled I was. Of prime importance then, was whether I was managing to maintain my smiling pretence of coping with my new life. My insecurity was probably transparent to Magda and Ruth. All the while I continued pretending to myself that my minimal efforts at adapting to my new home were sufficient.

My scary dream on the big wheel returned and I woke trembling. As the dawn crept beneath the curtains and lit the wall nearest the window, I chided myself in my mother's sternest voice. I had to make more of an effort to adapt. I knew almost nothing about Melbourne other than the streets around the house, the library and what I had read in travel books. And that didn't amount to much.

I had a whole day off work to look forward to. I went into the garden barefoot, stepped amongst the flowers and fed the birds. The dew on the grass and the warm, cloudless morning was a balm to my emotions.

Later, a quick check of my inbox confirmed the sale of the house in *Weintraubengasse* and that the money was deposited in my account. Though I was richer, I had lost a chunk of my past. At least my memories still lived in my childhood home.

My dream was not forgotten. I found the road map that Richard had put in one of the cupboards and placed it in the car next to me. Similar houses and small shops lined the route. When I saw a turn off to a nursery I followed it. Nearly all the plants originating from Europe I ignored, and continued viewing the large "native plant" section. There I noticed grevilleas and a red tinged plant called kangaroo paw, that grew in our garden. I sniffed, recognising the fragrances. The nursery man was near and I talked to him about the plant scents. He pointed to another shrub with yellow cup shaped flowers and light green foliage. 'Boronia. Very popular around here. Come closer and you'll smell it.'

I inhaled the aromatic lemony scent and smiled. I bought two Baronia plants and chose six more aromatic natives. I intended to place them in pots on the porch and take them with us when we moved.

At a suburban shopping centre along the route, a dress shop advertised a sale and I went inside. At the library each day I wore the formal but understated clothing I had always worn. The other women wore pants and colourful, casual, summer tops but I clung to what I called my European identity. I was in a buying mood and the bright cotton shirts on sale caught my attention. I bought a yellow, green and a blue one. All the way home the radio was turned on to a music station and I sang for the first time since arriving.

Anton passed me on the stairs wearing only a pyjama bottom and was carrying sandwiches and a cup of coffee to his room. With head down, he muttered his greeting. I dumped my shopping on the bed and followed him to his room, to find his door already closed. My first soft knock on his door was drowned by his loud music but when I persisted and knocked more forcefully the door opened with just enough space for him to stick his head out.

'Just wanted to know if you're okay. I hardly see you these days,' I shouted above the noise.

He shrugged. 'Things are fine. Don't panic.'

'You sure? No problems?' I persevered.

He shook his head. 'Na. Everything's fine. I like it here.'

'Right then, I leave you to it.'

I went into the kitchen disgruntled. He had flicked me away like a mosquito. It was difficult to tell but he did not look happy. I told myself that he had always been moody. Gabe was the more even tempered of the two. Was he purposely keeping me in the dark about the way he felt and how he was managing, I wondered, as I poured myself an extra strong cup of coffee and tore open a packet of rich chocolate biscuits. I felt useless as a mother. There was no point in turning to Richard for support. He had not spent time alone with his son, explored the city or taken him to a football match.

Anton had been transplanted from one comfortable life into another. When he came home each afternoon, he turned on all the lights upstairs and his music blared as loudly as it did in Vienna. When he enrolled at university, he did not ask about the cost. It probably didn't cross his mind.

'That we could afford it isn't the point. I don't want him to be concerned about money but he ought to know the cost of things if he is to become a responsible adult,' I said to Richard.

'Ah, leave him alone and let him enjoy his life,' Richard replied.

By then I had finished two- thirds of the biscuits and was nauseous.

Joan Zawatzky

How conveniently Richard forgot things. Two days earlier he had complained about the bills Gabe had run up in Vienna – excessive food and clothing bills and electricity.

'He's living in fine style while we're away, with not a thought of what it's costing us. He was sulky on the phone last time we talked too, carrying on as if we left him, while it was definitely his choice. He knows he can join us at any stage if he wants to.'

Most of our conversations with Anton were a battleground. He had separated himself from us and I was as much at fault as Richard. I had not spent enough time alone with him, asked detailed questions about how he was settling in, or if he was managing his university studies. I had closed off, not communicated with him for so long that he probably felt I didn't care. When he needed me, I had not made myself available. In my defence, in those early days of our arrival, I did not have the emotional strength or even the interest to extend warm, loving arms towards him.

Anton talked to me in snatched monosyllables. As he was on his way out of the door, I'd receive a truncated wave. I'd shout out after him, 'where are you going now? Who are you going with?'

Usually the reply yelled back at me was, 'I'm not a kid anymore, you know, can't you leave me alone?'

He had been an adorable baby and a loving child, but hormones and modern life had turned him into an unpleasant stranger with jaw clenched and mouth turned down in defiance. It was easier with Gabe. At a distance on the end of a telephone line, I could not see his anger. We talked for twenty minutes or half an hour at the most, and in that capsule of time I could send genuine caring and warmth in his direction. Gabe's confidence bordered on arrogance and he thought he knew best about almost everything. Anton, being younger and less independent, needed a steering hand. With barely enough energy to keep myself afloat, I had cut him loose to fend for himself.

Late one afternoon, I found Anton in the kitchen, his head cradled in his arms on the table. I touched his shoulder gently.

112

He sat up slowly and after clearing his throat he sighed. 'A German historian, Professor Schroeder gave a lecture today and I decided to go.'

'What was it about?'

'Mmmm the war... the Holocaust.'

'Oh!'

His face was pale, his eyes red rimmed.

'He talked a lot about Germany and Austria's role in it all... based his talk mainly on Vienna. I had no idea.'

'By the look of you, it must've been harrowing.'

Anton nodded. 'Of course I've heard about and read about it but hearing it again at the lecture today was...'

I nodded.

'It's hard to believe it happened a few years before I was born.' He shook his head and rubbed his eyes. 'And in our own country... our city. The things the Nazis did to Jews are unbelievable.'

'To our family, too.'

'I know! I know!'

'I tried to tell both of you boys the details but...'

'I didn't want to hear it or believe it then. I think Gabe probably felt the same.' He thumped his fist on the table.

'When you're ready, we'll talk.'

'It's weird, I haven't thought of myself as being Jewish until now.' He walked to the fridge for a coke, slammed it closed and opened the can.

The garden was my refuge. I sat under the gum tree on the grass, dotted with tiny white daisies and thought of the many conversations about religion I'd had with Richard. He denied his background and publically called himself an atheist. When the boys were born he thought it best to bring them up as Christians. On his insistence, we sent them to a school where they met only gentiles. When they turned thirteen they did not have barmitzvahs and though they were aware of their Jewish inheritance, neither of them had been inside a synagogue. He had not consulted them and I thought it wrong of him to make that decision for them. I was equally to blame. I ought to have stood up to him, insisted that we tell them about their family history and provided them with choices about their religion. Whether Richard liked it or not, now I would tell them all I could remember.

I grasped a handful of yellow, fluffy wattle balls and let them slip through my fingers as I recalled a late afternoon conversation with Ernst.

'One can't escape who you are. In Vienna, many Jews were baptised and converted to Christianity but their Austrian gentile identity made no difference to Hitler. Assimilation did not save those born Jewish from the gas chambers.'

'How did the Nazis know who the Jews were?' I asked.

'Records, birth certificates. Germans have always been excellent record keepers.'

Ernst was in a talkative mood and his passion was history. Whenever he talked about the past he usually revealed worthwhile and new information. The expression on his face was so serious that day that I could tell he was in his lecturing mood.

'For centuries there was terrible discrimination against Jews. In as early as 175 B.C. in countries that later became part of the ancient Roman Empire, Jews were persecuted because they refused to worship Hellenistic gods. Later as Christianity spread the difference between Jews and Christians became more apparent. By the fourth century they were a despised people throughout the Christian world.

'In 1096 after the massacre of thousands of Christians, the Christian knights began a crusade against Muslims to claim access to the city of Jerusalem, the birthplace of Jesus. They travelled through the Rhinelands and along the Danube killing Jews in their path.'

'How awful.'

'Yes, the persecution never stopped. Over the centuries that followed most Jews were driven from Europe and settled in Poland and Russia but pogroms or persecution occurred there too.'

'And here in Vienna?' I asked.

'Way back in 1624 Emperor Ferdinand the second, forced all the Jews out of the city. A new Jewish ghetto community developed beyond the city walls of Vienna, on an island on the Danube and it was called *Im Unteren Weld.* Late in the 17th century this place was given the name of Leopoldstadt, after the emperor, Leopold the first.'

'Oh, that's interesting.'

Ernst explained that by 1850 life for Jews in Vienna had improved. The Emperor, Franz Josef allowed the Jewish citizens civil and political rights. With the new tolerant attitude, the population of Vienna and other Austrian cities swelled with the migration of large numbers of Jews from Hungary, Bohemia, Moravia and Galicia. Around this time Jewish culture began to flourish. In 1858 the elaborate *Stadttempel* was built in Vienna. Now if they studied and worked hard, Jews could become respected members of society.

Jews were living in a conservative bourgeois and mainly Catholic society then, largely indifferent to the arts and intellectual pursuits. With their emphasis on education, by 1912 nearly half the students in secondary schooling were Jewish. They entered universities preferring the professions of law and medicine. By then Yiddish, formerly the language most spoken, gave way to German. Jews loved the German language and identified with the Viennese culture. Many hoping to improve their economic and social status relinquished their tradition and religion and converted to Christianity. Both Felix Mendelsohn and Gustav Mahler were amongst the famous, to be born Jewish and later baptised.

Not only were Jews successful in the arts but in business and trades as well. They became wealthy and bought mansions in the Ringstrasse, once the home of the nobility. 'Their wealth and assumption of everything Austrian did not help them when Hitler came to power,' he said grimly. 'Hitler gained popularity during a period of high unemployment, when soldiers were returning from the trenches of World War One. The rich and powerful Jews were ideal scapegoats.'

Joan Zawatzky

Twenty-Five

R uth and I were eating our lunch on the grass in a shady nook behind the library. She put her sandwich down. 'I haven't told you a thing about my past.' She collected a few crumbs before continuing. 'My story is much like many others. All of us Jews seem to have complicated family stories, of struggle and moving from country to country. It's the way it was then.'

My mouth was full and all I could do was nod.

'My family came from Hungary originally. I've traced family lines back to the seventeen hundreds.'

I relaxed back to listen. Her great grandfather had been a wealthy landowner and his properties were handed down to her grandfather's three sons, one of whom was her father. All the sons fought for their country during the First World War but only her father returned. He took over his father's business and increased his wealth. Ruth spoke in her earnest manner, describing her family's fear when Hitler's popularity rose and his intentions became known. They were fortunate and all escaped to England, though after World War Two, when Communist rule swept through Hungary, they lost their entire wealth.

Her parents were unhappy in England with the culture too different from theirs, but they used the opportunity to study French and English. Once they had qualified as teachers they moved to Paris. She smiled for the first time, as she told me that she was born in squalid accommodation in Montmartre, amongst artists and writers.

'It wasn't at all romantic. Many of the artists drank too much or were on drugs when they painted. Once my parents found secure teaching jobs we shifted into a home of our own. My brother teases me, says I'm the lucky one born into the easy life.' She smiled wryly. 'Paris was my home for twenty-nine years. I married Paul there and my life was almost perfect.' Her voice softened and she looked at me. 'I loved the sophisticated simplicity of life in Paris and the way Parisians take their time about the important things – food, wine and sex.'

The move to Australia came during one of the long Parisian winters when her youngest son developed a serious form of arthritis and her doctor recommended a warmer climate.

'That's when I found a job at the library and I haven't moved since.'

'Was the move to Australia difficult,' I asked.

'I hated leaving Paris and I spoke English with what the Aussies called a "froggy" accent. They laughed at me behind my back. Things haven't changed that much since then. They're still complaining that foreigners take Aussie jobs.'

'But some of it's true.'

'I suppose it is.'

She crumpled her fruit drink container and leaned against the wall. 'At first I hated the dullness of Melbourne life but when I forgot I was an immigrant, things slowly improved. The children loved it here from the start. One of my proudest days was when we received our citizenship. It was on Australia Day and we attended a ceremony with about four hundred other new Aussies. I don't think Paul and I will ever forget it.' She tugged the tough kikuyu grass. 'But I still have days when I know that my roots in are Europe.'

I glanced at my watch and gave a start. 'We're running late!'

'I was so involved that I forgot the time. Sorry, I did all the talking. You haven't said much about your own life… your past.'

'I will… I promise,' I said shaking the grass from my skirt and tugging it into place.

Richard was home earlier than usual.

'I had a talk with our top management today,' he said, as he carried his beer from the fridge to the couch. 'We'll have to move out of this house within three months or pay the full rent.' He didn't seem to notice my wide smile and went on talking. 'I don't know about you, but I'd like a place of our own. Something smaller ... and as soon as possible. We won't need a lot of space, Anton will be leaving any day.'

I interrupted, 'Oh yes! Yes!'

Unexpectedly he stretched and put an arm around my shoulder. 'Maybe looking for a house together and settling in with our own stuff will help us, bring us closer,' he said tentatively.

Not wanting to dash his hopes I mumbled, 'Yes, I hope so.'

He threw his hands in the air. 'I have no idea where to start looking.'

I volunteered to do the research on the most desirable suburbs and promised to ask my colleagues for advice.

The next morning Ruth noticed my happy smile. 'Something good must be happening in your life. I don't think I've seen you beaming like that before.'

My excited words flew out. 'We'll be moving into our own house soon. The company house has been a great financial help and I'm grateful ... but our own house! I can't believe it.'

'I'm pleased for you,' She squeezed my hand. 'It'll make all the difference. You'll see.'

That evening, I found Richard anaesthetising himself with beer followed by whisky chasers. I sat next to him in front of the television while he was engrossed in a game of Australian Rules football. His hand dipped into a packet of pretzels and I might as well have been alone in the room. The footballer's skilful defence tactics and their high flying leaps for the ball caught my attention momentarily.

Suddenly Richard belched loudly and barked. 'Coffee... can I have some coffee?'

I handed him the cup of instant coffee and looked at him. Where was the man I had married - the lean athlete interested in politics and the arts? His collection of trophies was in the garage and he had given all the elephants away.

Twenty-Six

M ama would've enjoyed helping me look for a house. Once I started thinking of her and the past, I couldn't stop.

She was at her kindest, her most caring on my birthdays and her presents were always thoughtful. She knitted me a pink angora sweater one year. It was nipped in at the waist with a vee neck and lovely, but it itched and I broke out in hives. She gave me party dresses with flounces and frills and my first pieces of real gold jewellery.

By my twelfth birthday, I had waited long enough. I considered myself old enough to know more about my father. When Mama tried to fob me off once more, my fury frightened me. I yelled at her. 'Wait until I'm older! You're telling me I have to wait until I'm older to find out about my own father!'

'Shush! Quiet child! The neighbours will hear.'

'I don't care who hears! You're hiding one of the most important things in my life from me.'

Mama gasped, bent over a chair and covered her face with her hands so that I wouldn't see her tears. I ran up to my room and closed the door. She didn't realise that I understood more than she thought, that I knew about adults, about her and Ernst but it did not bother me. I was a logical child and her actions did not make sense. If I had such a courageous father, surely she was proud and wanted to tell me all about him. What if

119

something awful happened to her and I never ever found out about my father?

My desperation to know more and my tears eventually forced her to at least tell me how she met my father. They met at a fundraising dance for Jewish survivors of the concentration camps. My father was one of the few former Leopoldstadt residents who had survived the camps. With no home to return to since his family had all perished, he was staying at a Displaced Person's Camp outside the city. The overcrowded camp became his home for two years after the war.

Even though he was horribly thin and looked strained, Mama was attracted to him.

'It was his eyes…his firey eyes and fighting spirit that drew me to him,' she said. After their first meeting, Mama returned to the camp frequently with food parcels for the sad stranger. They became friends, and then fell in love. All they wanted was to be together. Their lives were in shreds and they had been through far too much to worry about little things. They grabbed life fearing that the next day it could be snatched from them. And so he left the camp and came to live with her in what was left of the house. Gradually he built up his strength and together they worked on repairing it until it was a comfortable home.

I remember Mama lowering her voice. 'We lived in the house but we didn't marry until much later…and that's when you came along. By your first birthday your father was very frail,' she said. 'He died about a year later. I could tell he was dying, weakening by the day and I watched helplessly. The doctors said nothing could be done for him. His body failed… he'd been through too much.' She covered her face and sobbed. 'I can't… just can't say more, it's too upsetting.'

Twenty-Seven

Every year, on a Saturday in mid-December the library staff had lunch together. That year we agreed to meet at a restaurant overlooking the bay and then spend what remained of the afternoon on the beach. The idea of a day at the beach appealed to me. All I had seen of Melbourne's beaches was a quick drive past. Ruth's offer of a lift eased my concerns about the long drive. As she drove, I surprised myself by being able to identify major intersections and landmarks along the route. At least I was becoming accustomed to my environment, I told myself.

'We're early, so I'm going to take a detour,' Ruth said. 'You haven't seen the side of the city where most of the Jewish people live have you?' she asked with a smile.

'I didn't know there was one.'

'Most of them have moved up here, across the Yarra River. I'm not sure of the numbers but around 45,000 Jews live in this part of the city. There are very few left in our area on the lower side of the river.'

I glanced out of the window at the inner suburban streets and older houses.

'We'll drive a bit further.'

We were in a street lined with small shops that reminded me of the streets around *Tempelgasse* in Leopoldstadt with its kosher butcheries, delicatessens, bakeries and cafés. Amongst the crowd of people, I spotted several men in black coats and hats and women wearing long skirts and scarves on their heads.

'Does it look familiar?' she asked.

'Oh, yes. It reminds me of Leopoldstadt.'

'I took a tour to the Old City when I was in Vienna. One of the places we visited was the Holocaust memorial in Judenplatz.'

Her description of the memorial drifted past me. I was bathed in nostalgia recalling the inner city and the train station close to Judenplatz. I realised just then that I had not looked closely at the Memorial, nor had I been inside the museum. The excavations of the medieval synagogue and the ritual artefacts found there had never interested me. Of course I knew that in 1938 eighty centres of Jewish worship in Vienna had been destroyed. But the huge number had floated over my head and somehow it didn't feel as if I was connected to the horror. It was to the cafés that I hurried, to drink in their aroma and ambience.

Ruth's gentle voice carried me back. 'I come here often to buy special kosher food that isn't available where we live,' Ruth said. Before reaching the beach, she pointed out a Jewish aged home, a religious study centre and a synagogue.

I looked at the flat treeless land and the streets crammed with houses. I liked the idea of living in a Jewish area but I found this part of Melbourne too congested.

'After The First World War, the pogroms against European Jews led them to seek refuge. When the USA closed their doors to them, they were forced to take less popular options... South Africa and Australia.'

'So they came here as early as that.'

'They lived in Carlton then, a suburb close to the city centre. We lived there too... a long time ago.'

She tapped the wheel. 'We're running late. It's a pity to cut our tour short. We'll have to come back here another day.'

When we arrived at the restaurant, the others were already seated and waved to us. We enjoyed a tasty meal together and talked over a few bottles of wine. After the meal we ambled onto the beach where people from all over the world were catching the day's last rays. Melbourne lived up to the brochures. It was indeed multicultural.

On the way home, Ruth took another detour and we chugged along in the traffic until a huge painted face grimaced at us.

'Luna Park, our Amusement Park. Does it remind you of anything?'

'Of course it does – The Prater in Leopoldstadt. This area is a home from home.'

'I thought so.' She freed her hand from the wheel and touched my arm affectionately.

Late that evening I logged onto my computer. There were three messages and I opened the one from Luke first.

> *It's icy in Vienna with a pile of snow in the garden. Even if you're not used to living in Australia yet, it has to be an improvement on Vienna right now. I'll have to dig myself out. Look at the opportunity you've got to feel out a new culture and meet different people in a warm climate. I'd swop any day.*
>
> *I've got a few things on my mind that I can't write about. We'll have to talk about them. You'll see me sooner than you think.*

Luke wasn't the moody type but I could tell that the cold weather was getting to him. I felt a surge of hope, the way I felt once as a teenager, when I was due to meet him at a movie or the Amusement Park. I warned myself not to expect too much. In his next message he could be his happy self again and decide to stay in Vienna.

The two other messages from friends in Europe were also about the weather. Surely something else was happening there, I muttered to myself as I headed for bed.

Joan Zawatzky

Twenty-Eight

In the build-up to Christmas, I missed Vienna. I missed my friends, the intense green and claret contrasting dramatically with the snow and the choirs singing on each street corner of the city. It was hot and humid in Melbourne and Father Christmas and his reindeers were incongruous in the bright light.

By December, Mama's baking filled a shelf in the larder with decorated baskets and boxes of *lebkuchen* or special gingerbread, slices of *stollen* or fruit loaf and homemade chocolates wrapped in coloured foils. Being thrifty, she made greeting cards by sticking pictures from cards received previously onto paper. Each year she gave gifts to her bank manager, hairdresser, pharmacist and others who had helped her during the year. The task of taking the gifts to the homes of non-Jews was mine. She made a point of giving hamper sized baskets to two old Catholic ladies in our mainly Jewish street. Trudie Dressler was a wizened spinster in her late seventies who lived three doors way. She cleaned our house once a month and Mama found her efficient. There were rumours that she had thrown in her lot with the Nazis and informed on Jews during the war but no one could prove it and those who could weren't saying a thing.

'People are nasty and they make up stories…I don't believe it. She's a hard worker and has always been kind to us. She's poor and still cleaning and taking in ironing at her age,' Mama said.

Though Trudie had not been unkind to me, I sensed her reluctance to be in the house and her dislike of me. Her only words to me were to ask me to move from a room she was cleaning or to open a window. When her chores were completed and she closed the door behind her, I felt relieved. My delivery of her gift was a duty, executed quickly and with reluctance. I wished her well over Christmas but did not linger.

By contrast, my visit to eighty-one year old Anita Neumann, who lived in the tail end of the street, was a pleasure. Mama worked full-time and until I went to school Mrs Neumann looked after me. She was a kind, round woman who felt soft all over when I hugged her. I loved Mrs Neumann with a warmth different from the love I had for Mama. For Mama, I felt respect tinged with a touch of fear, though she had not done a thing to hurt me. I could talk freely to Mrs Neumann while Mama was easily upset and it was hard to please her. If I said the wrong thing, she refused to talk to me. There was nothing worse than that aloneness.

When I was little, I called Mrs Neumann the "Kind Lady", the name Mama had given her. The name stuck. And she was kind. She played games with me, silly doll games when I was very little and helped me paint and make things when I was older. Best of all, were the puzzles she gave me. When I was about three and a half she began to teach me about letters and numbers and at four I could read simple words and sentences. I realised later how much I owed her. Mama read to me at night but she was tired and could only manage a few pages. Mrs Neumann stimulated my mind.

Once I was at school, I continued to visit Mrs Neumann regularly. Later, when I returned to Leopoldstadt to see Mama I often visited Mrs Neumann. She would put down her knitting or stop her work in the kitchen and give me all her attention. She was old by then, had a stoop and wore thick glasses but her mind was sharp. Like most old people she talked about the past. From her I learned about Leopoldstadt, and more particularly *Weintraubengasse* between 1938 and 1945. Most of the people I talked to who had lived in Vienna around that time were

Jewish and were either in hiding during the war, had survived the concentration camps or had escaped from the area.

The day I knocked on her door with her Christmas hamper, she had just finished reading a love story based in Germany during the war. It had triggered disturbing memories. She pointed to the book with a beautiful young woman on the cover. 'I've tried to forget about *them*. I should've put the book down long ago but I'd already got into the story.'

'Them?'

'The bloody Nazis.'

I nodded politely.

'It brought it all back…what it was like here during the war.'

'I'd forgotten that you were here then.' I hesitated. 'Did you ever meet my father?'

'Yes I did, poor man! What a state he was in, thin and nervous. Anyone would understand it after what he went through.'

I nodded again, hoping to hear more.

'And do you know, he still had time to be polite to me, to ask after my children. He knew them well before the war, but my two boys died on the front. He even said he was sorry to hear that they had died even though they fought for…his enemy. As I said, a gentleman…and when you think what they did to him.' She stopped suddenly and covered her mouth with her hand.

'I'm sorry…didn't mean to upset you.' I gulped and took a deep breath. I didn't want to stop her. 'But if you can…please tell me what it was like living here during the war.'

'I tried to hide from it and of course I couldn't, but I stayed inside the house and only went out for food or some other necessity. I watched them through there.' She nodded in the direction of a large bay window. 'Swarming into Vienna and goose stepping down the street with their *Heil Hitler* greetings!' She looked out of the window. 'A lot of Viennese cheered but I knew the Nazis were evil…not that one could say a thing about them to anyone. The streets were creeping with informers. '

I shuddered and looked away.

'It was a horrible time, so little to eat, people were very scared but everyone knows about it, has read about it.'

'That's true, but hearing it from you, from your own experience is different.'

She sighed and adjusted her glasses. 'This has always been a Jewish street and the bastards had a party here. At dawn, groups of them went from door to door dragging out helpless families. They're all gone now. The butcher and his family... I forget his name, the Kleins who owned the dairy, Polansky the other butcher, the Blumsteins and all their eight children...and...and they took them away at gun point...good people, fine citizens ... all of them...but I can't... One young man struggled and yelled at them. He was shot in front of his family.'

'I have heard there was resistance in Vienna.'

'Oh goodness, yes. There were groups of civilians who handed out pamphlets against Hitler. It is said that they carried out acts of sabotage on railway lines. I don't want to think what happened to them if they were caught. By about 1942 life here was intolerable. There were jail sentences for listening to foreign broadcasts or telling an anti-Nazi joke. Towards the end of the war, quite a large group revolted against all of this. A lot of houses had the numbers "05" on their walls, standing for Ostenreich (Austria).' She was crying now, wiping away her tears with a lace handkerchief. It was my fault for insisting she talk about it and reminding her of the horror she preferred to forget.

I took her hand and stroked it. 'Let's stop talking about it. I've asked too much of you and I'm sorry. It was selfish of me. I'll make you some tea with a spoon of Schnapps.' The mix had been her remedy over the years.

❧

The holidays loomed. Magda and Karl had left for Stuttgart to spend Christmas with their family. Ruth and Paul were taking their holiday at the beach and would be away until after Christmas. Anton had not been invited out, and so on Christmas day I decided to cook a family dinner.

In the lazy days that followed Christmas, I dipped into the piles of books that awaited me. I read under the loquat tree and fed brightly coloured parakeets with cut fruit until they became tame and sat on my shoulder. I was still on holiday when the weather turned disgustingly hot. An early heatwave, I was told. I had never experienced heat of that intensity before. Pounding rain followed. On every television station and the radio, the news was of vicious floods that had taken lives and property. I watched feeling helpless, concerned for the many people who were suffering. All I could do was donate money to the appeal and feel grateful that we were not living near a river.

Richard drank cold beer and appeared to cope far better than I did. I lay on my bed with the air-conditioner on full blast, unable to do much but listen to music, daydream and remember.

And there was so much to remember. Mama had died ten years earlier, two days after Christmas. I pictured her, sitting in her armchair next to the window with her silver head bent over a book. Curly tendrils escaped the tight discipline of her combs and formed a soft halo around her face.

She had turned eighty- eight and was still living in the house in Leopoldstadt, when she developed a series of coughs and infections. Her usually strong constitution began to fail and I sensed I would soon loose her. I packed a suitcase, left Richard with the two boys, and took the train to Leopoldstadt. Maria, a Russian widow, stayed in the house with her and looked after her. As Maria was poor and forced to live with a daughter she didn't get along with, she moved from house to house to nurse the elderly and sick.

Mama opened her eyes when I entered the room and attempted a brave smile. We kissed, pretending that I was there for a brief visit. She had taught me to pretend. Pretence she believed was invaluable to a young woman in many aspects of her life, especially in marriage. Of course she was right.

Maria carried in a tray with coffee and cake and drew up a table next to the bed. She plumped up Mama's cushions, muttered a few soothing words in Russian and left us. Between heavy breaths, Mama fingered her hair into place and drew her bed jacket together to hide her scrawny chest.

I was seated near her, drinking the last of my coffee with a piece of cake, when she put her cup down slowly and took a wheezy breath. 'We might've been poor but at least we had manners. Sit up straight Ella, darling…and don't gobble up your cake,' she said in her thin voice. 'Daintily…'

I smiled and corrected my posture. 'Don't worry about silly things Mama.'

'You tell me …often … that etiquette is dead and buried… Nonsense!'

'Never mind Mama, things are different now.' I said as I stroked her hand.' Try not to exhaust yourself.'

She put her cup down, flicked crumbs from the sheet and attempted a smile. Minutes later she closed her eyes and drifted into sleep.

The doctor visited daily. He wouldn't commit himself, but said that she was likely to rally briefly and then decline. On the morning of the third day of my visit, she coughed less and her speech was easier to understand. It was a warm morning and Maria drew back the curtains to let in the light.

I was as desperate as ever to know about my father and later that day I asked Mama about him again. 'Please tell me all you know about him… please, all you can remember. So many times you've promised to tell me about him and never did. Now you have to.'

Her voice was thin and whispery. 'I understand… you must know … but I'm sorry, I can't talk about it. Ask your father's sister, Gertrude…Gertie.   She knows and will tell you everything.'

A frustrated part of me wanted to insist she tell me my father's story but I let it go. There was no point upsetting her. I wondered if she remembered all the details of my father's past. Her memory had been patchy for years. When I was a teenager I noticed that she was having trouble remembering her shopping or what we had eaten the day before. In later years she forgot important experiences we shared. She could not remember a thing about my schooldays or Luke, who was a frequent visitor.

She patted the bed. 'Come sit next to your Mama.'

As she began to talk, I realised that she was trying to tell me another story, the story she had told me many times when I was little. She faltered, battling to recall the beginning.

'You've told me about our history in Leopoldstadt, Mama. Save your energy and we'll tell it together.'

'You must remember it and tell your children… so that their children will know.'

I reassured her and took over the story telling. She nodded as we shared the ritual that connected us. It was the same dramatic story that Ernst told, of the Jews who lived in and around Vienna and how in spite of discrimination and expulsion, the area became the centre of Vienna's Jewish cultural life. I continued telling the story of the rise of Jewish Vienna after centuries of discrimination. Her eyes were tightly closed, when I reached the part I knew she would enjoy most, about the *Jewish Renaissance*, as she called it, that had begun in Vienna in the mid eighteen hundreds. Her eyes opened momentarily and closed again. This time she drifted into sleep. The doctor was correct of course, by that evening she was wheezing and gasping for air again. With medication she was able to rest. Maria and I sat by her bedside. The night before Mama died she whispered to me in snatches. The gist of it was that she was born Jewish and even though she had not been observant during her life, she wanted a Jewish burial. I stroked her head, kissed her cheek and reassured her. For the first time, she told me that she loved me.

She died early the following morning. After kissing her cold forehead, I left Maria to attend to her. I cried a lot and I was to cry more in the days to come. I cried for all she had suffered during her life and I cried for my loss. I was an adult orphan now.

Days later I wrote to Luke about Mama's death. He was too far away to comfort me but telling him helped. He replied almost immediately.

I'm so sorry about your loss. I wish I could be there to comfort you. Even though your mother was ill for some time and the doctor probably told you to expect her passing, the shock is devastating. I know because I recently lost my mother. We weren't close but I felt the pain.

I remember your mother well and am grateful that she was kind to me. I will never forget her.

Twenty-Nine

The heat and heavy rain persisted. I could've been in the tropics. As the floods continued relentlessly, the television showed dreadful pictures of people's homes ravaged and lives destroyed. I ate little and drank only lemonade as I lay in the air conditioned room, slipping in and out of sleep or daydreaming.

Mama's funeral was held in the new section of the Jewish cemetery and a rabbi officiated. Most of the burial was a blur. Papa's sister Gertie arrived from Paris. She maintained that she had made the journey out of respect for my father. A few neighbours, some old friends and members of Richard's family attended as well. I had not attended a Jewish funeral before and Richard did the explaining. 'Cemeteries are purposefully stark and it's not the custom to place flowers on the graves. Rich and poor alike are buried in a plain pine box,' he said. 'Visitors place a stone on the marble.'

It was just as well he prepared me. There were none of the trees I was used to seeing, just grey and black marble headstones jammed together. As in life, there wasn't much space for the dead at the cemetery. The rabbi spoke in Hebrew except for a brief eulogy at the graveside. He had visited me at home and sat patiently listening while I told him about my mother's life and what I knew to be her personal strengths. I told him about her perseverance through a difficult life, the way she had cared for her elderly parents and for me. However, the person he spoke about at the graveside did not sound anything like my mother. He had turned her into a traditional Jewish mother and homemaker. She would've been appalled.

Following Richard's suggestion I had laid out cups and saucers, sandwiches and cakes before leaving for the cemetery. Nearly everyone who attended the burial came to our home afterwards and stood around talking about Mama.

A day after the burial, I was in the sitting room when I noticed a glowing blue light around the chair where Mama used to sit. The light hovered and deepened in colour. 'Mama,' I called out. The blue flickered and was gone.

'Mama, don't go, don't leave me,'

I was convinced that I was sleep deprived and hallucinating. Months later, when I heard a psychic talk on television of the spirit remaining around loved ones for the first few days after death, I accepted what I had seen.

Aunt Gertie had intended to stay with us for only two nights but ended up staying for ten. She was Papa's younger sister by about eight years. I calculated she was in her early nineties. Mama had told me that her sister-in-law was a busybody, a gossip and troublemaker. This was the reason she gave me for not visiting my aunt or even writing to her. Mama would not admit to an earlier falling out between the two of them. It was, I expect, her way of pretending things she did not want to talk about, had not occurred.

I hardly knew my aunt. During her previous visit I was a child and afraid of her sternness. This time I was with her long enough to reach the sensitive person she was. After the funeral, I was too upset to do more than attend to her basic comfort, but in the days that followed, we were alone in the house and we talked. She had not married and devoted herself to study. After the war she became a language teacher at a senior school and was proficient in German, Polish, French and English. She retired from her job in her late sixties and taught privately until recently.

She talked enthusiastically about her career. Though I listened politely, I was impatient to talk about my father. I explained how little I knew about him as Mama had found talking about him too painful. My aunt's response was diplomatic. She said nothing negative about Mama, but when she discussed her, she referred to her as "your mother" and refrained from using her first name.

When I asked her to tell me about my father she smiled. 'Your father was an exceptional person, not because he was my brother but when I tell you more about him, I know you'll agree.'

At last I would know.

'Before I say more, you must forgive me. I don't remember small details as I once did and sometimes I become a bit confused... however, I will do my best to give you an accurate picture.'

'Thank you, I understand.'

I sat up and concentrated hard. I knew that I would have to remember everything my aunt said as I wouldn't be able to ask a second time.

She smoothed her skirt and began talking. She described how early in 1937, before Hitler annexed Austria, my father and a group of his friends, predicting this would happen, formed an underground group. She had forgotten the name. They knew how powerful the Nazis were and there was already talk that Hitler had plans to deport the Jews and any dissidents. The underground group, with my father, as one of the leaders helped many to escape over the mountains to neutral Switzerland. He knew the mountains and was at home in the snow.

She smiled, remembering him skiing when he was as young as three and half years old. A tiny tot dressed in a red woollen suit and a blue hat. She continued speaking slowly in High German with a breath of vocabulary that amazed me. I still hear her voice as if she was speaking to me today. 'As soon as I could walk my father taught me to ski too. He played with me in the snow and built snowmen for me. When I was older, I went climbing with Walter, my father and some of his friends. I didn't like climbing but Walter went on to conquer the tallest peaks of the Alps. He knew the quick route from Vienna over the border to Switzerland so well, that he often spent a weekend there and came back the following day. As I said, he loved the mountains.'

I wanted to know more about the underground movement in Vienna and asked her about it.

'We called the Jewish resistance to the Nazis, the *Partisans*. She explained that the groups in Vienna joined up with other underground movements throughout Europe to help Jews escape the Nazis or engage in minor acts of sabotage. My aunt took a deep breath and rubbed her eyes. 'Enough for now! I must have tea, nice and strong and hot...with lemon and honey or I won't be able to continue.'

I placed the tea in front of her and she sipped it slowly. 'Ah, thank you. Much better! Now, where was I?'

I reminded her and she continued. 'Your father and his friends carried on guiding people over the mountains to safety well into 1939. They were in great danger with German soldiers everywhere. And that's where their courage comes into it. They could have escaped, taken the easy way but they continued their task, taking longer and lesser known routes to guide people to safety. There was always a chance of being caught...and that's exactly what happened. One afternoon Walter and a few others were near the border when the Germans spotted them. They were all seized and after several days in holding cells they were transported to Theresienstadt Concentration Camp.'

My aunt closed her eyes but she was not asleep. Her body rocked gently as tears dribbled down her face. She found her lace handkerchief tucked in her sleeve and mopped up her tears. Rising slowly, she walked towards the door. 'I'll have a little rest now.'

For a woman in her nineties, Aunt Gertie was astounding. She held herself straight and walked with certainty but more than that, she had an amazing memory and ability to explain and clarify. As a younger woman she must've been an intellectual force.

That night, after learning about my father's capture, I was too upset to close my eyes, let alone sleep. For the first time, I had an inkling of why Mama had refused to tell me more about my father.

Joan Zawatzky

The following day we were both spent, but rather than rest, I suggested a drive to the mountains for some fresh air. My aunt agreed. Initially avoiding the subject of my father, we talked only about the glorious weather, the fresh aroma of the forest and the view that fanned out before us.

As we were admiring the view, I plucked up the courage to approach her again for more information. I hated having to ask her about the past, to dredge up memories, but she was the only one I could turn to.

She sighed deeply and then placed her hands on mine. 'I understand how desperate you are to know all you can about your father and I will do my best. Tomorrow I will tell you as much as I can, remember.'

'Thank you. I can't ask more.'

'Our grandparents came from a *shtetl* near *Snagov* in Romania,' said Aunt Gertie, continuing the story. When the news of a society where our people were accepted and housing was affordable spread through to the community, my family left for Vienna. I was born in Leopoldstadt, in a small house off *Ausstellungsstrasse*. About ten years ago I revisited Leopoldstadt hoping to find it, but a block of flats stood in its place. I was curious about *Snagov* where the family originated and I took a trip there.'

'What did you find?'

'That part of Romania was beautiful with gentle countryside. Lotus flowers and waterlilies floated in the lake.'

'It sounds lovely.'

'This is where you'll laugh.' She paused dramatically. 'Count Dracula is supposed to be buried in the monastery that sits in the middle of the lake.'

'What! Dracula of all people!'

My aunt smiled. 'Don't worry our family lived in a *shtetl* quite a distance from the monastery. I don't think they would've believed in his powers.'

We both laughed.

'Aunt Gertie, can you remember your early years in Vienna?'

'Oh yes, the older one gets, the more one thinks of the past and forgets what happened yesterday.'

I nodded encouragingly.

We two children had a wonderful time. After school, while our parents were busy learning new acts or performing, we stole neighbours' washing from their lines, put our hands through windows to grab hot cookies. The best part was that we weren't caught. Most important to our parents was that we learned to play the piano and violin, to sing and dance. By the age of six we performed with them. I was shy and didn't like being stared at by the audience. Often I pretended I was sick or disappeared for a few hours rather than go on stage. After a while my mother told me to concentrate on my school work and didn't ask me to perform with them again. I proved to be a good scholar and enjoyed my schooldays.

'From a young age Walter was a showman. His talent was obvious. By the age of four he'd sing or dance and love the applause. I was sure it was a passing phase, and that he craved the attention, but after he left the polytechnic, he broke away from the family and went on to sing and play the piano in cafés around Vienna. He became well known. I don't know when he joined a Yiddish theatre group and branched out into acting. It was clear that he had a rare gift for comedy and by 1930 he played at theatres throughout Europe. All his shows were sold out.'

She smiled at me fondly. 'I don't think you realised how gifted your dear father was?'

I shook my head.

'When the Nazis stormed into Austria, he was already at the peak of his career. At first we Jews were forbidden to act on stage...and then they smashed the theatres. Students and lecturers alike turned against us, my scholarship was useless to me and I was forced to leave university. My academic future was in shreds.' My aunt closed her eyes and was silent.

My thoughts returned to my father's imprisonment in the concentration camp. It was too awful to imagine. As soon as she looked at me again, I asked how long my father had spent in Therisienstadt.

'He was there for almost three years, when the Russians marched in. They liberated the camp in time for him, or he would've been sent to the gas chambers at Auschwitz. When the Allies took over, he was in terrible shape, almost a corpse. Walter's stay in the camp is a long story that I can't face today but I promise to tell you about it. I was lucky, the one who got away. I left Vienna for Frankfurt and from there I managed to buy a passage on a ship to the USA. After the war I returned to Vienna.'

Gertie rubbed her swollen knuckles and then closed her eyes again. 'All these memories …they exhaust me.'

'Do you want to rest,' I asked.

'A cup of tea, please … and make it hot. I hate luke warm tea.'

She rested until I arrived with her tea and a plate of biscuits. She dipped a biscuit into her tea, sucked it. 'I remember a little more … but after that I'll have to lie down.'

I touched her hand.

'Do you know that your parents met after the war in the Displaced Person's Camp? After leaving Jana's care your mother didn't go directly to the old house. All her family were dead and she was too distraught to be alone in the house. She stayed in the D.P camp for a few months.'

It wasn't the story Mama told me but I didn't mention that to my aunt.

'She met your father at the camp. When she returned to the house, she took in a woman boarder and they tried to repair and clean it as best as they could. It was in a terrible mess, filth everywhere from the Germans who'd stayed there. Meanwhile she visited your father in the camp and took him food. She was in love with him and asked him if he wanted to live in the house with her. Of course the boarder was gone by then.'

My aunt's romantic story sounded like the truth and I preferred it as long as I ignored the dreadful circumstances.

'Your mother and I weren't close. I don't think it was my fault but one never knows if small things one says offend.'

I replied quickly. 'She didn't mention anything in particular.'

'More important is the loving way she cared for your father until the end. I could tell that they adored each other, hanging on every word the other said and their eyes followed each other around the room.'

'I know so little.'

'She loved him too much...she couldn't talk about him.'

I looked down to cover my surge of emotion.

'I have no doubt, your father's time in the camp affected him badly. He developed dark moods and there were weeks when he didn't talk, and then months when he left your mother and disappeared.'

'Oh!'

'I don't know if your mother told you that she wouldn't marry him until he had some medical treatment and became more stable.'

At last I understood why Mama did not want to bring a child into the world earlier. My aunt slipped back in the chair, her eyes closing.

'One last question...please, where is Papa buried? I can't find his name in any of the listings at the cemeteries.'

'There's a good reason for that. He didn't want to know about religion, about Judaism...turned his back on it all. Even though he knew cremation wasn't allowed in the Jewish religion, he asked for his ashes to be scattered over the mountains he loved.' She paused. 'Your mother was very upset about it. She would've preferred to visit his grave but she did as he asked.'

I kissed her cheek and covered her with a rug. The following morning I had trouble waking her. She slept most of the day.

Thirty

Two days later we took a slow drive along the Danube towards the *Wachau Valley.* We passed through ruins, old villages, steep, terraced vineyards and the castle where legend tells that Richard the Lion Heart was once imprisoned. At the town of *Krems* we stopped at an old inn. After Gertie's first cup of coffee with cake, she took my hand.

'I'm sorry my darling, I know how important learning about your father is to you but some of those things in the past still upset me. Thinking about it all tired me out. I'm feeling a little stronger today though. Before I leave I must tell you a few more important things. Let's sit here and we'll talk a while.'

We sat opposite each other on padded leather seats. The waiter filled our cups and slowly she began to speak. She had learned much of what she knew about my father's imprisonment in the concentration camp from his friend Jacob Koszinsky. They were in the camp together and later they remained close friends. Jacob died four years earlier and is buried in Vienna, close to where my mother lies.

When my father was seized by the Nazis and sent to Theresienstadt, it was his talent as a comedian and artist, as well as being very smart that kept him alive. He collected bits of paper and when he had enough, he wet it and shaped it into masks. He then let it dry. The children were allowed to draw and paint, so he stole paint and created characters on the masks.

He made costumes from torn clothing and taught his fellow prisoners comedy routines. Together they created a comedy team to amuse the guards.

'It's sickening now to think of the series of comedy acts...all hideous satires against the Jews. His masks were of long nosed, greedy Jews. They depicted the Jews in their worst light and the guards and the commandant of the camp laughed and laughed. In this way they gained the guards' protection and escaped the deportation list.'

In spite of the seriousness of the subject, she smiled. 'I asked Walter once how they managed to keep this horrible act going. He told me that he made one mask he named the *dybbuk.*

I must've given her another of my vacant stares.

She explained that prior to the war, my father had the main part in *The Dybbuk*, one of the most popular Yiddish mystical plays, written in the early nineteen hundreds by Ansky. In the play, a Talmudic scholar falls in love with a young woman and wants to marry her but instead her father finds a wealthy suitor for his daughter. The young scholar dies of sorrow and the woman becomes possessed by a *dybbuk,* a malicious spirit that due to former sins, wanders until it finds a haven in a living person.

'What Walter did was make a hideous mask...white and ghoulish. The guards liked it best and laughed loudest whenever he wore it. But to him and his fellow prisoners, it was an evil *dybbuk* they were setting loose to possess their captors.'

We both laughed.

Her smile lifted and she touched her forehead. 'He didn't tell me all he went through. He spared me the details. After the war your father refused to perform again in spite of constant requests. He said that putting on shows for the Germans had killed any pleasure he gained from being on stage and that the war had destroyed his sense of humour.' She tapped the leather seat. 'Well, that's all I know, my darling. I hope it adds to your knowledge of your father. He was a brave and resourceful man.'

It was fortunate that the traffic was light on the way back to Vienna as my thoughts were on the desperation that drove my father to create his vile comedy routine.

The morning before Gertie left, I heard her calling me from the bedroom. It was mid - morning but she was still in bed, attempting to recover her strength before she faced the journey home. She patted the bed, indicating that I should sit next to her. 'I've realised that I almost forgot to tell you something else.'

She stretched for her handbag on the floor and in the process almost fell out of bed. I helped her to regain her balance and passed her the handbag. She fumbled until she found a small notebook. 'You probably don't realise it but you have cousins.'

'Oh, I had no idea.'

'They're around your age…three of them and they all live in Israel.'

'My father…your grandfather had a sister Sheina. She married and had three children, two under three. Sadly, she and her husband perished in Auschwitz but she managed to ensure that her children survived. She handed them to their Polish nursemaid who lived in the countryside. I have no idea how the woman hid their identity from the Nazis. She and her husband cared for them lovingly and when the war ended all three went to Israel.'

'And have you met them?'

'During my last trip to Israel, five years ago. My niece Karla, the eldest, looks a lot like you. The boys are more like their mother and they're not interested in family. I keep in touch with Karla.' She pointed to my eldest cousin's postal and email addresses, written in her notebook. 'Contact her, I think you'll like her.'

Gertie slept most of that day but by the evening she was as bright and chatty as before. At the airport the next day, I promised to visit her in Paris.

'I live in the old Jewish area, *Le Marais*, you'll love it.'

We kissed and hugged briefly, trying not to prolong the parting. One wave and she disappeared.

The task of sorting through Mama's possessions and tidying the house awaited me. Maria had stripped the bed but the rest of the room remained exactly as it was when Mama died. Her slippers were on the floor mat where she left them and her dressing gown lay over the chair.

As an only child, the task of disposing of the items I didn't wish to keep was mine alone. That was the positive part. On the negative side, all the work and decisions fell entirely on my shoulders. I had no intention of turning the house into a shine. My intention was to clear the house, give most of my mother's belongs to a charity and install a tenant. She wasn't a hoarder and had few wants. The contents of the linen cupboard and all the cutlery and crockery fitted in to a few boxes. I placed two of her cake platters aside and the coffee percolator. They reminded me of Mama and I could use them. The items that were hidden in the house during the war, a carved rocking chair that belonged to my great grandmother and her ornate silver tea set, that I had loved as a child and that I pretended had belonged to royalty, I packaged carefully and placed them in my car.

I had left my mother's bedroom cupboards for last. Her clothes were easy enough to pack. I found her small jewellery box and placed it in my large handbag. When I scooped up Mama's underwear from one of the drawers I felt loose papers at the bottom – an old envelope and a single bent black and white photograph. I took the picture to the window and studied it. A thin, elderly man with little hair and sunken cheeks held a child in his arms. One of his forearms had a row of numbers on it. I could just make out most of them. The first three were 634. The next was a zero or an eight and the last a three or a five. Could it be my father and was the child me? I asked myself. I had seen Jews who had survived the Holocaust with

143

similar numbers on their arms. The child's face was turned away from the camera. Mama had said that he'd been desperately ill and died when I was two years old. Immediately I thought of the photograph of my father that had always stood on Mama's dressing table. It was already packed away but I found it and unwrapped its protective covering. When I compared the two I saw the similarity in the shape of the head, the nose and mouth. I had no doubt. He was my father.

I ignored my tight throat and opened the envelope. It contained two double sheets of yellowed paper, one more ornate than the other. Both were written in a text that looked like Hebrew. I wrapped the envelope and the photograph in tissue and carefully placed them in my handbag.

The boxes lay untouched in the boot of the car, until days later when I delivered them to the charity shop. I looked at the photograph often and cried as I imagined my father's suffering.

In Melbourne, I kept the envelope in a drawer, until one morning I decided to show it to Ruth. She could read Hebrew and possibly she'd have an explanation.

'Oh goodness, I know what they are,' Ruth said excitedly. 'They're *ketubas*, marriage contracts. I have one too. Every Jewish woman who marries in an orthodox shul has one.'

'Oh...'

'We got married in a registry office. Richard wouldn't hear of a synagogue wedding. I wanted it but...'

'It doesn't matter.' she touched my hand. She held up the more ornate document. 'It's beautifully decorated, hand painted I'd guess. Aren't all those flowers lovely?'

I nodded.

She looked perplexed. 'I read Hebrew well but I can't understand the writing.'

I wondered if one of the contracts had been my mother's, but I doubted whether she and my father had married in a synagogue.

Ruth took copies of the documents home with her and promised to ask a friend for more information. That night I went to my computer to do some research. I found that the *ketuba* was a contract by which a bridegroom undertakes to provide a financial settlement for his wife if he divorces her, or his heirs, if he dies before her. In Talmudic days the money changed hands was substantial – 200 zuzim for a virgin and 100 zuzim for a widow or divorcee. He was also obligated to feed, protect and work for her and provide her with marital rights. The main purpose of the contract was to prevent a husband from divorcing his wife against her will, which in Talmudic times he could do. When I read that the contract was written in ancient Aramaic I understood why Ruth was unable to read it.

Several days later she took the copies of the *ketubas* out of her briefcase with a huge grin. 'I asked a friend's husband about them. He lived in Israel and toyed with the idea of becoming a rabbi.' She slipped her hand into the pocket of her cardigan. 'I made notes…too much to remember. Both couples came from Hungary. The document in black and white is a contract between Dor and Avram. They were married in 1922 in *Miskolkz*. The colourful one with the flowers is a contract between Frieda and Chaim, dated 1919 from the same place.'

Mama had told me the names of my grandparents, Dor and Avram. The other two names sounded familiar but I wasn't certain whether they were my great grandparents or not. *Miskolkz* was a shtetl north-east of Budapest. It was likely that they were my great grandparents but perhaps I would confirm my suspicions in the future.

Thirty-one

The book I had started reading lay on the floor next to the bed. It was about a Jewish family that survived the Holocaust. I found the few pages I had read interested me but I had trouble concentrating. My thoughts drifted to my own father's experiences during that period.

My aunt had given me some background to my father's life and I was grateful for that. My work in the Vienna library gave me access to archived data. I could add to my knowledge with research. The Germans were renowned for their record keeping and this made my task easier.

It wasn't a pleasant task that I set myself. In my lunch breaks and after work, I sat at the computer and found the lists of prisoners at Theresienstadt. My father, Walter Tannenbaum arrived on 16 November 1942. He was listed as an actor and his captors were thorough enough to note that cigarettes and a bottle of whisky, both disallowed in the camp, were taken from him.

I printed out masses of material about the camp and took it home to study. Initially the details about Theresienstadt distressed me so much, that I found sleep impossible. The details rolled around in my head together with the gruesome photographs recorded. After working on the research for several weeks, as awful as it was, I gained a level of objectivity that allowed me to approach the task I had set myself.

The town of *Terezin,* about sixty kilometres from Prague, was once a garrison built in the late eighteenth century by Emperor Joseph the Second. The fortress was used as a prison. The original population was expelled when the Nazis prepared *Terezin* for its Jewish inmates. They transformed the barracks into a concentration camp initially to hold thousands of Czech and Austrian Jewish prisoners and they named it Theresienstadt. Between 1941 and 1945, approximately 154,000 people were incarcerated there. The intention was to hold their prisoners in the camp for a short period and then deport them to the death camps of Auschwitz-Birkenau, Majdanek and Treblinka.

A dreadful fact emerged. The camp was specifically intended to be a transport centre for older Jews, some as old as ninety. Amongst the elderly prisoners were men who had fought for their country during World War One, prominent Jewish businessmen, well known artists, writers and musicians. At times there were enough musicians in the camp to form an entire symphony orchestra, plus several chamber orchestras all performing at the same time. The camp was unlike Dachau, Auschwitz and others I had read about, in that it had none of the murderous gas ovens, but those prisoners who were too old and sickly to work, were deported to death camps. The prisoners were separated. Men and boys over fifteen were separated from the women and girls. All children under fifteen were removed from their parents' care. No communication was allowed between barracks and any infringement of these orders meant severe punishment. The younger, physically fit prisoners were a source of slave labour for the war effort. Men split mica for generators in the local forests, made shoes and coffins. Women worked in the kitchens, nursed the sick or laboured on the farm outside the camp. Prisoners were identified by their numbers but also by triangular coloured patches that denoted the prisoner's category. Political prisoners wore red patches, homosexuals, pink, Jehovah's Witnesses purple, black was for the work shy and criminals wore green. In Theresienstadt the majority of prisoners were Jews and wore yellow patches. Some wore more than one patch. The way in which the Nazis established control lines was ingenious. To carry out their orders and organise the day to day running of the camp such as distributing food, they chose a Jewish elder and a *Judenrat* or Jewish council made up from the prisoners. By 1943, the council had established a hospital, organised concerts, made sure the children had a makeshift school and encouraged drawing and the writing of poetry. However their most unpleasant task was to compile lists of names of those prisoners who were no longer able to work, for deportation to the death camps.

Discipline was another matter. The Nazis interspersed Czech police amongst the SS guarding the camp. According to the material I read, the Czechs were harsher and enjoyed their dominant position. A few photographs showed the SS guards wearing a special skull and cross bone insignia on their caps and sleeves. There were beatings and punishment and isolation cells for prisoners who would not obey their rules but I could not face reading those awful details.

One evening I stayed back late to view two films made about Theresienstadt. The introduction of the first showed the town as it is now, its neat cemetery with rows of graves, a shady park and the monuments erected since the war. The camera then panned onto archival material. It showed the separate men and women's barracks and children in the park with barely space to move let alone play. How had culture flowered in the unsanitary overcrowding? Plays and music was written and performed. There were photographs of concerts held in the camp and I questioned where they found the space. Apparently the guards turned a blind eye to the concerts and many were in the audience. As much as they enjoyed the performances they continued to deport these talented people to their death.

The second film was in German with English subtitles. It was the propaganda film the Nazis made to prove to the world that they were treating their prisoners humanely. I had read that after a group of Danish prisoners were sent to the camp, the Danish Red Cross had enquired about the conditions at the camp. The Nazis allowed them to visit but beforehand they made swift alterations, planting flowers and greenery, and adding a fake school and coffee shop. The film showed healthy prisoners wearing their own clothing rather than prison uniforms. They made handbags and pottery and sang while they worked. At night well-dressed adults attended concerts and lectures. Food was plentiful and nutritious; rather than the real usual single serve of watery vegetable soup with bread. The film was sickening.

For weeks after watching the films a dream recurred. I was a child in Leopoldstadt, outside the *Stadttempel.* A ghostly figure walked beside me through the cobbled streets and led me to the city square, the *Judenplaz* that was the focus of the city's traditional Jewish life since the thirteenth century. We passed a plaque with a Latin inscription dating back to 1497, reminding me of the roots of anti-Semitism. Translated it stated that the Jews deserved the fate that befell them. At the northern end we walked up to the Holocaust memorial, erected in remembrance of the Austrian victims of the Holocaust. I had seen the concrete cube often enough and its wall resembling piles of books in a library, but with the names of the books turned illegibly inward, representing the victims stories that will never be known. I saw again the doubled doors that had no knobs and could not open.

I awoke sad and unsettled. The message of the dream baffled me. If it was telling me that my research was unfinished, I knew that to be true. I knew too that I had yet to visit my maternal grandmother's grave at the old Jewish section of the *Zentalfriedhof* cemetery.

That afternoon, I took a tram to the cemetery situated in *Simmering*, outside the city centre. *Zentalfriedhof* is one of the largest cemeteries in Europe with thousands of graves. There are two Jewish sections and I headed towards the older one that was established in 1863. I walked down the tree-lined avenues of dilapidated graves hunting for my grandmother's tombstone. Some of the graves that had been smashed or defaced at the time of *Kristallnacht* had not been repaired. Others were so weathered that the writing was indecipherable. Would my grandmother's resting place be in ruins, I wondered. I found it covered in ivy but intact, amongst leaning headstones with trees and roots growing through them. Fortunately I could make out her name, Dorit and her date of birth and death. Though the rest was in Hebrew, I noticed the names Frieda and Chaim on the tombstone as well. I had found the answer to the question of the second Ketuba. Frieda and Chaim were my great grandparents. I set about ripping away the ivy. When I left, I placed my pebbles on the grave and walked away quickly.

While in the cemetery I took a long walk to see the graves of Beethoven, Brahms and Shubert. The well-tended cemetery was in stark contrast to the one I had visited earlier. I would wait before visiting the graves of my paternal grandparents.

Thirty-Two

The clattering of rain on the roof woke me. A door opened and I heard the sound of Anton's footsteps. It was 5.45, too early for him to be up. He was probably hungry, I thought. I yawned and placed my feet on the cold floor and felt for my gown and slippers. The only light in the house came from the kitchen.

'Hello Mutti,' he wiped his mouth and pushed the empty cereal bowl aside. 'Hope I didn't wake you.'

'No, the rain on the roof did that.'

He had turned on the kettle and water was boiling.

'Coffee?' he asked.

I nodded as I looked at him. He was dressed in jeans and a crumpled shirt. He must have just come in. Where had he been and why was he home so late? I wanted to ask but my tongue froze. He'd hate me asking. If I stayed in the kitchen with him perhaps he'd tell me. He drank his coffee and polished off a packet of biscuits. All the while his head was averted and not a word was said to me. My frustration was building. I bent closer to see him more clearly. He looked dreadful and he smelled.

'So, Anton, where have you been?' I finally asked.

He didn't reply.

'With the young man who own the sports car?'

'Yes. Listen Mutti, I don't like this interrogation. I haven't done anything wrong...I'm just meeting new friends and enjoying myself. You don't begrudge me that, do you?'

Before I could answer he stomped out of the room and was up the stairs.

A few days earlier he had insisted that he was "very happy" and that "life in Melbourne was far better than in Vienna". I doubted he was being honest with me. He lacked the joyfulness, the glow that the young have when they're happy. It must have been almost six months since we'd arrived in Melbourne but it felt longer. How excited he had been earlier about the adventure of living in a new country and attending a foreign university. Just as well I insisted on speaking English at home in the months before leaving. He mentioned that he was managing his lectures now and beginning to think and write in English. I noticed that he had picked up university slang too. He laughed when he told me that the other students were intrigued that he came from Austria, but apart from the one young man in a sports car, who picked him up for university in the morning and took him out some nights, no one popped in to chat or study.

At last the rain stopped and I pulled back the living room curtains to welcome the glow of dawn. It was time I had a long talk with my sons, told them all that I knew about their Jewish heritage. It couldn't wait. Gabe was hoping to visit us in Melbourne soon, but he wasn't certain of his plans. Somehow I would find a way of sharing the information I had gathered with them both. Even if what I had to tell them bored them now, they would remember it later. I thought of asking the Rabbi to talk to them, and to possibly invite them to a service. More knowledge about their background was vital, before they followed in my uncertain footsteps.

The sun was up and the moment of beauty that had gilded the room vanished, leaving it beige again. I thought of Luke and clicked on my computer. There was sufficient time to write to him before I showered and dressed for work. The longer we were apart the more I missed him.

Lately life with Richard is barely tolerable. If you were here with me, I wouldn't notice the holes in our marriage. I wouldn't care. In one of your emails you dropped little hints that you might come to Australia. I wish you would. Every day I wish it. Please write and tell me how you are and your news.

Thirty-Three

I threw myself into work. Late one afternoon, Ruth caught up with me. 'I've been trying to talk to you all day.' She changed her weight from one foot to the other. 'There's something I want to ask you.'

'Well?'

'I've been wondering if you'd like to come along with me to synagogue on Saturday morning.'

I was taken aback at first and did not answer her immediately.

'You don't have to give me an answer right away. Think about it.'

'I don't need time to think, I'd love to go with you.'

Early on Saturday morning I dressed modestly and drove to the synagogue. The exterior of the rectangular, brick building was ugly. It was designed with no decorative panels or spires reaching to heaven, and no plants or trees to break its starkness. I assumed that it was the inside that counted. I did not have to wait long, Ruth rushed up, full of excuses for keeping me waiting.

I followed her through the vestibule and up the stairs to the women's gallery. She greeted some of the other women and we found seats. She explained the layout of the synagogue and told me what to expect during the service. When she rattled off a list of Hebrew names for items in the synagogue or connected with the service I was lost. Any other questions, she said I would have to ask someone more knowledgeable.

As she handed me a prayer book, I berated myself for leaving the one Ernst had given me at home. As the service was in Hebrew, she suggested that I read the translation. My sense of being out of place could only be compared to my first day at high school. I stood when everyone else stood and sat when they did. Soon I realised that the congregation always stood when the curtains of the ark at the front of the shul opened. I observed the scene in the section below us. All the men wore prayer shawls and their heads were covered with yarmulkes. The reverberating sounds were of the cantor leading the prayers and the men joining him.

Light shone through the stained glass windows that told religious stories I did not understand. It wasn't that I didn't believe in a higher power, a God. But that God didn't appear to take the same form of the God I was reading about in the prayer book. My God was an amorphous God that controlled everything, plant animal, mineral and human, and also the dead. That my belief was in line with the Jewish faith and most others did not occur to me then.

I was aware that the layout of the synagogue, the prayers and rituals were ancient, perpetuated through generations of young men and their fathers. The idea of the history appealed to me, but I felt a mixture of sadness and anger that during my years of growing up in Vienna, Mama had deprived me of the opportunity to be part of all this. My thoughts tumbled and I was lost in them until Ruth's clear soprano joining the choir, carried me back. I heard her prayer book snap closed. The service had ended.

'*Good Shabbos,*' Ruth said giving me a kiss.

In bed that night I relived the morning's experience, the glimpse into my heritage. I held the prayer book Ernest had given me and turned the worn pages until I found the Sabbath service. The High German was difficult to understand and I was slow, but I read a few pages before closing it. If not for Ruth I might not have had this taste of my past.

※

As I drove home from work, the weather turned nasty, vicious winds flailing all in its path. Fortunately I was safe before the storm unleashed its torrent. I held my hands over my ears as rain and hail pelted the roof. Within an hour it was over. I checked the house for damage. All was intact, with the air crisp and the stars sparkling.

Richard and Anton were not home yet. I tried their cell phones and left messages but they did not return my calls. I could only hope that they were safe. Later, after my attempts to reach them failed, I left a note on the table that dinner was in the microwave ready for heating. I went to bed but lay there unable to sleep. Richard arrived first. When the front door banged and I heard my son's voice, I closed my eyes.

In the weeks that followed, communication with Richard deteriorated further. It was only in front of our son that we made an effort at civility. There was no point in sharing a bedroom. I moved out, leaving him the king size bed. The way he was expanding he needed it more than I did. I no longer feigned interest in his work. At least now if I chose to, I could read late into the night.

Work provided me with a routine and contact with people. When the librarian in charge asked for a volunteer to work late to cull old books cluttering the shelves, I was the first to offer. There was nothing for me at home and the extra money was useful.

Once everyone had left the library, I turned on the radio to a music station and worked happily. The time passed quickly and at 9.30p.m., the time agreed on, I doused the lights and locked the library door behind me. Tired and thirsty, I stopped at a bistro on the main road. Hungrier than I realised, I ordered a sandwich and a bowl of fries. By the time I turned into my street, it was well past 10.15p.m.

All the house lights were on and Richard was pacing outside the gate. 'Where the hell have you been? I was about to phone the hospitals and the police.'

His voice was more frightened than angry. I had forgotten to tell him that I was working late. I tried to explain but his complaints drowned me out.

'Did you find something to eat?' I asked.

'Yes, in the freezer but that's not important... I was worried about you.'

I stared at him. 'You were worried?'

'Of course. Just because we're going through a bad patch it doesn't mean I don't care about you.'

'A bad patch!'

'Let's sit down, have a drink and talk,' he said, his arm herding me into the sitting room.

I asked myself what we could say to each other, but I didn't argue. I sat on the couch. He handed me a glass of white wine and poured a beer for himself. While we talked, he paced.

'I know you've been unhappy. Your eyes say everything.'

'So?'

'We knew coming to Australia wouldn't be easy.'

'Mmmm.'

'It's not been a joy ride for me either. Maybe you think I just waltzed into the new job. Well I didn't. The systems they've put in and the plant aren't anything like the ones I was used to in Vienna.'

'Well?'

'They showed me into an office with a huge desk and plush carpet. All very nice... but I was handed two thick green manuals to read, listing all the Australian adaptations. My head was a mess and I couldn't concentrate. I still haven't got it all straight in my brain.'

'How could I know if you didn't tell me?'

'And how could I tell you? It was like coming home to a piece of wood. You weren't interested in anything I had to say. I don't blame you, it was too hard to cope with my problems on top of what you were going through.'

'Mmmm,' I muttered again.

He sat down next to me and clumsily placed his arm around my shoulder. I felt like the piece of wood he had described. I did not encourage him with a squeeze or a pat, nor did I push his arm away. His grip around me tightened as he pulled me closer and stroked my head. Practical as always, I allowed him to nudge me towards the bedroom. I wanted to turn away or make an excuse but I felt sorry for him. It was the first time he had been open with me since the move. Hurriedly he pulled off his clothes and slipped under the doona. I took a little longer and joined him. The sheet was cool next to my body and I shivered.

'I'll warm you up,' he said.

Breathing much harder now, he caressed my joy spots, as he called them. I surprised myself by responding. In minutes he rolled over and with a sigh, closed his eyes.

'Hope it was good for you too,' he murmured.

I did not have to lie. He was asleep.

Thirty-Four

There was one message in my computer inbox.

Dear Mrs Biederman

We hereby advise you of our contractor's findings while demolishing the house we purchased from you at twenty-three Weintraubengasse, Leopoldstadt.

In the downstairs room that served as a study, the contractors discovered a sealed compartment hidden in the wooden shelving. A wide space had been cut into the shelves and then covered by a wooden flap. Once books filled the shelves it would not have been noticed.

Inside the compartment we found a large metal folder (90 cms x 55cms). The size and weight of the folder and the cost of sending it to you, led us to believe that it was best to open it and ascertain the contents prior to sending it. I hope that you will excuse this liberty, taken in the pursuit of a practical solution.

We advise you that that the metal folder contains several drawings and paintings, each signed by Walter Tannenbaum. If we send the metal folder to you by sea post it will cost you approximately $150.00. Should you want us to send the material to you, we will be happy to do so.

We await your instruction.

Yours faithfully,

Daniel Ungaro

For R. R. Property Developers.

Paintings signed by my father! A secret panel! And inside a large metal folder! I could only think that my father had built the compartment when he and Mama were restoring the house. More secrets! No one kept secrets like that today. With cell phones, Facebook and Twitter some people revealed their every thought and activity. For a moment I allowed myself a touch of optimism that at last I might find out more about my father.

The library was quiet that morning and Ruth and I talked as we worked.

'You must still be missing your friends and life in Vienna… so different to life here,' Ruth said.

'Yes, I do miss them and the old city,' I replied as I placed a book on the shelf. 'This is such a new land with no history.'

'No history! I'll tell you a little about our history later.'

During a break, Ruth told me about the *Wurundjeri* people. I had no idea that at least 4,000 years before the Whites settled in the country, indigenous people called the *Wurundjeri* had inhabited a massive slice of land along the Yarra, the waterway flowing through the suburbs and beyond.

'One can just imagine them in their canoes making their way along the waterways of the Yarra River. The wild-life was plentiful, with possums, kangaroos and eels to sustain them as well as plants, roots and fruits. Your present house is probably built on *Wurundjeri* land.'

Clearly I had some history to catch up on.

I longed to move, but I had no idea where to start house hunting. The thought of finding a suitable home was daunting. Where were the most "liveable" suburbs in Melbourne?

When I caught up with Magda she made suggestions, but one look at the prices real estate agents were asking for homes in those areas, decided me against them. Over the weekends, I drove through streets in areas I thought might suit us. Tired and confused, I usually ended up outside an estate agent's office staring at a window display of houses for sale. Those that interested me were too expensive and the rest didn't tempt me. The memory of Ruth and Paul's house in a street with tall overhanging oak trees remained with me. It reminded me of our last house in a similar tree lined street.

Ruth suggested a real estate agent she knew and my hunt for a home became a more professional endeavour. It didn't take the agent long to provide a list of choices. Both Richard and I took a liking to a single storey house in dark brick and wood with a dreamy garden. Though we invited Anton to view the house, he claimed he was too busy and that his opinion didn't matter as he'd be moving into his own place soon.

We persisted through the ordeal of the auction and though the price escalated ridiculously, we secured the house. Richard had made arrangements with his company's bank for a loan and he didn't appear to be as perturbed as I was by the costs involved. The best part was that we could move in within two months. Once arrangements were made for the container holding our possessions to be sent to the new address, I waited impatiently, visualising the placement of our beds, tables and chairs and naturally my piano.

Mama was secretive about so much, yet she spoke openly about my grandmother and in the softest tones. I found this difficult to understand when she avoided talking about my father.

She relished telling me about this diminutive, gifted woman and I did not tire of the stories. My grandmother was a child prodigy, playing simple tunes on the piano by four years of age and more complex pieces faultlessly by seven. She chose to play Mozart and Beethoven and knew the pieces by heart.

By the age of thirteen she won competitions throughout Europe and began a career of concert performances, with her mastery reaching its peak a few years before the Second World War broke out. Luckily Mama had kept a few precious recordings of my grandmother playing at concerts in Berlin and Prague. Since then I'd had them enhanced. The sound was a bit scratchy but her skill amazed me.

'If you practiced every day for hours like grandmama did, you could be as good her. I'm sure of that. You've got her touch and the same feeling when you play. Like you she sang with a sweet voice,' Mama said. 'It was a treat to listen to her singing in the kitchen while I was preparing our meal or cleaning. Though my father wasn't as talented a singer, some evenings he would sing with her.'

Like my grandmother, I preferred playing classical music but no matter how many praises I received, I could not help feeling inadequate when comparing myself to her. I lacked my grandmother's perseverance and played the pieces I knew by heart for my own pleasure. To me music was like my breath. As my fingers moved over the keys, I was expressing the composer's intent and feelings as well as my own and I disappeared into a timeless, consoling space.

Richard, my mother and their friends enjoyed listening to me play, but entertaining them was not my intention. It was to be expected that my sons loathed my choice of classics. Now and again, they leaned against the piano and tapped their feet as I rolled out popular music to please them.

'One day you'll appreciate good music,' I'd say to them. I didn't realise then how important music was to a generation. I should have. I still hum to ABBA tunes on the radio while driving.

Thirty-Five

Early one morning we were woken by loud banging on the front door. Richard rushed downstairs. In seconds I was behind him. In the pale pre-dawn light, two policemen stood in the doorway.

'We're looking for Anton Tannen ... baum,' one policeman said slowly consulting his piece of paper.

Richard scowled at them. 'Tannenbaum. Yes! What's wrong?'

'We would like to speak to Anton. Your son?'

'Please come inside while my husband goes to look for him,' I said, uncertainly. I felt my heart race. I'd had nothing to do with police in Vienna. Was Anton at home? I hadn't heard him come in. And what had he been up to?

The policemen followed me inside and waited in the hall. The older one, a sergeant, shuffled his feet impatiently.

'I'm sure he won't be long,' I said, hoping to placate them.

After a wait, Richard marched down the passage with Anton behind him. He was dressed, though scruffily.

'Here he is ... Anton Tannenbaum,' Richard said a little too loudly. 'What do you want with him?'

'It's in connection with a certain Dragar Barboescu,' the younger policeman replied.

'Barboescu! A Rumanian?' There was a controlled shriek in Richard's voice.

I clutched Richard's arm. 'My God Richard! What's this about?'

'Let's keep calm and sit down,' the sergeant said.

Richard tightened the belt of his dressing gown. 'Yes, I'm sure we can sort this out.'

I ushered the policemen into the sitting room and Richard and Anton followed.

The sergeant leant forward, his expression grim as he faced our son. 'Do you know this man ... Dragar Barboescu?'

'Yes... I know him.' Anton looked at the floor. 'What's the problem?'

The sergeant tapped the table with his pen. 'Well then, where is he?'

Anton shrugged. 'How do I know?' he replied too quickly.

'You should know, you've been spending a lot of time with him. You've been seen together. Last Friday as it happens, at a bar in the city.' He referred to his notes. 'In Lonsdale Street to be exact.'

'Yes I was there. Aren't new migrants to the country allowed to drink in pubs?'

The younger policeman clenched his fist. 'Don't try to be smart.'

Richard glared at his son.

'Dragar has been good to me, showed me the scene,' Anton said.

'The scene eh! And he also took you to his lab in that fancy red sports car of his, did he?' the younger policeman said sharply.

'Lab? What lab?' Anton looked startled.

'Before we get on to Barboescu's drug game, I want the truth out of you NOW or we'll take you into the station for questioning. I'll ask you once again ... where is Barboescu and when did you last see him?'

Richard walked over to Anton. 'The truth now, son. No more mucking around.'

Anton swallowed hard and nervously eyed his father. 'I was with some guys at The Elephant and Wheelbarrow last night and saw him there. I greeted him and that was it... heard one of them say they were all going for a burger. It was at around 1.30 and I stayed on with friends for about half an hour or so. I didn't have a ride home and so I took a cab,' he added as an after thought.

'Do you know the names of these guys he was with?' The sergeant asked.

'They were heavy looking, with loads of tattoos. We were never introduced. Anyway, they ignored me.'

The younger policeman stood and stared down at Anton. 'That doesn't help us much.'

'Let's move on then,' the sergeant said impatiently. 'Did this Dragar ever give you any of his homemade feel good tablets?'

'You mean drugs?' Anton replied looking shaken.

'Yeah, drugs!'

'He gave me some E, if that's what you're getting at,' he said. 'Just a few tabs but I've already had them.'

'What I'm interested in is whether he asked you to flog his stuff?' The sergeant asked in his sternest voice.

'Oh my God!' Richard mumbled.

Anton was trembling now. 'Definitely not. I'm not a druggie or a dealer.'

'After all that time spent softening up a new boy and nothing's come of it, he wouldn't have been pleased,' the sergeant said with a grimace.

Anton stared out the window. 'Well if what you say is true, I'm not pleased either. I thought he was a friend,' he said softly.

'I don't wonder,' the sergeant said. 'We'll be checking your story with the barman at the Elephant and Wheelbarrow. He's a reliable bloke who knows who's who in his pub.'

The younger policeman looked at Richard. 'We'll have a quick look through the boy's room before we go, then, if that's OK with you?'

'Richard nodded. 'Go ahead.'

What was Richard thinking? God knows what Anton had in his room. Richard was lying down and rolling over. From my experience, police needed a warrant to search. It couldn't be that different in Australia. It was too late. Angrily I watched him lead the policemen up the stairs with Anton following reluctantly. I remained in the sitting room. My fear was so intense, that I heard the wall clock tick each minute until they came lumbering back down. Richard caught my eye and opened his arms wide miming to me that the police had found nothing. The sergeant beckoned to his sidekick and they moved to the corner of the room to confer. A few minutes later they joined us.

'That's it for now, but we may be back for more information,' the younger one said.

As they walked through the door, the sergeant stopped and looked back at Anton. 'A word of advice. You're new to the country young man, and green by the look of it, so watch out who you spend your time with in future.'

When the policemen left, I closed the kitchen door and waited in the sitting room for Richard's yelling to subside. Anton said little in his own defence. Once there was silence I joined them. Richard's face was sour.

'You used to be discriminating about people, Anton. This time you were so desperate to make new friends that your judgement went out the window.' I took a breath before continuing. 'Maybe this wouldn't have happened if Gabe was here.'

Richard nodded. 'Yes, pity he's not here.'

'But you're our son and we love you.' I said quickly.

Richard cleared his throat. 'Yes, of course we do.'

I put an arm around Anton's shoulder. 'And we wouldn't let anything happen to you, you know that.'

'Of course,' Richard echoed.

I walked towards the cooker. 'We've got to tackle this thing head on. Blame isn't going to fix it. I'll make some breakfast now and then we'll talk it through... make a plan. And Richard, if you're late for work today, it's too bad.'

No one spoke over the meal and the tense atmosphere eased only after Richard left for work. Anton and I talked about how difficult it was to find one's way in the new country and how important it was to fit in and make friends. It was a start.

In the past I had handled emergencies calmly and efficiently but this time I crumbled. By mid morning my legs shook. I lay on the couch and slept the day away. It was dark when I woke. Richard wasn't home yet, but reassuringly loud music emanated from the upstairs bedroom. I inhaled the sweetness of Lilly Pilly and wondered if the police would let the Dragar matter die.

The following weekend Richard and I decided to buy Anton a car. If he had his own transport he wouldn't be dependent on others for lifts. He clearly disliked taking the train to the university and had ignored our argument that it was only a short walk. Richard's secretary suggested a second hand dealer she knew personally and we followed her advice. A week later, Richard drove home with a small, second- hand Toyota for Anton.

Any mention of the *politzei* made Mama tremble. Sirens of any sort made her shake. She offered no explanation for her fears but she did not need to. I understood that in her past men in uniform were associated with unpleasant memories. She warned me to keep away from the police. I was not to look in their direction or make eye contact. I was also to be wary of strangers. The term paranoia could have applied to Mama if there hadn't been a firm core of rationality behind those fears of hers.

We were alone in the large house, a women and a girl without the presence of a man. No wonder she felt vulnerable. Back then, having a man around for protection or even to speak on your behalf was an important asset. I grew up during the years of the Cold War, when the presence of the *Abwehr* or secret police, anxious to protect Austria's neutrality was part of our lives. We all knew they were out there eyeing foreigners, or anyone who looked as if they were instigating an antigovernment disturbance. The trouble was that they looked like one of us and blended into the milieu. It was scary.

The family of a girl I went to school with had a *wachter,* a watcher. At first the family didn't take any notice of the ordinary looking man in a duffle coat who hung about outside their house smoking cigarettes. After a few days when he didn't move along, they realised there was something sinister about him. He was there mornings and evening when her father was home, and some days he followed her father to work. Her father was a Yugoslavian immigrant who worked on an Austrian leftist newspaper. I wasn't told whether he was questioned or threatened but nothing dreadful appeared to happen to him.

Mama had no cause for concern. She was more law abiding than most people. If a shopkeeper made the mistake of giving her too much change she would return it. She obeyed traffic lights to the second and always kept to the sidewalk. Poor Mama!

Late one afternoon, I saw a policeman walking along *Weintraubenstasse* and wondered where he was going. I had a shock when he knocked on our door. I thought Mama would faint. The policeman said that he was carrying out a routine door knock, asking residents if they had noticed anything unusual in the street that morning. There had been a robbery and the police were gathering witness statements. I can remember how relieved she was when she told him that she hadn't noticed a thing and he left.

During those years, we all knew that hidden eyes were watching us. Not only the eyes of the security police, the army and officials but members of our community. Vienna was a city of watchers who reported anyone or anything that offended their sense of order or did not conform to their views. People reported neighbours and even friends. Police on foot made their presence felt and consequently petty crime and vandalism was reduced. Graffiti was hardly ever seen on walls, unsecured bicycles were not stolen and sidewalks were easier places to walk along. But we paid for our orderliness and civic pride with the loss of our freedom.

Thirty-Six

Autumn in Vienna arrived with the smell of ripening grapes, long walks and the start of the music season. In the cool weather, I like others, turned to the cafés for hot chocolate and coffee. In sports mad Melbourne, the Autumn focus was on footy. I watched the strange, tough, but athletic game of Australian football and struggled to follow it.

The seasonal change marked the move to our new house. All we took with us were our suitcases and items of food. Our container was waiting for us with almost everything we had carefully packed intact. Richard and Anton applied themselves to lifting and prising open the tea chests, while the unwrapping of loved possessions and finding a place for each of them was left to me. There was pleasure in touching, and often caressing each item associated with memories of Vienna.

I was unwrapping an ornament, when Richard gave a holler. 'Ella, where do you want us to put your piano?'

Carefully I put the ornament down and ran to Richard.

'I know the exact position,' I said, pointing to a sunny spot in the corner of the room. My piano had always fitted neatly into a corner and there was no reason for a change. Richard and Anton cursed as they lifted the Baby Grand but together they placed it where I asked. I dusted it and opened the lid. My emotions flooded in so fast that I could barely contain my build-up of longing and joy. My old friend was back in my life.

After adjusting the height of the stool, I sat at the piano, took a deep breath and tentatively played a few notes. In spite of the long journey no tuning was necessary. I played the opening notes to Beethoven's Moonlight Sonata and satisfied, rested my hands on the keys. When all the unpacking was done I would play my much-loved pieces.

There were three chests of our books. Richard's professional and technical books went into the bookcase in the study and mine fitted nicely into the shelves in the sitting room and once again Simone de Beauvior, Virginia Woolf, Betty Frieden and my other modern favourites were with me.

Once the tea chests were piled into the garage and awaiting collection, the house looked and felt like ours. I hummed while making dinner as a new contentedness swept over me. Luke remained a loving shadow. Whenever I was happy I felt I had to share my joy with him. I wrote to tell him about our move, describing the house in detail, telling him where we had placed the piano and the furniture. This time he decided to phone us to express his congratulations. He asked for photos of the house as soon as possible.

I thought less of Vienna and at night my dream of the Big Wheel disappeared. The Australian accent no longer sounded as jarring and I was beginning to understand some of the slang. For the first time I appreciated my colleagues' easy humour, their non-conformism and the sardonic way they made light of their troubles. All in all, I was pleased with most things.

Soon after we moved, Ruth, Paul and their children visited. Ruth placed a package on the kitchen bench. 'A few items for a Jewish home - bread, salt and wine. May you never be without them,' she said with a kiss on my cheek.

Paul took a tiny box from his pocket. 'I've brought you something as well. It goes on the doorframe beneath the lintel... a *mezuzah*.'

 He removed a box as long as a toothbrush and as wide a man's thumb from its package.

'I forgot all about a *mezuzah*,' Richard said softly.

When Paul slid open the box a slim silver ornament lay inside. 'What is it?' I asked.

'It contains a piece of parchment from a Hebrew biblical text,' Richard replied.

'It's your spiritual helmet... to keep you safe,' Paul added.

'That's very thoughtful of you,' I said. I looked at Richard. It sounded important.

Paul fixed the *mezuzah* on the doorframe and said a Hebrew prayer to bless our home.

While I was in the kitchen, I heard Richard bragging to Ruth and Paul about my piano playing. 'Did you know that Ella is an excellent classical pianist?'

'She hasn't said a word about it to me. Please Ella, we want to hear you play,' Ruth said loudly enough for me to hear.

How could I refuse? I sat at the piano and after a moment's thought my hands flew over the keys.

'I think she's playing Beethoven's *Appasionata*,' Ruth whispered.

Then I was lost in the music and forgot I had an audience. When I finished playing, they applauded. I gave a slight bow and stood.

'Your playing is wonderful... just wonderful. You should be in the orchestra.'

'Absolutely!' Paul added.

'I've told her that so often,' Richard said but...'

'I play for myself and don't want the pressure of constant practice.'

The discussion about my playing continued all the way down the driveway until we said our goodbyes. I remained in the garden. Tall trees cast shadows and flecks of pink tinted the sky. The garden was traditional with old flowering shrubs and beds and I loved it. We had it all, a lovely garden and home with a mezuzah on the doorframe but I did not feel Jewish. What was it that made one feel Jewish?

The next day, Sunday, Karl and Magda arrived laden with parcels. Magda had baked her special chocolate cake she knew I liked and Karl brought a fine malt whiskey to toast the new house. We showed them every part of the house and their praise of our choice was genuine.

'It looks like a European house,' Magda said as she rubbed the toe of her shoe over the polished floorboards. 'I'm sure you'll be happy here.'

We drank a toast to our future in the house. Then the two men sat in front of the television and watched an overseas soccer match, while Magda and I went into the kitchen to prepare afternoon tea. It had been a busy weekend but Richard and I were both happier than we had been for months. We'd had our friends around us, their gifts and good wishes.

Thirty-Seven

Richard was asleep on the couch, his snoring competing with the din emanating from Anton's room. Though Anton showed no interest in the new house, he moved in with us. It was a temporary arrangement he insisted, until he was able to shift into his own place. Earlier that week, I noticed a small article in the newspaper about Dragar Barboescu. He had been taken into custody and was awaiting a trial on several counts of drug manufacturing and distribution. Out of habit I cut out the article and placed it in my diary. It was a relief to learn that he was out of the way for a while, at least.

The move had exhausted me. I had taken a few days off work and needed recovery time. Instead of doing necessary cleaning, I gravitated to the established garden. There was time to explore and enjoy the many shrubs, flowers and the tall shady trees the former owners had planted. A row of peaches and nectarines ran along the one side of the fence. That delighted me. I would bottle the fruit for the winter months.

The spot I chose to relax was under the lacy foliage of a shady silver birch, close enough to the roses to smell their perfume. In the summer warmth my thoughts travelled to the garden I knew as a child.

Grandmama had selected tall tea roses and fragrant damasks for her garden, boldly coloured, hardy plants with vicious thorns. When the roses bloomed, I picked a small posy to put in a vase in my bedroom. During the summer months of my holidays I hid amongst a heap of rose petals tucked under the trees. There I read undisturbed. My favourite book and one I read many times, was Heidi by Johanna Spyri. I became the child living in the alpine cottage with her strange grandfather and with no one to talk to except her shepherd friend. Heidi was a lot like me and I understood her plight. I imagined that Luke was the shepherd.

The plump ginger cat from the next door house found me each day. I saved a piece of meat for her from dinner the night before and kept it hidden from Mama. After a snack, Snoookie, as I called her, would cuddle up next to me. I thought it a fair exchange. I longed for a cat or dog of my own but Mama wasn't used to animals around the house.

The aromas from the kitchen competed with those of the garden. Mama baked once or twice a week in those days, and I could identify the cakes that would soon grace our table. The sweetness of *Apfelstrudel* and tart smell of *Zwetschgen Torte* were my favourites. My mouth watered at the mere thought of a strudel or plum tart. Often I watched mama go through the complicated process of making the strudel. She mixed the dough, rested it in the fridge for a while, and then came the hard bit of tugging and spreading the dough. When it was thin enough, she filled it with apples, raisins and walnuts and then delicately placed it in the oven. The plum tart was made with the first and sweetest plums of the season. I had the job of slicing the plums in half and removing the pips. I ate a few before Mama laid the halves in the tart case in a circular pattern and then sprinkled sugar over the lot. The tart came out of the oven with a tangy aroma and we ate it with beaten cream. I thought it tastier than the strudel and always asked for a second slice.

A sudden downpour disturbed my reverie. I gathered my rug and book and ran indoors. I was unexpectedly hungry, not for a sandwich but for something sweet like the cakes I had recalled. The small delicatessen near the library satisfied some of my wants but none of the foods were fresh, and I soon tired of them. I checked the pantry. I had all the ingredients for a strudel. Mama's strudel board, the wooden board she used for making the thin strudel dough was in one of the rooms and after hunting I retrieved it. No recipe book was necessary, the ingredients were firmly planted in my head. The mixture was soon made, the base in shape. Within minutes it was filled and in the oven. When I bit into the succulent layer of dough, I was home in Vienna. After three large pieces with cream, I was bursting. I covered the rest of the strudel and left it as a surprise for Anton when he came home. Strudel was by far his favourite.

⁂

In my excitement over the new house, I hadn't paid Anton much attention. He spent most of his time alone in his room. He hadn't spoken to Gabe on Skype and brushed aside my attempts at chats over breakfast. As the police had not contacted us again and Anton didn't mention their visit, I assumed that it no longer bothered him. When I noticed him hanging about the house instead of attending university I began to worry. I went up to his room. At first, he didn't answer when I knocked on his door but after persisting he peered out at me through a chink of a few centimetres.

'Yes, Mutti?'

'Let's talk,' I said hesitantly.

'Not now,' he said, closing the door.

An hour later he was still in his room. I knocked again.

'What do you want?'

'Just to know if you're okay.'

He muttered something inaudible but didn't open the door.

'Dinner's almost ready!' I called loudly.

He ignored my call and did not come downstairs to eat.

The following day his coffee cup lay on the bench but no cereal bowl. I knocked on his door again.

'What is it this time, Mutti?' he said through the closed door.

I stood there wondering what I could say.

'I want to talk to you... that's all.'

He opened the door far enough to poke his head out.

'What do you want to talk about? The door was wide open now. I saw the heaps of dirty clothes, unopened boxes of books

174

and CD's. I stopped myself from commenting on the mess. Instead I hunted for words that would draw him out of the room.

'I'm lonely. Please come and have a cup of coffee with me downstairs.'

He moved from one foot to another. 'Oh, alright, I'll be down in a second.'

The kettle had boiled and coffee was cold by the time he arrived.

He plopped into the chair and scowled. 'Well then?'

'I wanted to catch up. There hasn't been much time... with the move.'

He scratched his thigh and shrugged. 'Never mind.'

I placed a hot cup of coffee on the table and he nodded his thanks.

'And so, Mutti, are you getting the house into shape?'

'Sure. Everything is fine.'

He was looking pale and tired in spite of sleeping his days away. I searched for the right words.

'Have something to eat.'

He shook his head. 'I'm not hungry.'

'That's not like you. Something must be worrying you.'

He looked at me. 'Wouldn't you be worried if the police turned up to question you?'

'Of course I would... and we are concerned but...'

'There's been talk on the campus that Dragar has been charged... but no details.'

I remembered the newspaper cutting and stretched for my diary. 'Have a look at this.'

After reading the article, he looked up. 'Thanks, reading that helps a bit.'

I put my hand on his. 'He'll be out of the way soon.'

The memories won't be... out of the way. It's the police. '

I put my arms around him and hugged him.

My throat tightened. 'Perhaps you need to talk to someone... professional.'

'No, no. I'll be okay.'

I stroked his hand. 'Are you sure?'

'I could do with some toast and jam.'

'What is it with the police?' I persisted.

'Ah, nothing.' He shrugged me away.

'No, no, it's important.'

He sipped the coffee and nibbled his toast.

'I've always had a thing about them... since I was little.'

'How come?'

'I think it started when I was with grandmama. If she saw a policeman we avoided him by walking down the next street. She told Gabe and me some horrible stories about the Nazis. She warned us to keep away from all policemen and be careful... that all men in uniform were Nazis inside. It stuck in my head.'

'Yes, I know. She told me the same thing.'

I had moved my chair next to his by now and my arm was around him. 'Are you sleeping okay?' I asked.

'No,' he snapped.

'Why didn't you say something?'

'What, beg to crawl into your bed like I did when I was three?'

'Adults get scared too,' I said gently.

'But nothing bad has happened to me.'

I gave him a hug.

'Our family dying in the Holocaust... since that lecture, it's still in my head.'

'You've known about their terrible suffering during the war for a long time... about the Holocaust.'

'Of course, I've known,' he snapped. 'But I don't know the details... don't want to.'

That night I told Richard about my talk with Anton. He put down his bottle of beer and stroked his chin. 'Yes, this unsettling move hasn't helped him... and the episode with the police.'

'It could've caused all these other worries to surface.'

'Maybe.' He stroked his chin again.

'And neither of us has spent enough time with him. He's had to cope alone.'

He sighed and then nodded.

'I think it could help if you explained your reaction to the koalas... like you did to me. He'd understand how the past can rise up and affect one.'

'I'll talk to him. Maybe knowing it can happen to others… even his own dad, will help.'

Anton continued to spend most of his free time in his room. When he did go out at night, he didn't volunteer information about where he was going. I hated asking.

'Visiting friends,' was his usual reply but he didn't mention the friends' names.

When he came home late I worried. If he didn't go out I worried too, thinking he might be lonely. I tried to keep our conversations in the kitchen going. When I asked how he was, he glared at me.

'Sleeping better?' I asked as casually as I could.

'Much better,' he replied. 'Whatever was bugging me has gone.'

I hunted for an appropriate word. All I could come up with was, 'Great. That's great.'

Though his answer was positive there was not evidence to support it.

'How's Anton?' Richard asked, as he ate his withered meal.' He had come in late again and I heated his meal in the microwave.

'It's hard to tell. He says he's alright but he doesn't look good.'

'With young people these days, one never knows.'

He topped off his meal with a beer. That night he didn't fall asleep in front of the television. I was reading on the couch when he sat next to me.

'I appreciate all you do for me and Anton, you know,' he said moving closer.

In seconds his arms were around me and he was planting his kisses. My book fell from my hand.

'The bedroom,' he whispered.

My body stiffened in revolt. I looked up past the stairs. The light showed under Anton's door. What if I refused and Richard began to argue? Anton had been upset enough. I followed Richard towards the bedroom.

When I woke, the room was dark. The clock told me it was 4. 20 a.m. Richard's scent was on my body. I tiptoed out of bed and not wanting to wake him, showered downstairs. There was no point going back to bed, I would not sleep.

In the sitting room, I waited for the first signs of dawn. I was living with a man I no longer loved, trapped in a country that meant nothing to me. Luke was on the other side of the world and so was Gabe. There wasn't even a coffee house to run to. If not for Ruth and one or two of the others, I could've left my job. The pay was dreadful and all it did for me was fill my time.

As strips of rosy light crept into the room, I drew back the curtain and stretched my arms to greet the day. At least I had the weekend off work. It came to me in an instant. I would leave... Richard, Anton, all of it. I would drive until I felt able to face it all again. I wrote a quick note for Richard and left it on the kitchen table. I took a road map, my handbag and left.

Would I head for the mountains or the sea? I asked myself. Both, if I was lucky, came the answer. I consulted the map and drove in the direction of Apollo Bay. It was a longer drive than I anticipated but I didn't stop, and arrived just before midday.

One look at the fishing town and I loved the small harbour, the wide rocky beaches and the backdrop of mountains. In part I felt like a naughty school child who had run away from home, but at least I felt free. I wandered through the town, stopped at the wharf, bought fish and chips and a bottle of wine. Apollo Bay was one of the windiest towns I had come across but with my coat zipped and my hood down I walked and walked. Impulsively I decided to stay the night. I found a motel and booked a room. I left messages on Richard and Anton's phones, letting them know where I was. After I'd eaten a plate of sandwiches and drank the entire bottle of wine I had bought earlier, I was asleep in minutes.

The sound of a breakfast tray rattling at the door woke me. I consulted the brochures I had collected from the reception area. The Otway Ranges covered an extensive area but I had the time for a brief drive through the national park and the rainforest. The drama and magnificence of the massed ferns, winding streams and waterfalls astonished me. I wished I could've explored further. In the cool, moist air, I made a promise to myself to stop hankering for the past, dipping into old stories. Instead, I would try harder to seek out the beauty of this new land.

A few days later I made a late appointment at a hairdresser Ruth recommended. If I was to change, then my long hair worn in an old fashioned French twist or bun would have to go. It didn't take me long to decide on a natural style that would be easy to care for. When the hairdresser at last finished, I smiled at my image.

Joan Zawatzky

Thirty-Eight

When I received notice from the post office that a parcel had arrived for me from Vienna, all I had to do was to provide proof of my identity and collect it.

Early the following morning, I waited excitedly for the post office to open. I was handed a heavy package that I battled to lift from the counter and drag to the car. Though I had intended to go to work that morning, the parcel took precedence. I drove home and rushed indoors. With a sharp knife I sliced through the cardboard wrapping. Once the outer protective layers were freed, a battered aluminium portfolio lay on the kitchen bench top. It was the type of portfolio I had seen artists carry in Europe.

I unfastened the straps around it, drew back the foam lining and stared astounded at an etching of the old house in Leopoldstadt, as it had been when I was a child. I could tell that the portfolio held much more, and hurriedly I turned the etching over. Beneath it were several etchings and water colours of the house from different angles. There were also oil paintings of the Vienna Woods, the mountains and of lakes in Tyrol, as well as portraits of people I did not know. In the bottom right corner of each was the name *Walter Tannenbaum*– my father's name. What a thrill it was to see his signature on a painting. These had to be the paintings Mama had talked about but said she could not find. I propped a few of the paintings on the couch to appreciate later and continued emptying the portfolio.

Close to the bottom, I felt something hard-edged. It was a cardboard folder and a canvas bag with a zip containing black and white photographs. Hurriedly I put the folder aside and spread the photographs on the dining room table. Mama! I recognised her first. What a beauty she was then, with her shoulder length hair in bangs and curls. She posed with her hand on her hip and her head tilted back like a movie star. No wonder my father fell for her. Then Mama and Papa together. There were several photos of Mama's friends, whom I remembered seeing at the house when I was very young. In one of them, Papa as a young man, healthy and smiling, stood next to his sister, my Aunt Gertie. They were flanked on either side by two elderly people. I wondered if they were my grandparents. I had no doubt now that I had inherited my father's eyes and high cheek bones but my curly hair came from my mother. I collected all the photos of Papa. While examining them, I wiped away my tears as I thought of the photograph I'd found of him as an old sick man.

I left the photos on the table and carried the cardboard folder to the sitting room, where the light was brighter. It contained my parents' birth and marriage certificates, his diplomas from senior school as well as his studies at the Vienna Polytechnic. The documents were all in German apart from the marriage certificate or *katuba* in Hebrew. I would keep it with the other two, I thought. There were numerous letters and accounts and I placed them in a drawer to examine later.

Exhausted, and too emotional to evaluate the contents of the portfolio any further, I collapsed into an armchair. While admiring my father's painting of the Vienna woods, I fell asleep.

Richard shook me gently. 'What's going on? Paintings against the couch, photos on the table?'

'They're my father's... his photos and paintings. A package arrived today...' I rubbed my eyes.

Richard peered at the photos. 'You look the image of your father and Anton looks a lot like him too... the way he smiles.'

'Yes, he does and he has Papa's small frame.'
'I wouldn't have believed that your mother was that glamorous when she was young.'

I ignored his comment. Richard and my mother had managed their relationship by keeping their distance from each other. I stretched and stood. I hadn't even thought of cooking dinner.

'It's late. Either we'll have to go out to eat or have sandwiches or cereal,' I said.

'Let's go out... find a nice restaurant.'

In the car we agreed that we would show our sons the photos and paintings and I would do my best to answer their questions about their grandfather.

Thirty-Nine

The following week an email from Luke appeared in my inbox. He had been asked to present a paper at a geoscience conference in Adelaide. After the conference, he intended to visit Sydney and then spend some time with us in Melbourne.

> *I'm so excited I can't wait to see you, Liebchen. I have so much to tell you. Your life has changed since you left for Australia, and since my mother's death, mine is not the same either, but that won't alter the way we feel about each other. I will write soon with more details. I can't wait to put my arms around you.*

'Of course he'll stay with us,' Richard said, taking a gulp of beer. 'Write to him with an open invitation.'

I half turned to look at him. 'You're sure?'

'He's an old friend.' He gave me a quizzical look.

Richard must've been blind or an idiot to be unaware of how close Luke and I were. Of course I hadn't told him how crazy we were about each other as teenagers or he wouldn't have encouraged me to attend all those concerts with Luke in Vienna. Possibly all the beer he was drinking had dulled his judgement.

Richard and Luke were friends. They had met through me, but liked each other immediately. They were both sport crazy and enjoyed sailing. They even went to the same movies and when we formed a foursome with Hilda, picnicking or hiking we all had a grand time. It was understandable that Richard wanted to entertain Luke.

'Take some time off work and show him around, and I'll free myself up over the weekends.'

'Right, I'll answer him immediately.'

As I began the email to Luke, a fluttery sensation crept from my stomach to my chest. I typed the message with a mixture of dread and excitement. Richard was throwing me into Luke's arms. Our move to Australia had made me more vulnerable and needy for affection than I could remember, and Richard's excessive involvement with his work hadn't helped. I left the computer and went on to the porch. In the cool breeze I stared at the crescent moon and shivered.

Within the hour Luke responded to my message.

Yes and yes again! Thank you! I can't think of a nicer way of the three of us spending time together.

Luke confirmed the date of his arrival. It was sooner than I imagined. He would be in Melbourne in five weeks. I wondered if I had made a mistake in allowing Richard to persuade me to invite him to stay. It was the friendly thing to do and Richard had insisted, but was it right for me? It was about time I faced the truth as hard as it was. The image of myself as an adulteress was one I managed to gloss over most of the time, but that's exactly what I was. Admit it, I told myself. After the concerts we attended together in Vienna, we talked for a while over coffee and then we went by taxi to Luke's friend's apartment.

The apartment was in a non-descript but well maintained building on the city fringes. Luke said that the apartments were owned by wealthy business people and top civil servants, who slept there but were away all day. The inside of number 1240 was more than comfortable. Supportive chairs and a sofa were placed in front of a huge television set, but the greatest effort was taken to create an air of relaxation in the spacious bedroom. It was an ideal spot to make love and it was conveniently empty at the times we needed it. Only occasionally, we came across tell-tale signs of someone else living there. An empty coffee cup might be left on the table or a cushion was out of place on the couch. On each visit we changed the bed linen when we arrived and again when we left.

We had an hour together. By then we knew each other's bodies well and we aroused each other immediately. Our lovemaking was so intense and pleasurable, that I feared each time would be the last. It did not end though, not until I left for Melbourne.

Though I cared about Richard's wellbeing, he no longer interested me sexually. Without Luke, I could not have endured Richard's fast fumblings in the dark. My excuse to myself was that anticipating meetings with Luke allowed my marriage to last. It had to last for the boys' stability and emotional wellbeing, but this hardly applied to my sons now. They were adults and about to leave home.

I wondered again about the invitation I had just made to Luke. He must've thought that Richard was clueless about our *liaison*. Instead of accepting readily, Luke ought to have thanked us politely and refused our offer with an excuse. Surely he realised that having him so close would be difficult for me. It would have been so much easier if he stayed elsewhere. I kicked one of the ceramic flower pots. I longed to spend intimate hours with Luke. Since he had accepted the invitation, my body tingled and I felt warm even though the weather had cooled down. It was where all of this was leading that concerned me. How would I continue my pretence while he was in the house with both of us and what was I going to do about Richard? I tried not to think about that.

Forty

On the Friday of Luke's arrival, the house sang with flowers and the fridge was packed with food. The joy I felt could only be equalled by memories of our meetings during our teenage years. I fixed my hair in the new style and dressed in my most flattering casual outfit.

Luke's plane was late and we waited for what seemed ages. When I caught sight of him walking towards us, I wanted to run and hug him but I restrained myself and gave him a kiss on the cheek.

He brought gifts of wine for Richard and chocolate and perfume for me. He sat in the front of the car with Richard, while I had to be satisfied at the back, listening and chipping in with questions and comments. Melbourne was Luke's third stop and he talked exuberantly about what he had already seen of Australia.

'The people are wonderful, so friendly.' He stretched and sighed contentedly. 'And it's so light and bright here. I love it. The conference in Adelaide was wonderful and my paper on geothermal energy went well…lots of interest.' He laughed and said that he was flattered by the job offered to him by the head of geology at the university. After the conference he went on to Sydney and I could tell he was taken with the harbour and the suburbs. I hoped he would find Melbourne as appealing. I was taken aback when he mentioned that his next stop was Darwin. From there he was to travel on to geological sites near Alice Springs. He was uncertain whether he would return to Melbourne after that or fly home via Sydney.

When Richard showed Luke around our new house, he appeared to be impressed and made appreciative noises. Though Richard had intended to take the Friday off work, that afternoon he was called into the office to attend to an urgent meeting. I calculated that we had at least an hour together before he returned.

At last we were alone, and all I could think of was making love to Luke. I stood on the tip of my toes and threw my arms around him. He tightened the embrace and we kissed gently at first, and then hungrily. We pulled off our clothes and fell onto the narrow couch. Our eyes met. He kissed my neck, my breast and then he was inside me. Minutes later we lay facing each other. He stroked my hair and kissed my face. Reluctantly I sat up and moved away.

'Let's not take chances, Richard may come back sooner than we expect,' I said, as I scooped up my clothes. 'I must tidy up... won't be long.'

When I returned, he was dressed and seated on the couch with a wrapped package on his lap. He grinned as he handed it to me. 'I've brought you something special... to celebrate your move into the new house. Hope you'll like it.'

I tore at the package. Beneath the paper and tissue was an enamel hand twice the size of a man's hand. I stared at its white background with tiny colourful squares and at the Hebrew writing, meaningless to me.

'Thank you *Liebchen*, it's lovely and so artistic but...?'

'Ah! It's from Israel and called a *Hamsa*. It's goes back to ancient Jewish beliefs of protection against evil spirits.'

It was a strange gift and I looked at him questioningly.

'I wrote the translation of the Hebrew down somewhere.' He flipped through the pages of his pocket diary. 'Yes, it says, *Shalom al Israel*, Peace upon Israel.'

'How do you know about the... *Hamsa*?' I enunciated the word carefully as I placed the hand on a side table.

'I've been doing a lot of reading lately... about Judaism.'

'Oh?'

'I found it in a shop in Vienna that sells magnificent art and home ware from Israel.'

From the decisive tone of his voice and the way he rubbed his hands together, I could tell that he had no intention of saying more about the gift.

❧

Richard and I planned Luke's ten day stay in Melbourne meticulously. I arranged leave from work and planned to be with him most of the time. Richard intended to make himself available in the evening and weekends and Anton, who regarded Luke as an uncle, would spend time with him after his lectures. The following weekend we put aside for camping.

During that first weekend, all Luke asked of us was to be allowed to unwind and catch up on sleep. When he was rested, he spoke about the impressive offer of employment he had received. I listened but said little, daring not to hope for too much. At least we might be on the same continent. Late that afternoon, Ruth and Paul dropped in to meet Luke and stayed on for a light dinner. I had my friends and all my men with me, eating the food I had lovingly prepared and drinking the fine Australian wine we had discovered.

At odd moments I eyed Luke, the familiar tilt of his head, the way he swept strands of hair from his forehead, hardly daring to believe he was back in my life even if it was briefly. I warned myself several times about my intense feelings for him, and that the strong rational part of me would have to keep me in control. Years ago, I had given up cigarettes and stopped eating fat laden food, but could I rely on my willpower to keep my longing for Luke in check?

On Monday morning we were alone in the house for the first time since our lovemaking on the day he arrived. The sky was a pristine blue and it was too sultry to sit indoors.

'Let's sit on the porch, we can see the garden from there,' I said taking his hand.

He stretched lazily. 'Good idea. It's lovely out there.'

'Do you want to do some sightseeing today?'

'No. Now that we're alone I want to talk.'

But we didn't talk. We held hands and sat so close that we could feel each other breathe. I realised suddenly how hungry I was.

'Something to eat?'

He nodded enthusiastically.

When I returned he wore his serious face. 'I can't tell you how much I've missed you,' he said, holding a hand out to me.

I took his hand and squeezed it. 'Come on, the coffee will get cold.'

I gave him a mug of coffee and a slice of Linzer torte that I'd made especially for him.

'Umm... s*ehr, sher gut!*' he said with an appreciative sigh, as he cut a second slice.

After we had eaten, he talked rapidly. 'I can't believe it, twenty- two years of marriage to Hilde. We had our wedding anniversary only a month ago ... and not a thing has changed.'

'Ah hah!'

He swallowed. 'Boring and passionless.'

I felt my eyebrows lift. I knew what he meant.

'We stayed on in the marriage, living together, doing our own thing, for the children but I don't know if it was such a good idea.'

I nodded and he continued. 'I found out that she's been having an affair with her art teacher. Not that I care. Our daughters know that things between us aren't working and Jeanette, the older of the two, suggested we split up.' His laugh was sardonic. 'How stupid we were to think we were fooling them. So yes, Ellie, we will have to separate. We can't carry on like this.' He slapped his thigh and then looked at me. 'Sorry, it's all about me. What's happening in your life?'

'Richard and I haven't talked about where our marriage is heading for months, virtually since we arrived. I know I'll have to talk to him, make some decisions, but I'm not ready. Too much has happened with the move... and I'm waiting to feel more settled before looking at any further changes.'

'I wonder some times how much he knows or has guessed about us. He's self absorbed but no fool,' Luke said.

'He hasn't said a word about it. Not now or ever.'

'That's it then.' Luke moved closer. 'Let's forget about it.' He made a dismissive gesture with his hand.

A wave of desire rippled through me. 'I think we should go out for a bit.' My decision was instant. We had to leave the house. I didn't trust myself. It would've been too easy to suggest going inside and up the stairs to the bedroom. But I could not allow that to happen... what if Richard decided to return early or my son turned up. Reluctantly he followed me to the garage. He held the map while I drove towards the mountains. He had not said much about his life in Vienna and during the journey I asked him to tell me his news.

'I've been too busy to do much else but work and I've tried to spend as much time as possible with the girls on the weekend. There's nothing to tell.'

I knew Luke's appetite for sex. Logic told me that he must have a girlfriend or more than one. I was too far away to be possessive and hated the idea of him even touching another woman. I knew he would answer me truthfully if I asked.

'Do you have a girlfriend in Vienna?'

He glanced out of the car window before answering. 'Yes, in a way. I suppose you can call Eunice a girlfriend. We have sex.'

'I see.'

'Are you happy now that you know? I'm not a monk, never have been and you know that.'

'Eunice, a strange name.'

'She's quite attractive. Long dark hair, a wide mouth, long legs.'

The sound of her wide mouth and long legs was a little disturbing.

'You shouldn't think twice about it ... it's just sex.'

I tried to explain how differently women like me viewed sex, but he placed a finger on my lips. We were together and we were enjoying each other as we always had. He was right, I had nothing to worry about.

We stopped near the foothills and decided to follow one of the trails along the Yarra River. Holding hands, we picked our way through the long grass. We had been walking energetically until he stopped and looked up at the tall Eucalypts.

He took a long breath. 'I like their long grey trunks and their smell... absolutely wonderful!'

He was impressed that I could tell him about the trees, that I knew the names of some of the plants and could spot galahs and a kookaburra. I didn't mention that before he arrived I had been reading. I tried to ignore my lust for him by walking faster. When we heard the sound of water we followed it to a stream rushing over smoothed rocks. Near the water, he found a grassy spot, surrounded by bushes. He threw his jacket on the ground and pulled me down on the grass with him.

'*Ich liebe dich*', he mumbled.

'*Ich* ...' He covered my mouth with a kiss. Neither of us could wait. I wriggled out of my clothes and pulled him towards me. The animal and bird life may have watched as we melted together. Afterwards we laughed as the tough grass scratched us. We rose slowly and brushed off the dry leaves that stuck to our clothing.

'We'd better get back to the house, wash and change,' I said, looking at the grass stains on my shirt.

I drove home faster than I should have. It was a toss up between breaking road rules and bumping into my son in a dishevelled state. After a wash in the basin and a change into fresh clothing I went downstairs. Once the evidence of sex in the forest was chugging away in the washing machine, I breathed more easily and I busied myself with preparing dinner. There was no time to feel even the tiniest bit guilty.

Forty-One

Luke's eyes opened as I entered the bedroom. I had waited patiently to show him the contents of my father's portfolio. He shielded his eyes from the light and complained that I had disturbed his sleep. Then with a loud mock sigh, he good naturedly followed me downstairs.

As I spread out the photos on the dining room table he shook his head in amazement. He pointed to a photo of my father. 'Heavens Ellie, apart from the different hairstyle, this could be you. You looked exactly like him at your present age.'

My father had been a handsome man. That was before he suffered during the war.

'Have you noticed there's not a single photo of any of them after 1940?'

He grimaced, nodding slowly. 'Still, you're lucky to have these,' he said as he examined the photographs.

I took his hand and gave it a tug. 'Come, I want to show my father's paintings. I've put them against the wall so that we can see them properly. You appreciate art, have a look at them and give me your opinion.'

Slowly he examined the paintings. 'Your father was a talented artist; his colour and composition is good. You should be proud and frame a few of his paintings. They'll look good on your walls.'

He was selecting a few, when he called out. 'Ellie, come and look at this!' His voice was high with excitement. 'This small one can't be your father's.' He separated one painting from the rest and placed it on the sofa where the light was good. The spring landscape of trees in a meadow with delicately painted foliage and a mottled sky was iridescent. 'I missed it. It's small and it must've been caught up with the one in front.'

I looked at it closely. 'Isn't it lovely?'

'Oh, yes!' He ran his fingertips over the painting. 'It bright and light. Not at all like Viennese work.' He peered at it again. 'It looks French Impressionist to me. Look at the brush strokes and how the paint shimmers to create a sense of light.'

'French Impressionist! Don't' be ridiculous!'

He squinted. 'Here, look carefully. One could easily miss the signature... in the water... *Mein Gott*... Camille Pissarro.'

'I've never heard of him. Have you?'

'Yes, I have, but I'm going to have a look on the internet... see some of Pissarro's other work so that we can compare it.'

I stood next to him at the computer.

'Have a look. I'm right. It says here that Pissarro was a French Impressionist, born in 1830 and died in 1903. He worked with Monet, Renoir and other young artists who became known as Impressionists.'

'It must be a copy or a fake, my father probably liked it and he kept it.'

'I doubt it,' he said placing a kiss on my cheek. 'It looks like an original to me but then I'm no authority. You'll have to ask an art expert... but let's keep positive.'

Luke went to the bedroom to read but I stayed and stared at the painting until my eyes closed. When I woke the bright morning sunlight was replaced by banks of clouds. A splash of water on my face and I was alert. Perhaps it was the shock of cold water that made me realise that I had not examined the remaining contents of the folder. I retrieved it from my desk drawer and placed it on the table near the photos. My nose crinkled at the musty smell.

Though I felt uncomfortable reading my father's correspondence, I approached the task methodically, putting accounts to one side as I searched for letters. I found two postcards from his friends who were on holiday and had written to him with their news. There was a birthday card and two letters from my mother. Her style was flowery but her words of love sincere. The last letter in a buff envelop, lay in the flap of the folder. It was addressed to me. Astounded, I opened it, tearing the envelope in my haste.

To my daughter Ella, on her 18 th birthday.

My dearest Ella

You will be an adult when you open this letter. I asked your mother not to give this portfolio to you until you were eighteen and I hope you will understand my reasons.

I must explain to you that I have been unwell for many years but now my health is deteriorating rapidly. I am certain that I will die soon. That is why I have made arrangements for you to receive it. Your mother has promised to make a note of it in her will, in the event that she dies before you turn eighteen.

You will find a small painting in the portfolio by a French Impressionist. It is a valuable painting and will fetch a large amount of money at auction. I have kept it for you my darling, rather than sell it now.

I fell in love with you when you were a tiny baby and now that you are almost two years old, I can see how much you resemble my side of the family. You will be beautiful when you are a woman and I hope you will have the love of a good man.

In this envelope you will find a letter from Mr Nachman. He is the person who gave me the painting.

May you have a life of good health and happiness.

Your loving father,

Walter

My heart thudded and tears trickled down my face, as I opened the letter from Isaac Nachman.

10 November 1949
343 Rampe de Cologny
Cologny,
Swizerland

> *Mr Walter Tannenbaum*
> *Displaced Persons Camp*
> *Rothchild Hospital*
> *Vienna.*

Dear Mr Tannenbaum,

I hope that this package finds you in good health. Friends told me that thank God you survived the war and that you are presently staying at the Rothchild Camp. Please God you will not be there for long and will soon find a home for yourself.

First of all, I am writing to thank you for guiding my father, myself, my wife and our three children to safety over the border. May God bless you! The weather was terrible that day and it was too dark to see more than a few metres ahead. Without you helping us we would never have made it to safety. I don't even want to think what would have become of us.

Secondly, I have placed this letter inside the package to explain a few things to you. When you remove the layers of protective paper, you will find a painting. It is not an ordinary painting. It is an original by Camille Pissarro, one of the French Impressionists whose work is well known by collectors. My father collected paintings all his life and knew a great deal about art. Each piece he bought was a gem.

Before we left Vienna in a terrible hurry, he found a hiding place for his paintings in the mountains. He packed each one well and made sure that they would be dry. Unfortunately he died during the war, but I knew where they were hidden and when peace was declared, thank God I found them. There were many of them, all in fine order. Together they are worth a fortune. I have kept half to sell later and given the rest of the money received away to those in need.

Since that dark night you assisted us, I have wanted to express my thanks to you, and now thank God, I can do that by giving you a painting. The reason I have sent you a painting instead of money is that a picture is pleasant to look at and also the longer you keep it the more valuable it will become.

May you be well and safe in God's hands.

Yours with my sincere gratitude,

Isaac Nachman

I sat back in the chair and wiped away my sweat and tears. It seemed ridiculous that no one knew about my father's paintings or the treasure he had hidden away. Was there no limit to the secrecy of the generation before me?

My father must have concealed the painting in the study all those years ago. He obviously told Mama to be sure to give it to me on my eighteenth birthday, but she did not. There was no mention of a painting in her will either. Her memory was patchy. I could only ascribe her omission to that.

All the information I had gleaned about my father had seeped out painfully. I thought of the sequence of events–the flooded old house, its sale and the demolition that had brought the paintings to me. Though some people believed in the workings of spirits, fate or religious intervention, I could not credit my finding of the photographs and paintings to any of them.

Forty-Two

I was almost as much of a tourist in Melbourne as Luke. To become more familiar with the city we decided to take a city tour and then return to places that caught our interest. The tour provided us with an impression of the city as well as the parks, river, beach and the mountains. For the first time, I felt a budding pride that Melbourne was now my home. Luke insisted that he had seen enough of the city and exhibitions and asked to go to the beach. We consulted brochures and maps and decided on Portsea.

The day was clear but blustery when we drove to Portsea. The town lies on a peninsula with two beaches. Instead of the calm and protection of the bay, we chose the wilder ocean beach. From grassy dunes we looked down on the stretch of empty sand and raging sea.

Luke beamed. Apart from one or two walkers we had the beach to ourselves. We zipped up our parkas and walked along the water's edge with the surf roaring and a bracing wind behind us. Luke rubbed his chest, threw his head back and took deep breaths as he stopped to admire the white topped waves. Hand in hand, we played like children, kicking at bits of driftwood and dancing away from the incoming waves. Warmed from the long walk, we tramped back to the car through the heavy sand. On the back seat was a wicker basket with a picnic lunch I had prepared and a flask of hot coffee. We finished the lot. After the meal Luke rested his head on my shoulder.

'All of this,' he said pointing to the vista, 'warmth, food and you with me, what more could a man want?' he sighed contentedly and kissed the nape of my neck.

I squeezed his hand.

'We know each other well... at least we think we do,' he said, planting another kiss on my neck.

'We should by now,' I said with a laugh.

'And yet there's so much I haven't told you... about the past.' His tone was serious.

'Oh!'

'I'm sure you know that my parents gave me a hard time and I was happiest away from the house.'

'Of course I know that,' I said, remembering the welts I had seen on his legs.

'Poor Gunther, he had the worst of it being the eldest.' Luke's forehead was creased in memory. 'I didn't understand then and I still don't know what rules we broke and why we were beaten so often. There were so many rules. The corners of our beds had to be exact, our shoes shining as if we were in the army and nothing could be left lying around in our rooms. We could count on my mother's nightly inspection.'

'Oh, Luke.' I stroked his bent head.

Gently he removed my hand.

'I think it has made me stronger but I wish I didn't hate her.'

'I had no idea it was as bad as that.'

'It's still in my head and it won't leave me.'

Luke was an optimist and I had not known him to dwell on the past. I wanted to tell him that I had been living in the past too, but he was too troubled. It was not the time to talk about myself.

'Your mother's hospitality was a godsend. I spent more time at your house than my own'

I smiled remembering.

He swept a lock of hair from his forehead. 'I haven't talked about it but I'm sure you realised that both my father and my grandfather fought with the Germans during the war. Though my grandfather was Austrian, he joined up as soon as the fighting started, but my father was too young then. In 1943 when he turned seventeen, he was drafted and sent to Kursk on the Eastern Front. I asked him about the war many times but he wouldn't say a thing... closed his eyes and pretended to be asleep. Once I nagged and nagged for an answer for so long, that he eventually snapped back at me, "I nearly got frozen to death in that bloody snow." I wasn't satisfied with his answer and kept on nagging. He glared at me. "One didn't argue if Hitler or one of his generals gave an order. Now leave me alone about the war."

'He was a soldier and was expected to follow orders. It's like that in any army,' I said.

'I didn't know my grandfather. From what I've heard he was one for following orders.'

I looked at him waiting for him to tell me more, to explain but his eyes were fixed on the sea for some time before continuing.

'What a family I come from! My mother was so pro-Nazi when I was little that she talked about Hitler as if he had been an uncle.'

I didn't interrupt.

In a quiet voice he insisted that his father was nothing like his mother. Every now and again his father would praise the Third Reich's values and compare them to what he called "the lazy, immoral attitude of modern youth." For all of that, he couldn't recall his father making derogatory comments about the Jewish family, Ella's family, living across the road or their next door neighbours.

'I felt awful, I couldn't tell you then how bigoted my mother was. Do you know, she even tried to prevent me from visiting you. If I had been at your house during the day, I heard all about it from her that night.' He moved about uncomfortably. 'Let's get out of the car for a bit.' He put his hand out of the window and was satisfied that the wind had died down enough for another walk.

I thought of his mother and swallowed hard but didn't reply. Though his mother's dislike of me had not been spelled out, I noticed that she turned her back on me when I passed her or greeted her in the garden. I watched Luke a few paces ahead. Why was he upsetting himself about his family, and after all these years? It was the first time he had spoken against his family. He was betraying the unwritten rule of not revealing family business to outsiders.

He turned around and called out, 'Come on, you're falling behind.'

We followed the walking track that took us along the cliff's edge with its glorious view of the ocean, that was interrupted only by seagulls.

'I think you'll be happy in Melbourne.' He drew an arc with his arm. 'This is marvellous,' he said inhaling the salty air.

When we returned to the car, his face had tensed.

'What is it, Luke?'

'I'm here with you surrounded by all this beauty but I can't get rid of the drumming in my head.'

I waited for him to continue but he remained silent. He would struggle with himself until he could talk about it.

He stretched for the thermos. 'Is there any hot coffee left?'

'You finish it,' I said gazing up at the dying sun.

Luke spent most of the next day in the bedroom pretending to be asleep, but when I peeped, he was sitting up with a vacant look on his face. We met for lunch but he did not mention what was bothering him. His pensive mood hung heavily in the house. It was like waiting for a storm to break. Restlessly I busied myself cleaning crockery and cutlery that had been cleaned only recently. Activity helped when there were things I didn't want to think about.

Late that afternoon, he found me in the kitchen and watched as I chopped vegetables. I was rinsing them in a colander when I felt him behind me. He spun me about to face him and his arms encircled me.

'I've been watching you, longing for you. You won't get away from me this time.'

I dropped the knife and pulled him closer. He was breathing fast as he kissed me. And then, I did everything I promised myself I would not do. I followed him up the stairs to the bedroom.

In my haste, I tugged at the bedcover. We fell on the bed and reached for each other. Afterwards we lay in each other's embrace for some time without talking.

'Beautiful *Liebchen*... wasn't that just beautiful,' he said.

Instead of replying, I kissed his forehead, his cheek and his lips. I did not spoil my pleasure by talking. Our lovemaking was the closest to perfect it had ever been but I wished it wasn't. He was leaving soon and all I would have of him was this memory. It would make the loss even greater.

I forced myself from the bed. 'Come on, let's get up and dressed. Anton will be home soon.'

'Oh alright,' he groaned. 'It's a pity, I'm so comfortable.'

'We shouldn't have allowed this to happen in the house,' I said, as I snapped my bra shut.'

He was dressed and standing near the door. 'I'm going into the garden for a while. I need to clear my head.'

'Right then, I have some tidying to do.'

I smoothed the bedspread, changed into a fresh shirt and went downstairs into the kitchen. The schnitzel had defrosted and was waiting to be beaten. When Richard had not arrived by dinner time, we ate.

'Thank you for a lovely meal,' he said, as he stepped behind my chair and kissed my head. 'And thank you for listening yesterday. You don't know how much it means to me.'

It was just as well I hadn't told him what I'd learned about my father. The right moment would come.

Joan Zawatzky

Forty-Three

On Friday, Richard arrived home early with tents and borrowed camping gear packed into the back of his Land Rover. We were taking Luke to Phillip Island for the weekend. Apart from buying the food, I left the entire preparation for the trip to Richard. My memories of the dead and injured koalas in the bush were still raw and camping was my last choice, but Luke had hiked and camped throughout the Alps and for him a weekend in the bush near the sea was a novel experience. I did not want to spoil it for him

Anton did not join us on the trip. A university get-together he described as "essential networking for new students" took precedence. I could tell that Luke was disappointed that Anton had not put his socialising to one side for him. While I sealed the food in plastic containers, I muttered to myself about Anton's decision. I had been looking forward to a family weekend and having him there would have created a buffer between the three of us.

We left for Philip Island before dawn with the car packed so full that Richard could just about see out of the back window. The men sat in the front and by now I was accustomed to my seat in the back. I did not mind relaxing after the rush of the early start, as long as they did not forget me. Luke sat stiffly, his repartee less keen than usual.

'What's up with you?' Richard asked him.

'I'm tired ... reading late.'

'Come on you two, look at the glorious morning,' I said, hoping to lift the flat mood

202

I was wondering if Luke felt uncomfortable about breaking the code of "friends wives are off limits" or whether he was concerned that he had talked too openly about his parents. After all these years, I still could not work out what was worrying him. Before he left Vienna he wrote to me that his life had changed since his mother's death yet he provided no details. In the past week he hadn't said a word about these "changes".

While the two men chatted, I thought about our lovemaking in Luke's friend's apartment in Vienna. Afterwards, I would return to my life at home with Richard and the boys, knowing that in spite of boredom and dissatisfaction, there would be a next time with Luke. It was easier to deal with than our recent moments of passion, knowing he would be leaving soon.

We drove across the bridge connecting the island to the mainland. The sun was up and the island glowed in the soft peach light. I heard Luke sigh deeply and then slap his thigh decisively. Once we neared the campsite, his moodiness had disappeared. He pointed to plants that were foreign to him and to rocks of geological interest.

After the men set up the tent we spent the day exploring the island. Richard happily followed Luke as he examined plants or counted the ridges on a rock face. I watched Richard's transformation from the boring man who came home to me each night to an inquiring, vital person. In the late afternoon, we joined international tourists at the seafront to wait for the parade of fairy penguins. People from all over the world came to the island to watch the plucky little bids return to their nests in the sand. We waited as the sky darkened. Enthusiastically Luke identified the first few fairy penguins breaking through the waves and then toddling up the beach to their burrows in the dunes.

Later, alone in our tent, Richard's grumpy self returned. I slipped into my sleeping bag, grunted "goodnight" and turned my back on him. I stared into the darkness. Surely he was aware of my deception and our lust for each other, I asked myself.

The next morning during a long hike, we were admiring the coastline when Richard's cell phone buzzed. He answered and looked irritated. 'It's about bloody work. Problems with the plant.' He walked away to continue his conversation.

Luke beckoned to me. 'Have you told him about us yet, Ellie?'

'No. I think I'd rather wait until you've gone home.'

'Yes, I suppose it may be better that way.'

Richard stuffed his phone into his pocket and joined us. 'Thank goodness it's nothing serious...they'll settle it without me.' He stretched and smiled. 'Hasn't this been wonderful? Just us... old friends together. In a way I'm pleased now that Anton didn't come along.'

After our walk we returned to the tent. Richard settled into a chair and picked up a newspaper he had bought at one of the kiosks.

'I'm tired out! Why don't you two go for a walk while I catch up on the news?'

I wondered if I imagined a sardonic smile play on Richard's lips. It was late afternoon, the breeze was up as Luke and I walked along a path of swaying blue gums and listened out for calls of birds returning to their nests. Luke was observing a mutton bird, while I thought about Richard. Had he purposely used the newspaper as a ploy to throw us together? He could have joined us for the walk and read his paper later. I toyed with the idea that Richard was intentionally drawing us together. If this was the case, he had been doing it for a long time.

We passed a young couple wound around each other in embrace.

'They should go behind the bushes and get on with it,' Luke said with a laugh.

'Give them time and they will.'

He ran his hand along my thigh and kissed me. I felt a shudder of desire.

'Come on, let's keep walking.' I said.

The temperature had dropped and we returned to the campsite shivering and hungry. Richard and Luke put the *bratwurst* I had brought along on the barbeque, while I fried precooked potatoes for *rosti* on the electric plate.

'When are you two going to eat real Aussie food?' Luke asked laughingly.

'I don't think we ever will,' I replied, stirring the coffee. 'Anyway what's wrong with this food? You've eaten it all your life.'

'Nothing, it's delicious.'

The meal sealed our enjoyment. We all agreed to stay on an extra night, to prolong the pleasure of having the stars above us and being surrounded by the scent of the forest. As my eyes closed, I imagined Luke beside me instead of Richard. It was Luke's easy going friendliness as well as his desire to explore each part of the island and visit the wildlife sanctuaries that made the weekend enjoyable. Koalas, possums and kangaroos replaced my thoughts of the waters of the Danube.

Forty-Four

Luke was in the garden surrounded by birds vying for breadcrumbs.

'Are we alone?' He asked softly.

I nodded.

He rubbed the last few crumbs from his hands, put his arms around me and kissed me. I tasted fruit as his lips pressed mine. He had been eating plums. We stood arm in arm watching the birds fly off into the tall trees.

'Only three days left before I fly to Alice Springs. We'll both have some thinking time...and then I should be back here in Melbourne.'

There wasn't any point in begging him to stay on or in expressing my fear that he wouldn't be back. I knew how easily he could change his plans and fly home from Sydney.

'The weather is perfect, let's go out and explore,' I suggested.

He looked up at the sky. 'I'd prefer to spend the day here with you. We need to talk,' he said giving my hand a tug.

'Fine, but breakfast first.'

He carried the breakfast tray to the covered porch, where we had the warmth of the morning sun and a view of the garden. We ate slowly enjoying our croissants, raspberry jam and coffee.

'Ah, a delicious breakfast,' he said wiping his mouth with his napkin and relaxing back in to his chair.

Right then, I was content in the pleasure on his face and his smile of satisfied fullness. We exchanged parts of the newspaper and chatted over news items. When he threw the paper to the floor and turned his chair to face me I was surprised.

'There are a few things I couldn't bring myself to talk about before and I'll be away soon so...'

'Come on then, tell me, I'm listening.'

'Ellie, I've found out something awful about my family. I've told you some of it but this is really awful.' His body tensed and he clasped his hands behind his head. 'I know you won't like what you're going to hear.'

'It doesn't matter. If it's upsetting you I want to hear it.'

He took a deep breath. 'Right then, here goes. My mother was in her nineties when she died in a retirement home. She hated it there but they looked after her well enough... but what I have to tell you isn't about that. After she died, her solicitor phoned me about her will. She didn't have much and all of it was left to me. I must've told you that my brother Gunther died in a motorcycle accident two years ago. Anyway, when I went to the solicitor's office he handed me an envelope of my mother's, he had been keeping in his safe.' He stared at me silently.

'And?'

'I wish I hadn't opened it. It would've been easier if I hadn't. We don't know our parents. We think we know them but... no.' He stretched out his arms helplessly.

I nodded eagerly.

'What I found changed my life but you won't like what I have to say.'

'Come on tell me.'

'Well... I'd always thought my grandfather was a soldier in the German army, like any other soldier and that my grandmother was a housewife, but it wasn't like that at all.' He took another deep breath. 'My grandparents were both involved with Hitler's SS,' he said in a tight voice.

My stomach leapt and I looked away. This was something I didn't want to hear. I wanted to cover my ears with my hands or yell out *stop* but how could I? I loved Luke. He needed to tell me his story and I had to listen.

It was a long story. Amongst his mother's papers was his grandfather's military service record. After Germany's annexation of Austria, Luke's grandfather joined the German army. He rose in the ranks after acquitting himself well on the front and was inducted into the SS.

'Now, here comes the worst part. As ashamed as I am, I'll tell you about it now ... all of it.' His eyes closed as he spat out the words. 'My grandfather became a guard at the Theresienstadt Concentration Camp.'

'Oh no!' I regretted my shocked response as soon as my words were out.

'Can you imagine it... my own grandfather a prison guard in one of those camps? The worst imaginable place.' He cradled his head in his hands. 'I wouldn't have believed it if I hadn't seen his service record and medals.' He sighed and continued. 'There was a letter amongst my mother's papers from the army to the Commandant of the camp explaining that both my parents spoke Czech well. They'd lived in Prague for a short while after they married. You see, many of the prisoners were Czech and most of the camp guards were drawn from the Czech police.' I stared at him speechlessly.

'And my grandmother. I can't be sure how it came about, but she became one of the few female overseers at the same camp. According to her records, she worked in an armament factory until 1942. Later they both took up positions at the camp. Being a woman she couldn't be a member of the SS, but she was directly linked to it through my grandfather and her job.'

As a child, I had seen his grandmother hanging out the washing or cutting back plants in the garden. She was old and bent then and wore only black.

'When I think of my grandparents now, I feel ill. I imagine him in his Nazi uniform with his SS insignia and tags. And all those prisoners, *Mein Gott*! He stared at the garden. 'They did a good job of indoctrinating my mother. You know only too well my mother's attitude to Jews.'

'Oh yes.'

'At least my grandfather on my father's side was a soldier. He died in action in 1944, fighting for his country and wasn't in the SS.'

'How long have you known this about your grandparents?'

'My mother died last year and I discovered it shortly before you left Vienna. You had so much to deal with then that I didn't want to add to your stress. I suppose if I'm being honest, I was as ashamed to tell you about it then… as I am now.'

'But we were talking about your family a few days ago when we were down at the beach and you told me that your grandfather fought at Kursk on the Eastern front.'

'Yes, he did but I couldn't tell you the rest then … the truth about them.'

'You didn't say a word on the afternoon we went to the concert at the Vienna Philharmonic… our last afternoon together before I left. And then there were your emails. I had no idea something like this was bothering you. How could you've kept it to yourself for so long?'

He sighed.

'Yes … very nasty news,' I said searching for words. 'But I'm glad you've told me.'

'I've felt and still feel such shame when I think of you, your mother and the other Jewish people I've met.' He wiped his eyes with the back of his hand. 'I tell myself that it had nothing to do with me, that the guilt belongs to my grandparents and their generation but it doesn't help a bit. All those people herded to the camps in cattle trucks and then sent to their death… I can't even describe how bad I feel. '

'Hold on. You're not to blame for what your grandparents did. It's not like that.'

'But I carry their genes, their blood.'

'Luke… Luke!'

'I locked myself indoors and drank until I'd consumed all the alcohol stored in the cellar. Then in fury I destroyed anything and everything that had belonged to them. I chopped up my grandmother's antique chair into firewood, smashed their ornaments that were above the fireplace and stamped on their precious gold rimmed cups and saucers. But my anger did not lessen.' He moved his feet restlessly.

I should've made supportive, caring comments but I couldn't. I was frozen. He must've noticed my horrified expression.

'What can I say *Liebchen*? You had to know, I couldn't keep my shame from you any longer.'

Luke's words settled on me. There was no escape from the horror of it. It didn't stop with Luke's family history. Intertwined with his family story was my own. I asked myself over and over if it could be cruel fate or just coincidence that my father had been a prisoner at Theresienstadt, the concentration camp at which Luke's grandparents had been guards. I had no idea whether the dates they were at Theresienstadt coincided, and I thought it best not to make any attempt to find out if there was a link.

🦥

After breakfast I suggested a walk in the garden. 'Let's sit on the grass. I have something important to tell you. It's my turn. I've hidden something from you for ages, but now I have to tell you about it. '

When I finished telling him about my father's imprisonment in Theresienstadt and all that followed, we were both trembling. Neither of us spoke.

That afternoon, we avoided each other. Luke went for a long walk and I busied myself in the kitchen. Working frenetically, I attempted to block my thoughts but it wasn't successful. After hours in the kitchen I had baked several cakes, made the dinner and meals to freeze. A full fridge somehow eased the ache inside. When at last my frenzy abated, I sat on a kitchen stool and wrung my hands.

Forty-Five

I heard a door open and footsteps along the passage. It was 3.30 a.m. Luke was on his way to the kitchen. When the cupboard doors banged, I guessed he was looking for cocoa to make hot chocolate.

When he joined me in the kitchen the next morning his eyes were dull. I offered him breakfast but he shook his head.

'Bad night? I heard you in the kitchen.'

He nodded.

'Anything else you haven't told me?'

'I have a lot to sort out. The two of us are in an impossible situation. We have to find a way.'

I didn't answer.

'We've been apart far too long and we're getting older,' he said with sigh.

Dread gripped me. Were our difficulties too great to overcome…was he going to suggest we part?

'I'm going to sleep for a while…I'm so tired,' he said.

He was snoring softly. I closed the bedroom door and went to the piano. Playing the piano soothed me, and I played my classical pieces until my hands ached.

I was in the kitchen, making a sandwich when I heard Luke's footsteps. He was dressed and though he looked refreshed, his expression was tense. I cut another slice of bread and buttered it. He put his arm around my shoulder. 'As bad as things are, it doesn't alter how I feel about you, how much I love you and always will.'

I nodded, too emotional to speak.

'I'm thinking of leaving Vienna and coming to live in Australia.'

I put the knife down and faced him. 'Escape doesn't always work.'

He cut in. 'Sometimes moving away can help. I've had several offers here in Australia. I need to think them through.'

'Take it from me, leaving is a huge decision,' I added.

'I love Vienna and the academic life in Europe and I have my two girls there... but there's plenty on the down side. The weather for one. And there are other things too.' He took a bite of a sandwich and swallowed it. 'It was bad enough having to come to terms with the events of the Holocaust. Now there are Austrian neo-Nazis with their right wing extremism yelling out their hate slogans, brandishing swastikas and giving heil Hitler salutes. If they had their way it would all be happening again. There are thousands of them and their anti-Semitic rallies have been gaining ground since 1979. The police have been rounding them up but that doesn't stop them.'

'Yes, it's starting up again or perhaps it never really went away. Magda told me that there are neo-Nazis here in Australia too. One can't escape them. '

'I know.'

He finished the sandwich and ran his hands under the tap. 'I suppose one has to look on the positive side too. Synagogues in Europe have been rebuilt and that's good. I've been inside some of them.'

'You've been to synagogues?'

I looked at him. I knew even less about Luke than I thought.

The Third Generation

Forty-Six

Luke had packed his bag in advance and it stood in the hall as a reminder of his imminent departure to Alice Springs. Neither of us wanted to stay in the house or be reminded of our discussions of the past two days. We walked through the front door together, when Luke placed a hand on my shoulder. 'I see you have a mezuzah on your door. Was it there when you moved in?'

I dropped my handbag. 'How do you know about mezuzahs? He smiled but didn't reply.

'Paul arrived with it as a gift for the new house and I had no clue what it was. Richard had to explain. You know he's not interested in following his religion, but he allowed Paul to knock it on to the lintel for us and say the special prayer.'

Luke steered me away from the door towards the car and I had no time to ponder on how he knew about *mezuzahs* until later.

I drove towards the mountains and he followed the map until we reached a sign "to Lake Emerald". He liked the idea of a bright green lake and wanted to see it. We reached the wide expanse of sparkling water, green from the reflection of the trees on its banks and agreed that his choice was an excellent one. We took the path through a chestnut grove, breathtaking with its huge overhanging trees. Past fern gullies we walked, and on to the verge of the lake framed by spruces and birches. Rainbow lorikeets twittered from high in their branches. The stillness of the water, the birds and trees were so familiar, that we agreed we could've been transported to Austria. Engrossed

213

in the natural beauty, we had almost forgotten that this was our last opportunity to be together.

After the long walk my legs ached and we turned back. Luke pointed to a grassy, protected spot. Carefully he picked his way past bushes and a fallen tree and turned around to see if I was following. I moved slowly. He stripped off his parka and laid it on the grass but I was still fully dressed.

'Come on!' he urged.

'No... no, Luke... I can't.'

'But it will be our last time before I leave.'

'No... I'm sorry. There's too much floating around in my head after our talks.'

'I suppose I've been kidding myself, thinking things would stay the same.'

We sat on his parka silently and I took his hand.

I knew I would get over the pain. Reason told me none of it was his fault, it had nothing to do with him, but I was not responding to reason.

🐝

We all pretended to eat breakfast as usual. Anton called out his good-bye to Luke as he rushed out, already late for early lectures. When Richard crumpled his napkin and left the table to collect his coat and briefcase, Luke and I wrapped ourselves in a quick hug and kiss. Neither of us spoke. He moved into the hall and stood next to his luggage, waiting for Richard, who was taking him to the airport. I remained in the kitchen, hoping I wouldn't cry. I swallowed hard when I heard Richard's footsteps down the hallway. The two men walked to the car. Luke loaded his suitcase into the boot. I waved and they were gone.

All that was left of Luke in the house was a discarded paperback. I had intended to go to work, but the build-up to his departure had left me drained. I phoned the library with an excuse. The head librarian's response was cool. I had taken too many days off work lately.

Later, I heard a buzzing noise and then a thud outside the front door. Propped up against the doorpost was an elaborate arrangement of orchids. A note was attached.

> *Thank you so much Richard, Ellie, and Anton for your generous hospitality and for the wonderful time we spent together. See you soon. My love to you all, Luke.*

I buried my face in the flowers and inhaled their fragrance. In spite of Luke's revelations about his family, my ache for him was unbearable. Already I was grieving. Whether he returned to Melbourne for a while or not, ultimately he would leave for Vienna. I could not help being resentful. He had gone off to tour a distant and intriguing part of this new country, while I was left with a husband I was just tolerating and a son doing his best to reject his nest and gather the strength to fly off.

When Richard saw the orchids in the sitting room, he smiled and nodded to himself as he looked for the card. When Anton saw the flowers he looked concerned. 'It's a thank you and good bye gift. I wonder if he will come back here after his trip. Our home has been a comfortable hotel for him but I'm not sure that he'll be back.' he said.

My waking thoughts were centred on Luke, where he was and what he was doing. At last an email from him appeared on my screen

> *Ellie, I am missing you terribly already, and the wonderful times we had together are in my thoughts. I wish you were here to share this with me.*
>
> *I am so excited. I arrived in Darwin yesterday and immediately walked about the city. It is on the coast and more modern than I expected. But it is hot and humid here, like the tropics. Tomorrow I'll hire a 4WD and slowly head east to Kakadu National Park. I intend to stop off along the way if something grabs my interest. I've read quite a lot about the area and I'm*

looking forward to the adventure. I expect to be here for some time and will write and tell you all about it. I've never been anywhere like this before. I'm sure you would love it. It's such a pity you can't be here with me.

As with all of Luke's emails, I deleted it immediately after reading it and emptied the recycle bin as well. I went into the sitting room and looked at the bowl of orchids in their prime position on the dresser. Almost all the blooms had lasted. Luke knew about flowers and it was likely that he had specifically chosen orchids to last and remind me of him while he was away. If only I was with him. He might be missing me but he wasn't suffering. Not like I was. There were too many distractions to allow him to think of me for long.

Before I married Richard, I toured Europe and made friends with several fellow travellers. We were all strangers but a camaraderie developed between us as we told stories and sang silly songs. I could picture Luke, looking younger than his age in his jeans and colourful tee shirt, carrying his bag of geological equipment over one arm and his camera over the other. For all I knew, he might have linked up with one of the female tourists. It was hard not to let my imagination run wild. Later that day, another email arrived from him.

I had to write and tell you this. You won't believe who I've just run into at the hotel bar– Magda and Karl Weber. They're here on holiday. Magda told me that they lived in the house across the road from you when you arrived in Melbourne.

We were talking about our families and people we both know and the name Eddie Leismuller came up. It turned out that we are both related to Eddie. He is my third cousin and Magda's first cousin. So Magda and me, we're related.

I'm fond of Eddie and see him often. He's a taxi driver like the rest of his family. After the war the whole family moved from Stuttgart, to Vienna, where there were better job opportunities.

Maybe you remember him driving us to the apartment after concerts back in the old days. You liked him and laughed at his silly jokes. I should've told you he was a relative but I thought it better not to. You'd have worried he'd gossip about us amongst my family.

Eddie's grandfather, Joachim, is regarded as a hero. He was given a medal by the Jewish community of Stuttgart. At the beginning of WW2 he risked his life driving Jews from Stuttgart over the border. No one knows how many he saved from the Nazis but there are many people whose families owe their lives to him.

It's a lovely story and Magda is very proud to be his grandchild.

I'm off to bed now. Let me know your news.

I clicked off the computer but didn't move from my desk. Why hadn't Magda mentioned her grandfather? I thought about it for a while. It was family secrecy. It had to be that. I was tired of it all.

Forty-Seven

Nothing had changed. My promises to myself that morning in the rainforest were forgotten. Without Luke in my life, my despair returned with greater ferocity. My marriage continued to drag along, the new house was no longer a thrill and at work I went through the motions of a repetitive job. At least Anton appeared to be more settled.

I wished I had listened to Luke years earlier, when he suggested we have a child. It would've been our ultimate deception. Richard was the sort of man who would've considered any child I carried as his. In any event, we were still having a sexual relationship at the time and he would never have guessed. But that was years ago when I was younger. Though I told myself that dredging up the past was fruitless time wasting, I couldn't let it go.

❧

Anton ate at the university canteen and Richard had lunch at work in addition to whatever I left for him in the oven at night. He didn't complain or question my renewed lack of interest in cooking or my sour mood. I could only deduce that he did not care or was too caught up in his own concerns. He was coming home later than ever but I did not bother to ask questions.

I could have easily stayed in bed most of the day but knowing that I was expected at work forced me to shower and dress. If not for Ruth's caring support, I doubt whether I would've managed to last the long days at work. I have no idea how I performed the repetitive tasks but no one complained or appeared to notice my lack of enthusiasm. If they did they were too polite to comment.

The house was usually quiet when I returned after work each night. Anton had found a part-time job as a waiter at a bistro near the university and was rarely home. Boxed into emptiness and without even a nearby corner café, my refuge was the piano. I lost myself in the music I was taught as a child, Beethoven, Bach, Mozart and occasionally Chopin. When Richard returned, I served his dinner and with nothing to say to him, buried myself in bed.

Luke had been away for over a month, when I began to sleep more peacefully and thought of him less often. There was space in my head for other thoughts and my energy gradually returned.

One evening, laughter emanating from Anton's room was a pleasant change from the music he usually played. The door was open and I entered. A young woman with short brown hair and a face red from embarrassment averted her eyes.

'Hello there,' I said in my friendliest voice.

'Mutti, this is Jodi,' Anton mumbled.

'Pleased to meet you, Jodi.'

I edged towards the door. 'If either of you are hungry, help yourselves to food. There's plenty in the fridge.'

Much later I heard whispers in the entrance hall and the front door closing. Anton must be taking her home, I thought.

I was still up when he returned.

'Before you ask, she's not my girlfriend ... just a friend,' he insisted.

'You can bring your friends home any time. I'd like to meet them,' I added.

As we talked, I noticed a change in Anton's speech. He had already picked up a slight Aussie twang and his speech was flavoured with a sprinkling of new expressions.

'Uni is great Mutti... just great.'

He was looking different too, sloppier than before and he no longer combed his hair in the slicked down style he had favoured in Vienna. None of it mattered if he was finding his place with the university herd.

❧

I found Anton staring forlornly at the open fridge.

'Hungry?' I asked. 'We had dinner an hour ago.'

'Mmmm. Just looking for a snack while I finish my work for uni.'

'I'll make you toasted cheese.'

'Mmmm, lovely, thanks.'

The weekend that Richard and I had earmarked to tell my sons more about their family history and their grandfather had slipped past and I did not want to leave it any longer. Richard was attending a crisis meeting at the office. With him away, I could talk freely to both of my sons. After all, the story I had to tell them was about my family and it was best, I thought, that I did this without Richard.

'There are some things I want to tell you both... family stuff.' I said as I placed the toasted sandwiches on the table.

'Important?'

'Yes, it is,' I answered while nibbling my sandwich.

'You've got me interested,' he said.

'It's a pity Gabe isn't here, but at least we can all talk on Skype.'

'Anton glanced at his watch. With luck he'll be home now,' he said as he finished the last sandwich.

We moved extra chairs to the computer. 'Right, get comfortable and I'll dial your brother,' I said.

Gabe was home and he answered. When I explained the reason for my call, he replied tersely, 'It's about time you told us about our background.'

I hesitated at first but I had to tell them all I knew. I had no choice but to put up with the boys' resentment. I began by telling them both about the courageous role their grandfather had played during the war and how he'd put his own life at risk.

I didn't expect either of the boys to react with such awe and pride. It was the first time since Anton was a child that I noticed tears in his eyes.

'Thanks for telling us this, Mutti. I know it must be hard for you,' Anton said.

I coughed to ease my tense throat. 'Well yes, it is difficult ... but let's move on.'

'You sound sad, Mutti,' Anton said.

'I am sad and I can't help that, but it's important that both of you hear the rest of what I have to tell you. You can ask your questions later and I'll try to answer them... if I can.'

'Right, I'm ready,' Gabe said.

I told them how their grandfather was apprehended by the Nazis and then sent to Theresienstadt Concentration Camp. I explained how he managed to stay alive by keeping the camp guards amused. Both boys were crying now. Anton was sitting near me and I could comfort him but Gabe was so far away. As he battled to stem his tears, I watched helplessly. All I could do was talk to him gently. Both boys looked tense and pale.

'It's almost unbelievable that our grandfather survived the war. He did it through his wits and his courage,' Gabe said.

My moment for tears came when I apologised to my sons for not being able to tell them more about their grandfather.

'I wish I'd known your grandfather and that I could tell you more about him. All I can share with you are the bits and pieces I've put together about him. Mama told me almost nothing but Aunt Gertie helped me by filling in many of the holes in my information.'

Anton kissed my cheek. 'Thanks, Mutti from both of us.'

After both boys recovered from their initial shock, they asked for details... names, dates and places that I was unable to supply.

'There is more. I have photographs to show you both and some of your grandfather's paintings that were sent to me recently but we can look at them another time.'

'I don't know about Gabe but I can't handle it now. I'm wiped out,' Anton said.

221

'Me too,' Gabe said. 'Let's talk again later... in a week... and thanks Mutti.'

His voice faded and the screen went blank. Anton and I returned to the kitchen.

'I could do with a strong cup,' Anton said as he poured ground coffee into the plunger.

'Me too.' I stroked his hand.

'I hope Gabe is okay,' he said looking worried.

'Phone him a little later and have a chat.'

'Good idea.'

He refilled both our cups and sat with a sigh.

'Of course I'm glad you told us all this, but it's a bit of a shock, that's all.' He gave me a weak but reassuring smile.

I sprawled out on the sofa. Talking about my father again and watching my sons' reactions upset me more than I had anticipated. When Richard returned that evening, I told him that I had at last told the boys about their grandfather.

'It's about time they knew... and it was better that you handled it.'

I was surprised that he asked no questions about our discussion. Instead of lounging in his chair and drinking as he usually did after dinner, he went to the study.

By the following weekend, I had copied all my father's paintings and photographs onto the computer and emailed them to Gabe. It was a laborious task but I thought it only fair to ensure that Gabe would be able to see them too.

Once again the three of us clustered around our computers. This time I began by reminding my sons how I had received my father's portfolio.

'I've kept all of this from you boys for too long. When the portfolio arrived after a long sea voyage, I knew I had to tell you both about it but it's taken longer than it should've.'

The boys studied the photos carefully and were struck by family resemblances.

'Anton, you look like mutti and like our grandfather,' Gabe said excitedly.

Anton called out. 'And you're a lot like our grandmama when she was young.'

The images of Mama intrigued them. They had only known her as a sick, old woman.

'I can see our grandfather's strong character on his face,' Gabe said.

Both were surprised when I told them that all the photos were taken before 1940. Gabe's face crumpled in concern. 'He must've been quite an old man when they dragged him off to Theresienstadt.'

'All the more incredible that he survived,' Anton added.

'He survived but he was very ill.' I said, thinking of the photograph I found in Mama's bedroom. It would be best not to show it to them, I thought.

Both of my sons were fighting back tears again.

'I know this is terribly painful for you both but at least you will be able to tell your children how proud they should be of their great grandfather.'

'You're right, Mutti,' Anton said.

'Absolutely,' Anton said, agreeing with his brother.

'Let's take a break and then look at your grandfather's paintings and etchings,' I said, hoping for a change in mood.

Both boys had taken courses in Art at their school in Vienna and they could discuss the colour and composition of each piece. They agreed that their grandfather's art work was of a high technical standard, but more than that they enjoyed his choice of subject matter. He had painted the mountains and lakes, the vineyards and valleys they knew well. Gabe was thrilled when I offered him a few paintings for his apartment. Anton would have to wait until he moved out.

'We had an amazing grandfather and I'd like to find out more about him,' Gabe said. 'I'd like to do some research about his time in the theatre and his painting too.'

'Yes, we could check the archived records in Vienna,' Anton said enthusiastically.

My sons would discuss their family at length now and hopefully they would discover more than I had about their grandfather. I decided not to mention the painting that Luke had discovered. There I was, holding something back again but I did not want to build up their hopes. I intended to tell them about it later.

🦂

During breaks at work, Ruth and I chatted as before. My dark mood had lifted and I was able to tell Ruth more about my relationship with Luke. She was more understanding than I expected. She'd had a lover many years ago and still missed him. When I mentioned the discovery of my father's water colours and etchings she was intrigued. I showed her some of the photos of the pictures and she commented on their fine style and colours.

The following day I brought a photo of my special painting to show her. I said nothing and waited for her reaction. She was taken aback. 'A French Impressionist painting, I love the Impressionists.'

She scurried off to the art section of the library and returned with a tome of a book about French Impressionist Painters. Hurriedly she turned the pages in her search.

'Here's what I'm looking for. Have a look at these,' she said pointing to two landscapes by the artist Pissarro. I gasped. They were so similar to the picture at home that they could have been painted around the same time.

'How wonderful, you might have a jewel of a painting at home,' she said, giving me one of her warmest smiles. She told me about a family friend, a dealer in antiques and paintings, who had connections with art auction houses overseas. Kindly she offered to phone him and arrange for me to show him the painting.

🦂

Hiram Greenberger was a plump, balding man with a resonant voice. His office at home was crowded with antiques and every spot on the wall was adorned with a painting. I thought of the cost of his insurance and shuddered. There were no offers of coffee or tea but he was eager to see the painting. As I unravelled the outer coverings he restlessly tapped the table with his toe. He wore a pair of white cotton gloves to examine the painting. Handling it carefully, he placed it on an artist's easel. He then turned on a powerful overhead light and took a magnifying glass from his breast pocket. Once he had inspected the canvas from several angles and touched the brushstrokes, he examined it closely again.

'It could well be an unknown Pissarro,' he said cautiously, as he withdrew a book from the bookshelf. After paging through it he found what he was looking for. 'Have a look. Here we have a similar Pissarro.'

It was the identical picture Ruth had found in the library.

'Use my magnifying glass to compare the brushstrokes and you will see the similarity. Notice the colour range too, the exact shades of blue and green of the artist's palette.'

After comparing the paintings with his magnifying glass, I had to agree that my painting was similar to the one in the book.

'Do you think it could be an original, Mr Greenberger?'

'In my time I've seen many paintings from the French Impressionist School, but whether it is an original Pissarro... I can't say for certain. I'm a collector, an art dealer... not an authority.' He shrugged and opened his arms in a gesture of uncertainty. He walked to the window and then turned towards me again. 'All I can say that is that if it isn't an original, it's an excellent copy.'

The next step, if I wanted to take it, Mr Greenberger said, was to take the painting overseas to have it authenticated by experts. He talked of an art historian he knew, assessors and some large dealers overseas.

'How much will that cost?' I asked warily.

'Don't worry about that now, I have a lot of friends in the field who owe me favours.'

'And how long do you think all this will take?'

'The process of confirming the authenticity of a painting varies. I can't give you an answer on that but it depends how interested a dealer is.'

My head was spinning. The painting could be valuable, but on the other hand perhaps it was an excellent fake. Mr Greenberger was going to a lot of trouble for a fake, I thought.

'If it is an original, how much do you think its worth,' I asked tentatively.

'There's a huge demand for the French Impressionists with the scarcity of them these days... but... I can't say. However, I am certain that if it is a Pissarro, you won't be disappointed.' He tapped his foot again. 'Do you want me to go ahead with enquiries? If so, I have to take some photographs.'

I had nothing to lose and agreed. While Mr Greenberger was setting up the bright lights and camera, he asked how I happened to have the painting. I told him my father's story.

'What an incredible story. Do you think your father hid it, knowing it was valuable, but later forgot to tell your mother?'

'Unfortunately I'll never know.'

As I drove home, I thought about Mr Greenberger's comment that my father had forgotten to tell my mother about the painting. This was a possibility I had not considered. My father was dying and he may have thought he'd told Mama about the painting and its hiding place, but he hadn't. It may have had nothing to do with Mama's selective memory.

Forty-Eight

Luke continued to write regular emails describing the wonders of Kakadu. He phoned once at the start of the rainy season, and talked in his fast, excited way, allowing me barely a word, as he complained about unbearable humidity, nasty insects and afternoon storms. He was travelling through the area in his 4WD, sleeping in camps with the locals, prepared to put up with discomfort, in view of the area's beauty and geological importance. Talking in "geology speak" that was difficult to understand, he marvelled at rocks that had developed 3,000 million years ago when sea covered the land, or described zircon crystals he had seen, when the earth was formed.

When the phone call ended I felt empty. There had been no talk of missing me. Kakadu had engaged him to such an extent, that he had put aside his earlier guilt about his family's involvement in the Holocaust. Enraptured by the brilliant, blue sky, coloured birds and the array of native animals, he overstayed the five weeks he had planned. Once I had seen photographs of Kakadu and the surrounding area I was able to picture him in the setting, and an email provided some of the answers I was seeking

> As I am writing to you, Ellie, my glasses are covered with a film of mist and I find it difficult to see the keys on the laptop. We've just had one hell of a storm here that swept right though the plains and the world is still underwater.

Yesterday morning I went out with my camera, chasing a photo of wild geese. I'm an idiot and should've looked where I was driving, because I got stuck in spongy mud. The wheels of the 4WD spun and wouldn't shift. In minutes there was thick mud up to the door. I'm usually not the sort who panics but this was very scary. If not for the rangers who drove past an hour later and pulled me out with ropes, I'd have been stuck there overnight, or worse, sucked into the mud.

I'm not a pessimist, you know that, but late that afternoon while I waited for help, my thinking turned negative. I weighed things up, sifted through all the dreadful family stuff I'd found out lately and I asked myself what was really important to me. My answer came fast. My two girls and you are the ones I cherish. There are others I care about too, like my wife and close friends. I was taken aback that I didn't put much value on my home, possessions or my profession.

Existence in Kakadu was more hazardous than I had realised. Luke was adventurous but not foolhardy. I could only hope he would remain safe.

A week or two later, Luke tired of his nomadic life, the absence of hot showers and good food, and booked into a hotel. He had left his investigation into the area's thermal energy for last and spent a few days in discussion with Geoscientists at the Darwin University. He wrote to me giving me details of his meetings at the university.

This whole area around Kakadu is like a toy shop for a geologist. My talks at the university went well. It was good of the Professor to set up a meeting for me with the CEOS of two huge companies who are establishing geothermal energy operations here. They're in the early stages but it was a thrill for me to see this happening on such a large scale. Deposits of energy are plentiful in the Northern Territory.

Apparently after our talks, the scientists at the university were impressed with my background and my knowledge of geothermal energy. So much so, that they offered me a definite position – to head up a new department in Geoscience at Darwin University. I'd be a fool not to consider it.

I was pleased for Luke. He was receiving the recognition he deserved. If he took the position in Darwin we would still be miles from each other. His emails that followed were filled with excitement about the job offer but he expressed no thoughts about our future. We clearly had no future, I told myself. For years, Luke and I had dreamed about our life together. Until recently, I imagined travelling almost anywhere to be with him, but now I was forced to acknowledge that he was still married to Hilde and though he talked and wrote about leaving her, he had made no tangible plans to do so. When I was honest with myself, I tore our fantasy apart and tried to accept the painful truth.

In the early mornings while hazy with sleep, once again I stepped along the streets of Vienna, rode my bicycle along the Danube and through the meadows of the Prater. Luke featured in most of my morning imaginings but when I opened my eyes and found myself alone in my bed in Melbourne I was disappointed, even sad.

When longings for Luke and Vienna interfered with my concentration at work, I knew that I was stuck. I had confined myself to daily work, shopping and an occasional meeting with Magda. I had to venture further and involve myself in my new home.

One Saturday, in an adventurous mood, I followed the route to the beach that Ruth had taken. Though the streets were packed with an early morning crowd, I found the café Ruth and I had visited. The comforting smell of coffee and the sounds of talk greeted me. From my corner table I watched people around me. They looked and sounded familiar – European faces speaking the mix of languages I was used to hearing in cafés. I had come equipped with a newspaper, sunglasses and sunscreen lotion. As I read the newspaper, I ate and drank steadily. One slice of strudel with cream was a decadent breakfast but the strudel was so delicious that I had another with more coffee. Ruth was right, one had to know where to go and one could find most things in Melbourne.

Forty-Nine

Though Richard had lost some weight and was looking healthier, he was snappy and morose. If I asked about his work or one of his colleagues, my questions were met with a surly response. Despite my promise to myself to be open with him about my lengthy affair with Luke, I had done nothing about it. I was hedging until I felt strong enough.

On a day off work, I rushed out of the house in search of the throb and pace of the city. I wandered through the elaborate, nineteenth century Block and Royal arcades and ogled at their highly priced luxury merchandise. The crowded city was new to me and I kept a street map in my handbag. At one particular corner I checked the familiar sounding street names against the map. I was almost certain that Richard's office was on the third floor of a building on the opposite corner. Impulsively I decided to pay him a surprise visit. The company's glass doors opened automatically and I announced myself to the receptionist.

'Mrs Tannenbaum, what a surprise,' the young silvery blonde said as she eyed my clothing and hairdo. 'I'll let your husband know that you're here. Please take a seat.'

The waiting area was not as well appointed as Richard had described it but it had a moneyed look. Leather chairs with endless studs, wood panels and a thick carpet contributed to that impression.

While waiting, I imagined Richard in his office. Not the grump he was at home but pleasant and charming to his female staff and assertive with the men. He'd be amenable and his door would be open to discussion.

After a few minutes, another young woman appeared. 'I'm Jennifer, Mr Tannenbaum's personal assistant,' she said with a flick of her long, honeyed hair. 'I'll show you into Mr Tannenbaum's office. This way.'

I recognised the conspiratorial look Jennifer gave Richard. It was the look I had noticed between the boys when they told a lie. Richard stood, and edged towards me from behind his huge desk. Dressed in his slimming, dark suit he looked imposing, almost handsome. He kissed my cheek and pointed to a chair.

'Good to see you. Lovely surprise! I had no idea you'd be in the city today.'

I glanced at the large, airy room and viewed the courtyard. He introduced me to the staff members and gave me a brief tour through the rest of the office. When his phone rang, I waved and left. Back on the street, I leant against a shop front. The giggle that I had muffled when I caught the look the two of them gave each other broke free and I laughed until I ached. No wonder he came home late and was tired each night. Richard had as much to explain as I did.

During the next week there was no mention of Jennifer or Luke. If not for a phone call from a stranger, we may have continued our civility to each other for months. Rarely did personal phone calls disturb me at work and when Helmut Schmidt phoned, apologising for bothering me, I couldn't place him He explained that he had attempted to phone Richard at home without luck. He did not have Richard's work number and none of his countless emails had been answered. Helmut had worked with Richard in Vienna and badly wanted to discuss a business matter with him. Satisfied with his explanation, I gave him Richard's office phone number. It took me a while to work out how he had obtained my cell number. I had given in to Anton's nagging and agreed to employ a house cleaner every two weeks. The cleaner had my cell number and must've given it to Helmut.

Richard arrived home around 10.00 that night but I made no mention of his lateness.

'I'll warm up some dinner for you.'

'Aren't you even curious about why I'm so late tonight?'

'No, you don't tell me anything about your work. In fact, these days you don't tell me anything at all.'

'I'm sorry.' His sigh was followed by a deep frown. 'There's trouble brewing. The workers at the plant are calling a strike tomorrow and I spent ages negotiating with their union leader to try to avert it.'

'Oh goodness!'

'They're blaming me, saying that my approach is unAustralian.'

'Why? What have you done?'

'I cut back five staff at the plant. They were clearly unnecessary.'

'You must have your reasons, I suppose. You'll sort it out,' I said not particularly convincingly. 'You're good at defending your position.'

I placed a wrinkled piece of steak and stringy vegetables on the table. 'It's hot ... eat.'

'Have you heard from Luke?'

'Yes. I received an email from him this week.'

'Is he having a good time in Kakadu?'

'So he says.'

When I told Richard about the phone call from Helmut, he winced. 'He's after a corporate job for his youngest son... just completed his studies but his grades are low and he's nothing special. I was supposed to phone him back but I didn't'

I nodded.

'I've been meaning to tell you for days, I've had our home phone number changed to a silent, unlisted number. I've also altered my email address. I'll give you the new address later, in case you want to send me an email or anyone asks.'

'Why did you have it unlisted without telling me? The number was mine too? Surely not because of Helmut Schmidt and his son?'

'No no. And I'm sorry, I should've mentioned it.'

'Why all the secrecy?'

'It goes back to the months before we left for Australia. Someone was stalking me.'

'Someone stalking *you*!'

'Yes.' He looked down at the floor.

'Who? You didn't say a thing!'

'It's no longer a problem. It's all sorted out. I've got too much to think about to discuss it now. Another time.'

I took his plate, rinsed it and stacked it in the dishwasher.

'More bloody secrets,' I muttered as I wiped the bench top.

'I will tell you about it later, I promise. I can't handle a long discussion now. I have a lot of negotiating to do tomorrow and a board meeting to prepare for.' He eased himself away from me.

Someone stalking Richard? It sounded bizarre. He would explain eventually but I wanted answers immediately. I waited until he went to bed to search his emails on the laptop he took to work. Unlike me, he didn't delete his personal correspondence. There was no sign of the stalker in his correspondence but there were several erotic emails from Jennifer, his P A. This was my cue. The timing was perfect to talk to him about Luke.

Fifty

When I received a matter of fact email from Luke, stating that he had decided to fly home to Vienna from Sydney, I wasn't surprised. He had been in the Northern Territory for almost three months. He repeated his declaration of love for me and his promises, but his words were dry from overuse. His visit had drained me. Though my love for him would not diminish, at least now our deception and dishonesty that made me feel grubby and adolescent would cease.

When I went up to Anton's room to tell him about Luke's altered plans, he was disappointed, even angry that Luke had built up his hopes.

He puffed up a pillow he was leaning against and then turned towards me. 'You must be upset,' he said.

I raised my eyebrows. 'Of course, we were looking forward to having him with us again.'

'I meant *you* must be very upset,' he said with a sardonic smile.

So, he knew. And I had tried so hard to keep up a front. Rather than feeling shame, I wanted to laugh. It was not my usual reaction but he was so pleased with himself. He had caught his mother out and was delighted by his discovery.

'Don't worry about it Mutti, I'm not blind or stupid.'

'At least you know I'm human.'

He chuckled. 'I'll say!'

Don't comment, I told myself, aware that he was winding me up.

'Everything going well with you? I hardly see you lately, what with your job and university.'

235

'I'm fine. Everything's cool. Nothing to worry about on *my* account.'

⚹

Conflict at work was telling on Richard. His skin was sallow and deep dissatisfaction lines had gathered around his mouth. I fed him and attended to his laundry but we might as well have been living in different continents.

I waited until the weekend, and over dinner I told him about the email from Luke.

'I thought he wouldn't come back,' he said with a slight curl of his lip.

'He has a lot to sort out in Vienna.'

'I should think so!'

I looked at him, hoping that our conversation would not blow up into an argument.

I waited for him to speak. 'So, your lover won't be back. That must upset you.'

I felt a sudden inner jolt. 'I suspected you knew... about us.'

'Of course I knew.'

'So why did you ...?'

'Pretend I didn't know... put up with it?'

'Yes.'

'It suited me. I had a thing going with Andrea back home, and now Jennifer, my P.A. here provides me with everything a man could want. I felt less guilty knowing you were doing the same thing.'

'How pathetic!'

He laughed. 'It worked for a long time, didn't it?'

I put my hands to my face. 'We're both at fault.'

'That's modern marriage, my dear.'

'Oh no! That's not as I see it ... with such deceit on both parts, there can't possibly be a marriage.'

'I agree, things haven't been the best between us. Remember when I had the phone number unlisted. It was because of my secretary, Andrea, phone stalking me from Vienna, insisting she

236

couldn't live without me, wanting money from me, telling me she was following me over here.'

I felt the tension in my face.

'Don't look so worried. Of course, I got rid of her.'

'I'm convinced... you needn't say another word. It's over between us.'

'*So ist das Leben!*', he said, placing his knife and fork on his empty plate. That's the way it goes.

Richard took his time about packing his clothes and his possessions. Two weeks after I had asked him to move out, his arrangements to move into a furnished apartment near his work were not finalised. The nuisance of it all made him stall, but I refused to help him.

'Don't you understand, I want you out of here?' I screamed at him one morning while he was eating a leisurely breakfast. 'It's over between us... you have to leave... move out!'

It was unkind of me but if I hadn't insisted he could've delayed leaving for months. Once the decision was made to split, I was keen to sell the house quickly, share the profit and move on.

That weekend, he borrowed a trailer, filled it and drove off. The organising of the sale of the house he left to me. One after another real estate agent visited and viewed the house until I decided on Geoff, a fast talking but pleasant Australian. He brought prospective buyers to view the house while I was at work. My side of the bargain was to keep the house tidy and fill it with fresh flowers. We sold privately, well above the price we expected and undertook to be out of the house within six weeks. I packed all my possessions in good time and left his.

By the day of the settlement, the house was empty and cleaner than I had found it. The new owners, a middle aged couple with a teenage son and daughter were polite and undemanding. They hadn't asked for extra viewings or nagged for any details. My welcoming gesture was flowers I picked from the garden, arranged in a large jar and placed on the shelf over the fireplace.

Ruth kindly offered me space for my boxed possessions and my furniture in her storeroom. Richard moved into a motel. Everything was in its place but I had no idea where Anton and I would eventually live. In the meanwhile, I rented a furnished apartment a few blocks from the university.

Fifty-One

Sixteen months later

I flopped onto the couch. It was the second time I had shifted the sitting room furniture, but now the room was as I wanted it. My new apartment in the inner suburbs was compact, white, modern and with every convenience. Though I was used to high ceilinged rooms with a classical design, the luxury and ease of care won me over. There was a view of the river from the front room and I could see the city from my bedroom. My father's paintings graced the walls, my pottery bowl was on the table and Persian rugs enlivened the wooden floor.

The best part was that I was free of Richard. He agreed to a divorce, and was more reasonable about the splitting of our assets than I expected. Through it all we had managed to remain civil to each other. The cream from the sale of our house enabled us to set Anton up in his own flat near the university and pay for a new car for Gabe. Both boys were delighted. Richard and Jennifer moved into the suburbs and from his reports, they were happy. It had all worked out well.

I had a new job too. My part- time job at the library had become boring. How many books could I stamp? How many shelves could I straighten? If my library job had a broader reach, by spreading the love of books and knowledge to children and teenagers, I would've stayed. Luckily, I found the stimulation I craved as a research assistant in the marketing department of a multinational pharmaceutical company. It was a full-time job working with the latest information in medical and pharmaceutical advances, a huge field. It was my responsibility to deliver vital research information to doctors and the media.

After a first few days of jelly legs, I gained confidence. The work was absorbing and I could not complain of boredom. Most nights I read to keep up to date with research material. The staff of about thirty, mainly scientists and doctors, formed a tight community. I was pleased to be accepted, but none of us had the time or inclination to socialise outside of work, apart from the Friday ritual gathering at the pub.

Over the weekend I continued to play tennis with the group I'd met initially. I had made no new friends but had coffee with Magda and visited Ruth regularly.

I hoped that I had moved on in the months that had passed, become more flexible and adult. I was determined not to carry negatives with me into my new and single life.

⁂

A cool evening breeze ruffled the curtains. I closed the porch door and buttoned my cardigan. The sitting room was tidy and the dishes in the cupboard after dinner with Anton. I cooked a simple fish meal that he enjoyed as a child. After an hour of intense talk and laughter he left. Since the divorce, he came for a meal once a week. I delighted in his company and without his father around, we were growing closer. He appeared to have adjusted to university life in Melbourne and to his part- time job in a restaurant. He had made new friends and talked shyly about a girl he was dating.

Gabe and I continued our regular calls on Skype but distance and the months of not being together made our conversations forced. I had no idea what was happening in his life and I felt him slipping away from me.

I poured a glass of wine. It was the chardonnay I once enjoyed with Luke. Remembering, I sipped it slowly and then stretched for a chocolate from the bowl. Scrunching the wrapper into a ball, I threw it into the corner of the room, the way Luke would've and smiled. I lifted my glass and murmured, *to Luke my love, to the past and our memories.* I chose one last chocolate and savoured it as it melted on my tongue. Before bed, I looked in the mirror. My hair was in need of a wash. Looking my best was essential at work. The following day, the marketing gurus would assess my appearance together with the material I presented. They would use part of it in focus groups to assess the public's attitude to a new painkilling medication. After a warm shower I laid out my outfit, an attractive suit and black pumps.

In the morning, I was ready early to avoid the crush on a tram to the city. As on most mornings lately, I made my way to my favourite café. There was sufficient time to scan the newspaper over a coffee. During a lunch break or after work I returned to the same café for another cup as a booster. I selected this older place with patterned wallpaper and velvet curtains as it reminded me of a spot in Vienna. The owners and some of the regular patrons exchanged greetings and smiled at me. I was comfortable in reverting to café life and the home away from home it offered me.

After months of silence, a letter that had been redirected to my new address arrived. It was from Hiram Greenberger, brief and to the point. He had studied the markets over all these months and written to several experts and dealers on my behalf. Each of them had studied the photographs he had sent and were prepared to say that the painting may well be a genuine Pissarro. Naturally they wanted to examine the actual painting. He suggested that I or someone acting on my behalf, take it overseas to be assessed as soon as possible.

🐎

Ruth visited carrying a bunch of flowers from her garden. I placed them in a vase in the sitting room and the fragrances wafted over us as we chatted. She liked the apartment and was always on the look- out for any new decorations I added.

She had stayed on in her library job with no thoughts of moving. We were sitting on the couch sipping cool drinks when she gave me one of her long, appreciative looks.

'You're looking happier these days. Changed your hairstyle and your clothes are more fashionable. I like it. You look like a modern business woman.'

She took my hand. 'You've only been in the new job a few months but I can tell you're not missing Vienna as much.'

'You're right. I hardly think of it, there isn't the time, but I still miss Luke… always will, I guess.'

I had waited far too long to share my news. I told her about the letter I had received from Hiram Greenberger.

'It looks like you'll have to take it overseas.'

'Yes, I'll have to, if I want to sell it.'

'That's something to think about, to plan… a trip to Europe.'

Fifty-Two

My longing to be with Luke persisted, though we rarely sent each other emails or talked on the phone. *I wonder if Luke would like this*, I would ask myself when I bought a new dress or enjoyed a movie. He featured in my daydreams and I could still recall his smell and touch.

When an email from him showed up on my computer screen, I was surprised.

I must apologise for my weeks of not writing. I think of you all the time but somehow, I can't bring myself to write. I am not well– not my usual energetic self. I haven't been sleeping much and I've lost a lot of weight. My research at the university has been tedious and results so far are disappointing. You can imagine that this is a big blow. I don't have the inclination right now to do any further research.

I know that you must be fed up with my promises. I haven't stuck to my side of our bargain. You've left Richard and I wouldn't blame you for thinking that I'll never leave Hilde. It's not like that at all. It's just that I've had so much to sort out.

I've been staying in the miserable little flat at the university, a garret of a place and I drop into the house on a Sunday to look through my post. I have consulted a solicitor and my accountant about splitting up with Hilde and I will see them again.

Of course I can understand that you must be disappointed in me, but I do love you. I want to talk to you, to explain. My hope for us to be together has not changed and never will. I will phone you one night this week.

The tone of Luke's email concerned me. He was the most optimistic and positive person I knew. Usually he fell asleep almost immediately and was a healthy eater. He did not sound at all well. We hadn't spoken to each other on the phone since my move into the flat, but now I looked forward to hearing his voice. Perhaps speaking to him would settle my concerns about his health.

The sound of his voice produced a rush of love. He explained that he was in the process of moving away from home.

'But even if you only spend Sundays at home, you're still with Hilda,' I insisted.

'Listen, Ellie. This is about money, not love. All our funds are tied up together and it's difficult to unscramble things. As I told you in my email, I have started the process.'

'That sound's fine but until you're free and we're actually together again, who knows...'

'How can I blame you for saying that?' He was silent. All I heard was a crackling noise.'

'You still there, Luke?'

I heard a cough. 'Yes, yes... I'm here.'

'More important... what's wrong, why aren't you sleeping?'

His voice was slow now. 'I think I have too much on my mind and I need to sort it out.'

'Talk to me, tell me what's troubling you.'

'It's my research, this thing with Hilda and...'

'And?'

'It's too much to cope with now.'

'Is all that stuff about the war we talked about worrying you?'

'Yes ... and no. I will tell you everything, I promise ... when I'm ready.'

'Sure.'

'The spring university break starts tomorrow and I've decided to go away... to relax... up to the Lake District for a while. I can ski there and when it gets a bit warmer, walk beside the lake.'

'Good idea. I know how you love that area. You'll unwind there.'

'I'll take my laptop and send you emails. Please answer.'

'Yes, I promise to answer.'

His tone was serious. 'And don't give up on us. Things *are* happening but very slowly. I'm just asking you to be as patient as you were in the past.'

I tried to laugh. 'We'll be old if this ever works out.'

Flashes of Luke skiing broke into my thoughts. As a teenager we had spent hours skiing in the Alps together over our winter breaks. He was an athletic skier and I could not keep up with him. We spent the night in inexpensive but warm ski lodges packed with young people.

I did not expect a message from him but he kept his word and an email arrived two days later.

I've rented a room close to the mountains and lakes. It's small but it has a bathroom and is reasonably comfortable. The view of the mountain from the window is the best part. I'm out skiing every morning, avoiding the lower slopes, already covered in slush. It's the higher fields I'm making for, where the snow is still firm. At least up there it is free from tourists at this time of year.

Do you remember how warm it can get here in the afternoons at this time of year? That's when I go hiking near the lake. The flowers are out already and the beauty of it is incredible. I wish you were here with me to see it all. As a second best, I'm attaching some photos.

I'm trying my best to be active but I'm slow and tire easily. I can't rid myself of a heaviness that feels like a dark cloud hanging over the mountains. Maybe it will go as the summer starts.

When I heard from Luke again, it was a brief message to say that he was feeling wretched. He described the dark skies and the Spring rains pelting down the mountainside. Though he was due at the university in a few weeks, he could not drag himself back there. To his surprise the dean of the faculty accepted his request for leave of absence and suggested he take the rest of the year "to heal whatever was ailing him." There were no further emails from Luke for a month. I had written but not received replies.

At last he wrote:

> *I've been confined indoors for two weeks due to the dreadful weather and I have begun to piece together fragments of my past that have been worrying me. You know what I'm like, understanding and analysing have been my way of solving problems.*

> *I promised to explain what's been happening. Well, here it is: I've been trying to come to grips with understanding Judaism. It's a hugely complex topic. You are Jewish and your mother was too, but neither of you practiced the religion. Religious Jews have always been a mystery to me but slowly I am learning. I've been studying the history of Judaism and this always implies the study of anti-Semitism. The two go together, back to early centuries, through the crusades, pogroms and so on until all that hatred spilled out in the Holocaust.*

> *Sorry. Here I go again. I must be boring you. I'll stop there.*

> *Take care of yourself, and write soon.*

I assumed that guilt about his parents was at the heart of his depression. I had read that many Germans and Austrians, who, when faced with family guilt and shame did something I found strange – they embraced Judaism and some even converted. Luke appeared to be acting similarly. I supposed that he had embarked on one of his intellectual "crusades". He had disliked a particular politician and I recalled him writing to the newspapers to point out the man's faults. He also rebelled against school rules that he believed were irrelevant, even though his rebellion resulted in severe punishment. Luke's intelligence could be his enemy at times like this.

When I heard from him again, it was to tell me that he had left the Lake District to return to Vienna. As he had taken extended leave from the university, I thought it likely that he had returned to his home. When I phoned, Hilde answered. She explained that she had been staying with her eldest daughter but when she found out how ill Luke was, she moved back to the house to care for him. When I asked to speak to him she was adamant, he was not taking calls from anyone. She told me how concerned she was. He was eating poorly, had hardly slept and refused to leave his room. A doctor had prescribed antidepressant medication but he refused to take it.

I paced my small sitting room. Too confined in the apartment, I put on a parka and went out in the cool, cloudy night. As I walked, I tried to make sense of what was happening to Luke. During his visit to Melbourne I had noticed his interest in Judaism. There was his comment about the mezuzah and then there was the gift of the hand. Recently while up at the Lake District, he had begun to study the subject. His guilt and shame mixed with the information he had unearthed about Theresienstadt, probably set it off. Whatever the trigger, I could not imagine Luke in such a low state. The thought of him ill but too far away for me to do anything to help him was disturbing. I had to return to Vienna.

Gabe concerned me too. We had been separated too long. He was an adult and the more mature of my two sons, but I could not help wondering if his light breezy conversations were concealing unhappiness or a problem. His studies were almost completed yet he had not mentioned future employment. Then there were the experts and art dealers Mr Greenberger had contacted, who were interested in examining the painting. This was an opportunity to take it overseas for assessment.

As I had only been at the company for a few months, I could hardly expect much paid leave. Lies do not sit well with me, but in my desperation to see Luke, I concocted a plausible story about my son living alone and sick in Vienna. Dana from human resources was sympathetic and managed to advance my leave due by the end of the year. Two weeks paid leave plus another two weeks of unpaid leave was surprisingly generous. Before I left, there was a project I had to complete and then I handed all my other work to a temporary replacement.

I phoned Hiram Greenberger to tell him that I intended to take the painting with me overseas. His advice on packing it was invaluable. He suggested I show it to three people in Austria who had already seen photos of the painting and were interested in it. I thought of phoning them to set up appointments, but I sent emails instead. All three answered and asked me to contact them when I arrived.

The day before leaving, I met Richard for a quick lunch. We spoke to each other occasionally about our sons and had managed to retain a reasonably friendly relationship. Over a sandwich we exchanged our news and each boasted about our newfound happiness. Though he made some pointed remarks about Luke, I ignored them. We kissed each other on the cheek and I left with his gift for Gabe in my handbag.

Fifty-Three

The two years away from Vienna had passed in a flash. When the taxi drove into the city that morning, I was aware of details in the architecture and laneways I had not noticed before. The light seemed duller than I recalled and the smell of the air less fragrant.

With Luke and Gabe in different parts of the city, I had made a booking at a hotel in a central position near the station. It was an older hotel with stucco embellishments, in the baroque style I liked. As soon as I was in my room, I dialled Luke's number.

'It's Ellie, I'm here in Vienna,' I said excitedly.

It took him a moment for him to respond, and then I heard the delight in his voice. 'Oh, my goodness, Ellie! You're here! Isn't that's marvellous. You should've let me know…and I'd have met you at the airport.'

'I wanted to surprise you.'

'I can't wait to see you, *Liebchen*.'

'I can't wait either.'

We agreed to meet at our favourite café within the hour. I changed into a floral skirt and blouse I thought he'd like, applied a little make up, and a dab of perfume. As fast as I could I walked to the café, only a short distance from the hotel. I warned myself that he wasn't well, that I shouldn't expect the vibrant Luke I was used to, but it made no difference. I throbbed with the joyful anticipation of seeing him again.

He was seated near the window, his head bent. As soon as he noticed me, he stood and rushed towards me. We kissed and hugged and the feel of his bones replacing his muscles was disturbing. Talking fast and interrupting each other, we caught up on our news since we had been parted. Suddenly aware of my hunger, we ordered sandwiches and coffee. He nibbled while I wolfed down two sandwiches at a time and then a second round. He was nothing like my Luke. The man sitting across the table was another Luke, who had lost his appetite for life. When I told him that learning that he was ill had prompted my trip, he wiped tears from his eyes. I hadn't seen him cry before. To help him overcome his embarrassment, I made conversation about the people around us and remarked on the view of the street.

He stroked my hand. 'Thank you. Thank you, *Liebchen*. I desperately wanted you to be here with me but how could I ask? Now that you are here, I feel better already. There's a lot I have to tell you… about Hilda and me.'

'It's okay, don't worry about it.' I was tired of his promises of leaving Hilda.

'But something *is* happening at last.'

'Oh?'

'I haven't told you… we're legally separated now. But she's an angel and I love her like an aunt or mother. She moved back into the house for a while to look after me. Do you know, she made pots of chicken soup and all my favourites to tempt me to eat?'

'Yes, she must have a good heart. Living with you hasn't been an easy ride.'

He nodded but didn't even smile at my comment. His mouth was set in a firm line that had not known laughter for some time.

He took a few sips of coffee and explained that since his severe spell of the blues while at the Lake District, his mood had barely lifted. He coughed and rubbed his hands. 'I'm a mess at the moment… crying too easily and dragging myself around without any energy. In the end I gave in to the doctor and I'm taking some antidepressant medication or other. I know it's early days but so far it hasn't worked any miracles.'

I moved closer to him and gave him a hug. 'Of course it will work and you'll feel better. Give it time.'

He sighed, and spoke slowly as he explained that his sadness was different to any other he had experienced. Even when I pictured him as a young boy he was in control. Though I wanted to ask what had tipped him into depression, I waited for him to tell me. Revealing his vulnerability had always embarrassed him. The mouth-watering array of cakes in the glass display cabinet caught my eye. I knew he could not resist cake and pointed to them. He smiled for the first time and walked over to choose one. We both ordered more coffee with incredibly rich slices, laden with cream and chocolate. Watching him lick the cream off his spoon was my pleasure.

He returned to the topic of his separation with Hilda, insisting that her brief stay in the house had not changed their plans. He explained that their lawyers and accountants were working on a fair divorce settlement, which included the eventual sale of the house and splitting the profit.

'My girls aren't at all happy about this but they're adults and it's our turn. They have no appreciation of how hard we've tried to stay together for their sakes.'

'Is Hilda as keen on the divorce as you are?' I asked.

'Oh yes, I was hardly ever at home. There was always the excuse of experiments at the university or research to keep me away. She met a man at her bridge class who has become more than a friend and I wish her luck with him, she deserves it. Now that I'm feeling stronger, she moved in with him.'

I patted his hand but made no comment.

'So Ellie, soon we will both be free to choose our future.'

'It's been a very long time.'

He sighed, placed his cup down and turned towards me. 'Now I want to hear the rest of your news before we talk any more about me. You look different...a sophisticated Aussie haircut and you sound more confident.'

I told him about Hiram Greenberger's research on the painting and outlined my plans to take it to the experts who wanted to assess it. I mentioned the names of the people Hiram had recommended but he had not heard of any them. We went on to discuss my sons and Richard. He questioned me on all the details of my separation from Richard. By the time I got to talk about my new job, the café was filling for dinner. He was tired by then and looked pale. I explained that I had to leave soon as Gabe was cooking a special dinner for me.

'Before you go… tell me is Gabe still studying?' he asked.

'He'll complete his master's degree in economics and law in a few months but I have no idea about his plans after that.'

'I think you'd better go now. You haven't seen him for all this time. It will be a great reunion.'

The sky was the pink of dusk as we walked slowly to the train station. I wanted to ask Luke to move into the hotel with me, to be there when I returned from my dinner with my son, but I stopped myself. The last thing Gabe needed was to be confronted with was his mother shacked up in a hotel room with the man he considered as his uncle. I would have to be patient and feel my way.

Luke sensed my conflict. 'After you've seen Gabe we'll discuss our plans. Whatever is best for you both will suit me too.'

We parted with a kiss and the promise to meet the following the day.

Fifty-Four

Gabe's apartment was a few blocks from the station. As I walked, I counted the numbers. His door was wide open and a gold fringed banner with *Willkommen* in large letters greeted me. The genuine delight on his face and his numerous hugs accompanied by squeals of delight astounded me. I pressed family gifts into his hands.

'Thank you! You have no idea how much I've missed you, how often I wanted to pack up and take a plane to Australia.'

'You didn't say a word about being lonely when we talked.'

'How could I… you'd have worried.'

'Of course I would've,' I said, taking a few steps back. 'Now let me look at you.'

In the two years since I'd last seen him, his slim frame had filled out and his face had lost its softness. My son was a man now.

'You look well,' I said, giving him another hug.

'Let me show you how I've decorated the flat… rather how we have decorated it.'

The three small rooms were all painted white, the sofa and chairs were beige and the table, glass and metal. The décor reminded me of our first house in Melbourne. I disliked the look but kept my views to myself and did my best to smile approvingly. Gabe was a capable young man but I doubted that he had much to do with the furnishing.

'If you have a girlfriend where is she?'

'Gina is her name and we've been living together for over a year. She's out with her girlfriends tonight so that we could be alone, but you'll meet her soon.'

'You didn't say a word about her. Why so secretive?'

He shrugged. 'I don't like talking on the phone, even Skype doesn't feel comfortable.'

He told me about Gina and his eyes shone with his love for her. Not only did he find her beautiful and sexy but smart, an excellent cook and accomplished in most things. I looked forward to meeting her soon. He surprised me with a tasty casserole he had cooked. The dessert, a combination of caramel, chocolate and meringue was so delicious that I had two helpings. Later he admitted that Gina had made it.

While we had coffee, he told me about his progress at university. He hadn't told me before that his professor had recommended he continue his studies.

'A doctorate?'

'Yes, but I don't know if I want to continue studying, if becoming an academic is what I want. The real world of finance has a pull.'

'Don't leave it too late if you want to work for one of those big companies.'

'I know.'

He asked after Anton, if he had settled down at university and if he had new friends. We discussed Anton's new girlfriend and then he wanted to know about my decision to leave Richard. I began explaining our split when he cut in.

'We knew the two of you weren't getting along... hardly talking to each other.'

I had no idea that the boys were aware of our trouble. We had tried hard to shield them. It was a relief when he stood, stretched and poured himself a glass of wine. It was an opportunity change the subject. We talked about my apartment and he asked whether I was still working at the library. I was certain I'd told him about my new job but I filled him in with the details once again.

'That sounds more like you,' he said, clapping his hands.

He looked out of the window and then turned to look at me. 'And my father, how's he doing?'

'He's well. I saw him briefly before I left. He's living with...' I stopped and looked down.

'One of his secretaries?'

'His personal assistant, Jennifer.'

He smiled sardonically. 'That's my father.'

'Have you seen Luke yet?' he asked.

'Yes, this afternoon. He's not well... suffering from a horrid bout of depression.'

'I'm sorry. I've always liked him.'

We were pussy footing around. Any second I knew he would say more about Luke and our relationship.

'When are you going to marry him?' he asked with a grin. 'The two of you have loved each other for ages and ages.'

I spluttered a reply as my face turned red. 'He's just separated from his wife and we haven't discussed marriage.'

'Don't be embarrassed Mutti, you've tried to hide it, but we have both known about you and Luke since we were little. We could see the love in your eyes.'

He grinned. 'You've changed so much from the Mutti you were here in Vienna. And you're looking wonderful.'

My eyes were closing. I tried to focus on our conversation but it was useless.

'You're tired mutti. It's jet lag. I'll drive you home.'

I didn't argue. As Gabe drove up to my hotel, he promised to introduce me to Gina soon.

❧

Luke woke me with his telephone call.

'It's 10.45, I thought you'd be up already.'

'I had to catch up on sleep.'

'Do want to meet for lunch?'

'Tell me where and when, and I'll be there.'

Luke suggested the *Café Schwartzenberg*, a traditional coffeehouse near my hotel and I agreed immediately. I took a leisurely stroll down the cobbled street, flanked by ornate buildings and across the, *Schwartzenbergplaz*, one of the main city squares. As I entered the café, I inhaled the powerful coffee aroma and sighed with pleasure. This was a café I had always enjoyed visiting. I was early and settled into a booth under the one of the chandeliers, close enough to the window to watch the people inside the café and those hurrying past in the street. I felt as if I had never left Vienna.

He had been rushing and was puffed. He kissed me and then removed his coat. 'Isn't this place wonderful? I've always loved it.' he said.

'It's a typical older, Viennese coffeehouse. It's like travelling back in time.'

The waiter greeted us with the traditional Austrian greeting of *"Gruss Gott"* and placed menus on the table. I was hungry and ordered lunch while Luke said that all he wanted was coffee.

I took Luke's hand in mine. 'How are you today?' I asked.

'A little better. It must be seeing you that's lifted my mood.'

'Please Luke, have something more to eat.' I pressed his palm persuasively.

'No, not now.'

We had not decided whether we would stay together or not and I broached the subject. 'I'm here for three and a half weeks. Some of the time I'll spend with Gabe but during the rest of it, I want to be with you.'

'I was about to ask if I could move into the hotel with you.'

'As soon as you can.' I laughed and kissed his cheek. 'Gabe surprised me, he knows all about us. I don't think we have to hide anything from him.'

We parted again, but only briefly, while Luke went home to pack a suitcase. He arrived at the hotel so exhausted, that he almost fell on the bed. While he slept, I read and watched television. I was content being near him again and listening to the sound of him breathing.

❧

Awake before him, I ordered him a full breakfast. If I couldn't cook for him, I would encourage him to eat well. I watched delighted as he ate part of it. It was much too soon, but I peered at him hoping for improvement in his energy and mood. I was rewarded with a thin smile.

Later, we strolled towards the Carmelite Square, once a market that had teemed with Jewish shoppers. It was a part of Vienna we knew well and each step felt as if we were following our own past footsteps. At the square we found a bench with a view of the fountain. He began to talk about the period he spent at the Lake District once the skiing season was over. He had read obsessively about the Holocaust and then turned his attention to Theresienstadt, its commandants and guards.

'There are moments when I wish I hadn't started studying it. Some of it is too awful to absorb,' he said, urging me to walk on. He described dreadful incidents of brutality and the photographs he had seen of emaciated, terrorised prisoners. Then he stopped, dropped his head and placed his hands on an old stone wall.

'I couldn't despise my grandparents more. They were criminals in my eyes. And when I think of that grandmother of mine harping about Jews, I shudder.'

There was nothing I could say.

'I read about a guard who was tried in court for committing sadistic acts against prisoners... and I was revolted... felt ill for days. Of course I was scared that the guard could've been my grandfather. It turned out to be someone else. I went through all the camp records I could find mentioning the guards but nothing was stated about either of my grandparents. And so I'll never know how they treated their prisoners. Were they sadists too, beating and humiliating prisoners?'

I pointed to another bench and this time we sat without speaking. After feeding the birds bits of leftover bread from my meal, I stood. It was easier to talk about difficult things while standing. I told him about my detailed research, and that I had also read about the camp in search of information about my father.

'Yes, there were brutal guards and there was punishment for infringement of rules but I found no mention of your grandparents either.'

He wiped his eyes. 'Thank heavens for that,' he said, looking up.

When we returned to the hotel, he was spent from his emotional outpouring and slept all afternoon.

That night over dinner, he had more to say about his stay near the mountains.

'It was through my guilt that I read about the Jewish people and their religion, and some good has come from my studies. I've learned so much.' His eyes glowed with enthusiasm. 'They're amazing survivors, only about thirteen million of them in the world now.'

I looked at him, surprised.

'I've always known that their influence on monotheistic religions was huge... and I had to know more.'

I placed my arm around his shoulder. 'I understand... but all this study has worn you out, leave it for now.'

'No, *Liebchen*, it's time I explained.'

I nodded. 'Alright then, tell me.'

'It's a long story.' He patted my hand.

I nodded.

'Well... once I dragged myself up and stopped drinking, I went to church. I hadn't been since the previous Easter and I hoped that prayer would cleanse and then soothe me. Each night I prayed and said the rosary but my Catholic prayers felt hollow. One night I was out on the patio. The moon was full and I stared at it begging for an answer. It came. It was a synagogue I should pray in and not a church.'

'Oh!'

'The first time I visited a synagogue I had no idea what was expected. All I knew was that I should dress respectfully and cover my head. A *kippah* was easy to find in the small shops in Leopoldstadt. I stood with the other men and mimicked their actions. Only after a few visits could I relax enough to listen to prayers, the Hebrew words and the ancient melodies.'

I thought of my first visit to the synagogue in Melbourne. I understood his confusion and then later his appreciation of the service. As much as I wanted to share my thoughts, I did not interrupt.

'I had to understand and so I read about the siddur prayer book, and then followed up the biblical and other references. The importance of the *Torah*, elaborately encased in satin and silver was a mystery until I read that it contained the five books of Moses. I went to the synagogue again and again and the more I understood the more involved I became.'

By the time we returned to the hotel he was at ease. We watched television and nibbled nuts and raisins instead of making love. I could not remember him passing up an opportunity for sex. All I cared about was to see his sad face replaced by a relaxed one.

Fifty-Five

My first appointment with an expert art assessor was at 11.00 a.m and I was relieved that Luke agreed to accompany me. I felt safer with him carrying the painting and in addition, he knew far more than I did about art. Our taxi had trouble locating Ivor Keranovic's studio in a narrow street near the city centre. Papers and rubbish outside his door was a rare sight in Vienna's streets. We knocked on the unusual bronze door with a dark design that Luke thought had been created with a blow torch.

Ivo was a tall man with an arty ponytail, dressed in paint spattered jeans. After introductions, we followed him into a long studio that was nothing like the classy office I expected. His paintings were displayed on easels or stacked against the walls and pots of paint and tubes littered the floor. He painted joyful abstract explosions of bright colour that I found attractive and uplifting. He led us from the cluttered studio into an elegant, modern office. He hovered at the entrance.

'Take a seat, I must change my shoes and pants before joining you. I'm covered in paint.' He returned in minutes carrying a sheaf of papers. 'I received Hiram's letter and photograph and what I saw of your painting grabbed my immediate attention.'

After discussing the painting, Ivor stood. 'Enough talk. I can't wait a minute longer, show it to me.'

He handed us both gloves. Together we unpacked the painting and carefully rolled it out on a long but narrow table. Once it was lying straight and weighted down at the corners, he switched on two spotlights.

'Ahhh!' He inhaled and exhaled slowly. After running his gloved fingers over it and staring at it for what seemed ages, at last he said, 'What a beauty!' He pointed to a large screen on the wall and clicked an appliance resembling a mobile phone. A landscape appeared. 'I've done some hunting and found this Pissarro...a lot like yours. If your painting is authentic it may come from the same period. It's hard to be more specific.'

'How can you be so sure?' Luke spoke for the first time.

'Pissarro is one of the artist's that interests me.' He adjusted the focus of the painting on the screen. 'He and his family is said to have moved to *Pontoise* in France in 1866. Many of his landscapes in this particular style originate from then.' He pointed to the grass and bushes. 'Elements of your painting tell me it's also likely to have been painted around that time.' He went on to point out the colours used and he compared them with Pissarro's usual palette at the time. He explained that when an artist had been painting for many years, his style often followed a pattern. The colours of his palette, the thickness of paint, the length and direction of brushstrokes and even the forms in the landscape were repeated in each painting.

Luke was intrigued by Ivor's explanation.

At last Ivor turned towards us. 'I will examine the signature now and then give you my final opinion.'

He placed so many copies of the artist's signature on his screen that I couldn't count them. They were taken from paintings throughout Pissarro's life. He photographed the signature of my paining and placed it up on the screen with the others.

'It looks the same,' I said.

'Yes, it does,' he agreed. 'So far so good.'

He explained how clever forgers were and until my painting had passed all his tests, it could not yet be considered authentic.

'From the letter I received from Hiram, I believe you are due to see James Talbot-Kerr, an Englishman who lives in Vienna these days. He specialises in scientific techniques of authentication. Though he charges like crazy, he's the best we have... with his infrared lights and all the spectroscopic equipment necessary.'

Ivor was pleased when I replied that I had already made an appointment to see James Talbot-Kerr. I explained that I was in Vienna for only a few weeks and that I'd appreciate a letter from him in time for my appointment with Talbot-Kerr in three days. He offered to write the letter while we waited.

'What do you prefer, tea coffee? I'll ask my wife to put the kettle on and while you're waiting for the letter, there are all these art books to look at,' he said pointing at the pile on the table.'

'You realise, don't you, that you'll have to see a solicitor... someone who can negotiate with these dealers for you?' Luke said.

'Richard mentioned the legal angle before I left but I didn't follow up on it. I'll phone the solicitor who looked after all our business in Vienna.'

Mr Zuckerman was busy but as a special favour to Richard he found time to see me during his lunch break. We talked about the painting and the legalities involved in its authentication and subsequent sale. When I showed him a photograph of the Pissarro, he sighed with envy. He admitted to being a patron of the arts in a minor way and ran off an impressive list of the pieces in his growing collection.

There were numerous contracts to be prepared and then signed. I agreed to pay him another visit the following day. He promised all would be in order before my appointment with Talbot Kerr.

※

Luke was up and showered before I opened my eyes. 'I'm feeling a little better... let me take the painting to Talbot-Kerr for you tomorrow. It will save you the trouble and make me feel useful again. You could do some shopping.'

'You sure?'

'Why not! I'm fit enough to carry a painting... and I am interested in the scientific assessment. I'll tell you all about it afterwards.'

'Why worry about it now, we'll talk about Talbot-Kerr and the painting later,' I said gently.

Luke shrugged.

I pulled back the heavy lace curtains. 'What a glorious day! Let's not waste it.'

Fifty-Six

We were back in the old city, near the most famous of Vienna's Gothic cathedrals, St Stephens. Luke smiled. It was a warm, amused smile. It was too early for a sign of his recovery but I was hopeful.

'This is an ideal place to tell you more about my trip to the Lake District and to talk about religion,' he smiled wryly as we stopped to admire the old church's tall gothic spire.

I tried to look interested. All Luke seemed to talk about was religion.

'Well then...'

'The mornings were warm and I hiked and swam in the lake. Every afternoon and evening, I read until I had a basic grasp of Judaism. Even with all the time I devoted to it, I have only a superficial understanding. There's so much more to being a Jew than reading the sacred writings of the *Tanach* or attending synagogue, you know.'

'Tana...?'

'You'd be bored by a long explanation but basically the *Tanach* is the Old Testament arranged differently...the laws of Moses, the Prophets...'

'I don't know a thing about that.'I looked at him, amazed.' I was staring at him a lot lately. When we were children, he was an altar boy at the Cathedral two corners away. He attended mass regularly and went to confession until he was about sixteen. After that, his interest in church waned but he never missed attending services over Easter and Christmas. I couldn't imagine Luke of all people, steeped in Catholicism, now studying Judaism.

My head spun as he described what he had read about the tenets of Jewish observance and ritual. He was obviously fascinated by the religion, my religion, but he had lost me. Instead of listening, I watched the cars and people pass us as he talked and talked.

'Enough of that for now,' he said, as he noticed my confused expression.

'I've always loved this cathedral... it's majestic,' I said looking up at the ancient, diamond patterned roof, so steep that I couldn't recall having seen it covered in snow.

He nodded. 'Let's go,' he said, taking my hand.

He did not admonish me for my lack of interest or knowledge of my own religion, nor did he encourage me to study the texts he had read. I felt strangely uneasy. As we turned down a narrow lane of old houses that led to a newly built, small synagogue, he took a deep breath. 'I've visited most of the synagogues in Vienna and a few in Germany.'

I felt a frown cross my forehead.

'I must still visit the *Stadttempel*. After all, it's the main synagogue in Vienna.'

'Really!'

'I've done my best... obtained a simple overview of Judaism and I've attended a few services... but if I take my studies further, it could take me a lifetime'

'Is that what you want?' I asked, puzzled. The change in Luke was too dramatic for me to grasp. He even looked different. His colourful shirts and jumpers were replaced by conservative navy and grey. The easy-going, pleasure-loving man I knew had become solemn and obsessed with the Jewish religion.

'I'm not sure what I want,' he said, putting an arm around me.

He was silent and all I heard was the clink of our feet on the cobbled stones.

'I've spoken to many Jewish people here in Vienna, some very old, survivors of the camps, and honestly I'm surprised how open minded they are. They're warm and accepting of me. Somehow they've moved on, put these terrible things behind them.'

'Yes, that is so.'

'I admire them so much. If I were in their shoes, I'd be burning with hatred.'

❧

After a sandwich from a delicatessen we turned into *Weintraubengasse*, to the former site of my family house. I expected to see a building where the house once stood but I was taken aback by the hideous, tall apartment block.

'Disgusting! Built on the cheap with a lousy architect, by the look of it,' he muttered.

'At least it houses many people, probably a better use of the plot of land,' I said, trying to come to terms with the change and see it in a positive light.

'There's something important I want to show you.' He led me to the paving stones on the corner of the apartment block.

'Look at these,' he said using his toe to indicate two bronze plaques.

I edged closer. Puzzled, I began to read the inscription set into the paving.

In memory of the people who once lived in this house but died in the holocaust.

I recognised the names listed - my aunts, uncles and cousins who had perished in the camps. The other plaque was dedicated to my grandparents who had owned the house and lived in it throughout their married life, that is, until they were seized by the Gestapo.

As I felt for the tissue in my pocket, Luke placed his arm around my shoulder. 'Stones of remembrance… I had them specially made…for you and… your family.'

I could not hold back my tears. 'Where did you find all the names?'

'A lot of research from old records but it was worth it. Plaques like these have been springing up all over Austria and Germany.'

I hugged and kissed him.

As we walked on, he showed me other commemorative stones placed by loved ones who still mourn their relatives.

'At least they won't be forgotten.'

I was aware of the silence between us.

'I have something else to show you,' he said placing a steering arm on my shoulder.

'Where are you taking me?'

'Be patient,' he said as we headed for the station. We boarded a train and I stopped questioning him. 'Let's get out of here,' he said helping me off the train. 'We can walk down to the Prater from here.'

I smiled happily. The Prater and the park had always been one of our favourite outdoor spots in Vienna. Soon we were in *Praterstrasse*, the street that linked the inner city to the amusement park. We stood outside the *Nestroyhof*, a once fashionable boulevard of theatres built in 1898. Luke drew my attention to plaques commemorating actors and actresses and even the coffee shops they once frequented. I thought of my father and his talented family but I was determined not to cry again. I didn't want to increase Luke's burden by telling him that my father had been on the stage in those theatres and probably drank coffee in the theatre coffeehouses.

Luke was a few paces ahead of me as we neared the Prater, when he slowed down.

'Are you okay?' I asked.

'I'm fine… just very tired,' he said.

'We've done too much for one day… let's turn back,' I took his hand. 'We'll go to the Prater another time.'

I looked back at the amusement park with its giant Ferris wheel, the stuff of my nightmares. From a distance the wheel was not at all threatening.

Fifty-Seven

The following day, Luke remained in bed and refused to eat. When I talked to him, he turned his head towards the wall. In the past few days he had taken on too much both physically and emotionally. I could only hope that rest would bring him out of the slump.

The next morning, I left him asleep and went to the city. Two years absence from a city I had lived in all my life had given me fresh eyes. I decided to pretend to be a tourist. When I spoke German but not the Austrian dialect, people were rude to me. My eyes were opened to the insularity of the Viennese. I dressed casually in the manner I had grown used to in Australia and wore jeans and tee shirts. Vienna had a dressy culture. Some called it sophisticated but to me, after living in Melbourne, it was precious. I became acutely aware of Viennese rules, spoken and unspoken, that I had once taken for granted. My tastes had changed, even my views were different. The impact of the move to Australia had left its mark.

For breakfast I stopped at another café I frequented when I lived in Vienna. Nothing had changed. They still served café melange, a combination of cappuccino and latte, with a soft boiled egg, a Kaiser roll with butter and apricot jam. I lingered over my breakfast, soaking up the cosiness, the *gemutlicheid*. I could give Vienna's elaborate architecture a miss but the music and cafés were its lifeblood.

My stay was too short to contact and visit old friends but I was determined to see Ernst. He invited me for lunch at his house in Leopoldstadt. It was smaller than his original family home, but he said there was a strong resemblance to it. The stone house was set off from the street with a narrow path and tiny but well-tended front garden. When he opened the door, I stifled my shock. He had been a slim man but now his frame was wasted, his silver hair, limp. We kissed and I handed him a bunch of yellow roses, his favourites. He sniffed the roses, thanked me and ushered me inside.

'I know I look like an old scarecrow. Cancer my dear, but the doctors are optimistic... as optimistic as they can be with someone as old as myself.' he said with a shrug.

As I followed him into the sitting room, I calculated quickly. He was in his nineties.

'I'm delighted to have you here. When I said goodbye to you at the airport, I didn't expect to see you again.'

'Well, I'm thrilled to be here.'

His eyes darted to the door. 'I'm expecting my old friend Jakov. He's heard me talking about you over the years and I found out he knew your father... thought you'd want to meet him. Listen out for me... my hearing isn't what it was.'

Ernst had always been thoughtful. He knew how long I had been gathering facts about my father's life and that I was still hungry for information. As we talked, I propped myself up against the satin cushions and glanced around the tastefully decorated room in the style of the 1940's. His blue eyes sparked with interest as I told him about my new life in Australia.

'If only I were younger, I'd come and visit you there.' After questioning me about my work and home, he stopped talking and looked at me. 'In that light, and now that you've cut your hair, you look just like him... your father.'

'Thank you, I've seen a few photos of him recently and I'll take that as a compliment.'

He stood and bowed in mock old fashioned courtesy. 'Madame, I have prepared a light lunch, something I know you'll enjoy. Let's carry on our discussion in the dining room.'

Ernst had gone to enormous effort for a casual lunch. He pointed to the tablecloth. 'This tablecloth was embroidered by my mother and I managed to hold on to it over the years.

Now, any excuse to use it and having you here is a good one.' He smiled and lifted one of the white and gold porcelain plates. 'We had porcelain like this at home but it was destroyed with the house when...' He swallowed and looked away. 'After the war, as soon as I could afford it, I bought *this* house and then the furniture and all the crockery at auctions. I wanted it to be just like my childhood home.'

He drummed his fingers on the table and eyed the clock. 'Jakov will miss lunch. It's not like him... perhaps he's forgotten.'

Ernst had prepared a meal of schnitzel and finely diced salad, followed by a delicious trifle and cream that confirmed his reputation as a superb cook. Over coffee, I told him about finding my father's paintings in the portfolio.

I wondered where all his paintings disappeared to. This is marvellous news. He was an outstanding artist.'

I thought it best to leave out the bit about the painting Luke had discovered and was thought to be a Pissarro. The story was complex and he would badger me with questions. I would tell him about it if and when I eventually sold it.

We drank coffee while he reminisced. I had photos of the paintings in my handbag and handed them to him. He smiled, as he looked at them, recalling accompanying my father to the wineries and lakes on his painting weekends.

'In those days I was impatient and restless. I helped your father to set up his easel and then I left him. When I returned from a long walk, there he was still sitting in the same spot and a new landscape was alive on his canvass. Your father was a fast worker and by the end of the weekend he had created one of his fine paintings. Ah! I wish you could've seen him paint.'

I was conjuring up the picture Ernst had presented, when he picked up a newspaper from the table next to him. 'So my dear, have you been reading the newspapers while you're here?' he asked as he sifted through the pile.

'No, I don't bother much with newspapers. I watch the news on television.'

He sighed. 'For months and months there have been articles about anti-Jewish feeling building up across Europe. Here in Vienna too.'

'That's awful.'

He pointed to an article in *Der Kurier*. 'Look... yesterday, here in Vienna... swastikas daubed on the wall of a Jewish school. And last week... more Jewish graves desecrated.'

I shook my head and looked down. 'It's hard to believe.'

He muttered to himself. 'Perhaps it's just as well you left.'

'But countries like Germany, Austria have gone out of their way to repair shuls and make reparation. Look at the Berlin synagogue. It's magnificent and there are monuments all over to commemorate those murdered'

'Ja. Ja. That's true.' He said dismissively as he turned over the newspaper pages.

'Don't tell me it's happening again?' I felt a stab as I spoke.

'I don't think it ever went away. Extremists... always the same.'

'It's horrible!' I could taste my disgust.

We were drinking our second cup of coffee when Jakov arrived. The short, stout man smiled at me and nodded politely.

'Glad to meet you... forgive me for being so late but I wouldn't have missed our meeting.' He mumbled his apology.

Ernst offered to heat the leftover food for his friend, but all Jakov wanted was coffee and cake. We talked politely about the news of the day until Ernst commented, 'I've been telling Ella about the rise of anti-Semitism.'

'The air we breathe here is anti-Semitic... always has been.' The room was charge with unsaid words.

The vehemence of Jakov's statement disturbed me. I felt my heart race and I wriggled uncomfortably.

Ernst looked away and then coughed.

'Eh, Jakov, I haven't told Ella yet that you were in Theresienstadt with her father.'

'Ja... Walter!' he sighed before continuing. 'Without him I wouldn't be alive and many others wouldn't either. I owe everything to him,' he said haltingly. 'It's an honour to meet his daughter... but it's the memories.' He stifled a sob.

'Oh, please don't upset yourself... I understand.'

'No!' his voice was unexpectedly forceful. 'You must know'

'Have a brandy, my friend,' Ernst offered.

'Ja, good idea.'

Jakov took a slug of neat brandy and sipped the rest as he spoke. 'Walter was a genius at making people laugh. Every day he had another thing... an uglier mask or new horrible joke about Jews to amuse the guards. And so he kept us alive. At night, they all came to watch our little show, even the commandant. They laughed so much that the cells near us could hear them. During the day we overheard them repeating our jokes and laughing. Sometimes they were so pleased with our performance that they threw us some of the bread and cheese they were eating. One of the guards brought Walter a *wurst* he'd made himself, another gave him a loaf of bread. Your father shared all the food with us... and so some of us survived.'

Ernst poured himself a brandy and handed me a glass.

'Have some my dear. You're trembling.' He nodded in his friend's direction. 'Go on, Jakov.'

'Every few days someone disappeared. We saw him in line with a miserable group of the sick, old, or those who were considered intransigent. We were upset but at the same time relieved. We were still in the camp... safe. Some mornings we woke to find a corpse, a death from exhaustion, malnutrition, disease. In the beginning we tried to bury our friends properly but the guards wouldn't have it. They gave orders for us to carry a body to a pit, a stinking mass grave... drop it in with the others.' He shuddered and took another gulp of brandy. 'Dark days then. Survival was everything and people did terrible things to stay alive. They stole food, collaborated with the Germans. I did things I'm not proud of either,'

'Ach no, Jakov, that's not true,' Ernst insisted.

Jakov ignored his friend's comment and turned towards me. 'It's most important that you know your father's strength... his determination, so that whether he was carrying bodies to the pit or working in the fields, he was thinking up ideas to please the guards... to keep as many of us as he could from being sent to our death.'

'You're just like him,' Ernst said with a smile. 'I should know. When you want to know something you don't give up.'

A little later, I thanked Jakov again for his insights about my father. I gave Ernst a hug and a kiss. At the door I waved, and then turned back for a last look at the frail man who had been almost a father to me.

Fifty-Eight

Luke's mood was still low. He badly wanted to feel useful, but he wasn't well enough to take the painting to James Talbot-Kerr for the final assessment. I left him in an armchair watching a soccer match, while I headed for the heart of the business district.

Talbot-Kerr's assistant led me into a small but comfortable room. He explained that my painting would be analysed in detail and that the results would follow soon after. I was left waiting in the room with a pile of magazines. About an hour later, a short man with only tufts of blonde hair on his head but a bushy beard, entered the room to introduce himself.

Talbot-Kerr spoke to me loudly in German with an English accent and I didn't interrupt him. He reeled off the number of scientific tests he had performed on the painting. Finally I asked for his findings. He coughed and smoothed his white coat before replying.

'It appears to be genuine but one never knows for certain.'

I took a deep breath before asking if he could give me a certificate for the dealer.' I explained my short stay in the city.

He cut in. 'No explanation needed. I already have it here for you with my bill.'

I glanced at his exorbitant bill and stuffed it in my handbag.

'Oh, and there's a form my solicitor Jacques Zuckerman prepared... I hope you won't mind completing it for me.' I added.

He nodded curtly and disappeared into his office.

❧

I met Gabe several times. We retained some of our earlier mother-child banter but the change in him was striking. He had become the handsome and confident man I had hoped to find. It was a new and pleasant experience to be invited for lunch and have him pay for the meal.

We arranged to meet for coffee late one afternoon. I was late and hunted for a blonde head amongst the crowd. He waved and I saw a blond and a brunette. He had invited Gina to meet me. She was a pretty and confident young woman.

I enjoyed the couple's company so much that I dreaded the thought of leaving Vienna. Luke was ill and he needed me. But there was Anton back home as well. If not for him, I could've easily sold my possessions, rented my flat to someone and resigned from my job.

Joan Zawatzky

Fifty-Nine

The morning was grey and cool. Luke was asleep when I took the painting on its final and most important journey, to George Barrineau. George was French and as charming as his name. His showroom, cluttered with paintings, was a feast. Once we had covered the topic of the weather, I handed him the documents from the two assessors. He read them carefully and then unwrapped the painting. He followed a similar procedure to Ivo's, of looking at it under bright lights and then with a powerful magnifying glass. I waited for his verdict.

'After all I have read and seen, Madame... I can only say... yes, it's most likely a Pissarro.'

'Most likely!' I was indignant.

'We are careful not to use the word "definitely". You have no idea how clever the forgers are, but we have had the top experts assessing it and... which makes the likelihood of a forgery extremely low,' he said with a smile.

'I'm pleased to hear that, especially after the time and cost involved.'

'And so, from now on we will assume the painting's authenticity. And Madame, we will speak of it only as an original Pissarro landscape.' His smile was even broader this time. He offered me coffee and it arrived with delicate melt-in- the-mouth éclairs.

'I have seen other Pissarros and this one is a lovely example, quite lyrical and luminous, not so?'

I nodded, my mouth full of éclair. I swallowed quickly.

'Do you know how your father obtained the painting, Madame?' He asked.

'Yes I do, but why is that relevant. It's a personal detail.'

His look was sardonic. 'This could be a stolen painting. I must ask.'

I sighed and filled in the details of the story, revealing that Mr Nachman had previously owned the painting and given it to my father in gratitude.'

'Nachman! Not Jankel Nachman?' he said excitedly.

'I don't know Mr Nachamn's first name.'

'Jankel Nachman was a famous collector. You must allow me to use his name, to market the painting, Madame.'

I shrugged.

'Of course you would have to trust me to keep the personal side of your story to myself … but just mentioning it was once in Mr Nachman's collection would add to the price'

'Really?'

'Absolutely. You have my assurance. You'll see Nachman's name sells.'

I was undecided.

'You have my promise of confidentially, Madame.'

'Use it then, but remember your promise. I don't want to read my father's story in the newspaper.'

'Absolutely, Madame.'

'What happens next?' I asked.

He gave me another of his most charming smiles.

'This painting is far too valuable to go to public auction. If you agree Madame, I will contact some of my wealthy collectors who may be interested and sell it privately. In that way you will avoid the cost of an auction and the publicity.'

'How much do you think it's worth?'

'Maybe your father knew it was valuable even then. Around a million, maybe more if you're lucky… depending on the market. French Impressionists, even the little known ones are … big these days.' He laughed at his joke.

I felt shaky at the sound of so much money. Instantly I told myself he was buttering me up, that there was no truth in what he said. When I regained my composure, I mentioned the name of my solicitor who would represent me during the process of selling the painting. I handed Georges the contract Jacques had prepared and asked that he use it. We discussed the mundane matters of security, insurance, a reserve price and his hefty commission. He promised to contact Jacques when he had notified the collectors he had chosen and had selected a date for a private showing.

Before I left, he promised to send me a large copy of the painting.

'It will look so real that you'll want to frame it.'

George was an ideal choice for the manipulations of a private sale.

Sixty

When I returned to the hotel, Luke gave me a bear hug and kiss.

'Get used to the idea Ellie, I think you're going to be rich.'

'I'm rich already. I already have what's most important and valuable.'

We sat together on the couch holding each other and kissing as we had years ago. Luke appeared to have emerged from his dark mood but I was concerned that he could easily slip into again if he became overtired or stressed. At least his improvement made me optimistic.

A little later, he went to his home to check his mail and collect a change of clothing. When he returned he waved a white envelope at me. Next to the stamp was the logo of the University of Adelaide.

'It's about a position at the University of Adelaide. I've been in touch with the Department of Geology there. They made me an offer that I turned down before. The salary was too low.'

He waved the letter in the air.

'But this is a revised offer... and it's good.'

I read the letter. They were offering Luke an excellent package, including housing and travel expenses. 'I'm accepting it. The money is one thing but I insisted on selecting my own staff and setting the syllabus for study. It's all agreed now. I'll start next year... provided they have the numbers for the course.'

I kissed him. 'Congratulations, my darling. I'm thrilled for you.'

Luke explained that South Australia had abundant resources of geothermal energy but was at a relatively early stage of production. He had been given an excellent grass roots opportunity, the sort of academic challenge he enjoyed. We looked at the map of Australia and found that Adelaide and Melbourne were about a days drive apart. It was not a perfect option but it was manageable. We could spend time together over weekends. He rubbed his hands as he recollected the warmer Australian weather and relaxed atmosphere.

'I'll want to look at accommodation and organise staffing and so on. So that means I can be with you in Melbourne again for a while before I start…that's if you'll have me.' We both laughed. He took my hand. 'It's been a wonderful day and we've both had good news. Let's go out and celebrate.'

I glanced at him. He was looking tired, too tired to go out. 'Let's wait a bit, darling.'

The rest of the week passed at a leisurely pace. Luke was eating well and had not slipped back into gloom. We chose Thursday evening to celebrate. I thought it strange but Luke preferred not go out on the Sabbath. I wore black, the only dress I had brought with me and adorned it with jewellery. Luke eyed me in the way he once did, taking in my breast and thighs. His appreciative kiss had more vigour than the sloppy pecks on the cheek of past days.

We chose a buffet at a top hotel. Luke filled his plate with sea food and ate it all. We ate and drank slowly, relishing our meal. Afterwards we stopped for coffee and rich cake. Once we were back at the hotel we made love, for the first time since I had returned to Vienna.

❧

He surprised me by mentioning his intention to attend a service at the *Stadttempel* on Saturday morning, and wanted me to join him. After so many years of exclusion from Jewish life in Leopoldstadt, he was offering me an opportunity to visit the main Jewish synagogue, a synagogue I had never been inside.

We walked to the *Stadttempel* in *Seitensttengasse.* It had originally been designed with security in mind, hidden behind a façade of shops. This is thought to have saved it from destruction during Kristallnacht. As we entered the synagogue's doors, I gasped. It was magnificent in its splendour, nothing like the virtually unadorned shuls I had visited in Melbourne with Ruth. I left him downstairs watching me take the stairs to the balcony. When I turned to look back at him in his dark suit and *kippah,* there was nothing that could differentiate him from all the other men. Thanks to Ruth, I knew my way around the synagogue. The prayer books were on a shelf in virtually the same position as in the Melbourne synagogue. The translation of the Hebrew was in German like the prayer book Ernst had given me. I sat at the end of a row and looked up at the oval, blue, domed ceiling scattered with gold stars. The double ark was impressive, surrounded by a dramatic burst of gold.

My eyes closed as I listened to the cantor and the all male choir. The pitch was perfect, the sound rich and resonant. Were angels singing? A powerful moment of spiritual calm spread through me. No words could describe it. I followed in my own way by reading the German translation. At least now I understood the order of the service and some of its meaning. I thought of Ruth again.

On the way back to the hotel, Luke gave my hand a squeeze and I returned it. It felt natural for the two of us to be walking home from Shabbat prayer together, as if it was a weekly occurrence. I shared my memories with Luke of observing black hatted men, women and children walking to synagogue in Leopoldstadt, from our tiny upstairs balcony. So many years later, I was joining them.

'I'm happy for you my darling. It is more important for you to understand and embrace Judaism than it is for me.'

I remembered his comment and thought about it months and years later. He had given me a precious gift.

That night, Luke slept while I lay awake reliving the morning's service. My earlier peacefulness was replaced by a rush of fury. My chest was tight and my hands went to my throat as I struggled to breathe. At that moment, I hated my mother. So what if she was brought up as a Catholic, she was Jewish and ought to have encouraged me to go to the *Stadttempel* and make up my own mind about my religion. I had been deprived of a connection with everything that the synagogue stood for.

I thought of my children. Due to my background and Richard's disinterest in his Jewish background, they had been deprived too. At least I had seen something of Jewish life in Leopoldstadt, while they knew nothing about their Jewish heritage. I ought to have asked Gabe to attend the service with us. Though my boys were adults, I would have to try harder to make amends. I forced back my tears and tried to sleep.

Sixty-One

The three weeks of our living together in Vienna was a fairy tale existence. When I looked up at the night sky, the stars shone more brightly and the moon glowed with a kind light. As the days grew closer to my departure, we found excuses not to discuss our future together. The present was far too precious to introduce reality.

Luke's spell of good health continued and our days were crammed with walks and visits to our once favourite haunts in the Vienna Woods. We even made love in the forest as we had years earlier.

On a particularly warm day, we returned to the Prater. I was determined to ride on the Ferris wheel once more. The old wheel moved so slowly, creaking as it rotated, that I could not understand what had frightened me. Up high the view of Vienna in spring bloom was breathtaking. This was the image I was determined to retain.

Luke smiled and laughed, but one never knew with depression. His recent bout was a warning. I had seen the blues lurking for years in others. Though he looked and sounded almost healed, his doctor insisted he continue taking the medication for a few months to ensure his stability.

❧

My brief stay in Vienna was slipping away. I spent my last Friday afternoon with Gabe strolling through the university gardens, talking about his future. He and Gina were considering marrying and then leaving Vienna. He wanted to join us in Australia, but she had family in Switzerland and insisted on going there. This conflict was a wedge between them.

'I love Gina... and I suppose I'll give in eventually and move to Zurich,' he said, looking away.

I gave him a hug. 'I want to have you with us but you must follow your love, darling.' I said, swallowing hard.

He nodded. 'Being together is what's important.'

I had not yet broached the topic of Luke's interest in Judaism with Gabe and this was my last opportunity. We sat amongst flowers and undulating lawns and he listened intently intrigued, as I described how Luke had become interested in Judaism, how he began his study of the subject and as a result had become a regular synagogue goer.

'It's the last thing I would've expected from him. After all he's a Catholic.'

'Yes, but these days he's more Jewish than Catholic.'

'That's very strange.'

'He's told me often enough that Catholicism followed Judaism... developed from it.'

'But still...'

'I think the religion makes sense to him. He's a logical thinker.'

'I wouldn't know. I'm clueless about Judaism... or any religion.'

I touched his arm and looked away. 'I know that and I feel awful about not giving you that important grounding... but I can't change that now. You could talk to Luke though, find out why he's turned towards Judaism. He goes to synagogue regularly and I'm sure he'd be pleased to have company. He is becoming an authority on the subject and could explain a lot to you.'

'I'll think about it and discuss it with Gina. She has Jewish blood on her grandmother's side but I'm not sure of details. She may be interested in all this.'

'Yes, talk to her. You never know how you'll feel until you go into a synagogue that first time. I went with a friend and was surprised by my reaction. I described how my initial sense of being out of place changed to comfort and peace."Okay, okay Mutti... enough for now!' he said, putting his arm around my shoulder. 'I promise, I'll think about it.'

❧

My need for rest was sudden and overwhelming. All I could think of was sleep. As I closed my eyes I heard rain lashing the window panes. I thought I caught a glimpse of Luke moving about the room, but turned over and went back to sleep. When I woke hours later, he had left. A note on the table next to the bed said, '*See you later. Back for lunch.*'

When he returned he was humming a tune I thought I recognised from the Sabbath service.

'Hello and *Good Shabbos*,' he said planting a kiss on my cheek. 'I knew you were tired and didn't want to wake you so I went to synagogue alone.'

'You went last week. Do you go so... often?'

'Friday night or Saturday morning when I can. Unfortunately I missed quite a few weeks when I was feeling down.'

'Oh, I had no idea you were quite so...' I searched for the word.

'Committed,' he finished my sentence. 'I've already made enquiries about synagogues in Adelaide. Apparently there are a few.'

I changed the subject quickly, trying to avoid the constant talk about religion. 'What do you want to do this afternoon?' I asked.

'We can't go to the gardens, it's still pouring but it's your last weekend in Vienna, what about a special lunch?'

'Let's order sandwiches and champagne in the room. I'm in a lazy mood.'

We steadily ate our way through a laden platter. I had emptied my glass of champagne and was about to refill it, when his forehead creased in a frown.

'While you were out with Gabe I met my daughters.'

'Oh, you didn't tell me.'

He shrugged. 'We intended to go to a silly movie, have a laugh, but we got talking. And the afternoon didn't turn out to be much fun. Instead we went into one of those hamburger joints.'

'Oh?'

'While we were eating Jeanette made a comment about my dull clothing... said they hardly recognised me lately.'

'What did you say?'

'I spoke to them... told them everything.'

'Everything!'

'I had to. They need to know what's important to me now and why.'

'Well, how did they react?'

'We all cried after I told them about their Nazi great grandparents. They were horrified. Poor Caroline threw up. Jeanette went paler than I've ever seen her. Of course they know all about the Holocaust and they've both visited the memorials in the city. Jeanette has been to Auschwitz.'

'Oh!'

'They were furious with me... that I kept it from them.'

'Well... yes. I can understand that.'

'I should've told them... and I'll have a lot more explaining to do. I'll try next time I see them.'

'At least you've started talking to them about it.'

We emptied the platter of food and finished the champagne. We had nothing left to say to each other, touch and loving said far more.

At the airport, our goodbye kisses lacked the frenzy of our earlier partings. Though the dates were uncertain, we knew that we would see each other within in a few months.

Sixty-Two

When I unlocked the door of my Melbourne apartment, its familiar smell greeted me. I placed my suitcase in the bedroom and sat on the bed. I was home but my head and heart were still in Vienna. If I closed my eyes, I could still feel Luke lying next to me. I forced myself to unpack and threw myself into activity–cleaning and dusting the apartment and then into cooking, but Luke remained with me.

The day after I arrived I was expected at work. I toyed with the idea of a few days sick leave but I had already taken more leave than my quota. By pretending I was involved and interested I managed to resume my usual activities, but as soon as my attention strayed, my thoughts were of Luke. Long hours at work filled my time but the nights dragged. I gained weight from chocolate, biscuits and wine - anything to blot out my fears that Luke would change his mind about the shift to Adelaide or that some snag in his contract with the university would prevent him from joining me.

When Anton came for dinner, he grilled me for details about his brother. Once I had described Gabe's flat in detail, the intricacies of his daily life and told him all I knew about Gina, he sighed. 'I love all the presents he sent… and his new life sounds great.'

'But?'

'I miss him. My life without him isn't the same.'

'Of course, you miss him, he's your big brother.'

'We're growing apart.'

As he pushed the gifts aside, I made an instant decision. 'I'm going to contact Gabe and invite the two of them to visit over Christmas... all expenses paid. What do you say?'

His arms were about me. 'Oh Mutti, that's a wonderful idea. Thank you!'

After coffee, Anton took my hand. 'It's been a lovely evening but I wish you'd play for me like you used to. Come on Mutti, please.'

I went to the piano and played Mozart's Concerto No.9 in E Flat Major. I delighted in stroking the keys once more. He clapped and then hugged me.

'Your love speaks when you play.' He rubbed his chest. 'I feel it inside.'

⁂

Magda visited, carrying a bouquet of flowers almost covering her face. She had been to my apartment before but as always she gave it a practiced scan to check if there were any changes. Her eyes rested on a small metal sculpture of a vase containing a flowering cactus, a gift from Luke while I was in Vienna, from the same shop as the Hamsa. We had chosen it together for its attractiveness as well as its symbolism.

'It's an Israeli cactus or prickly pear...spiky but strong and sweet inside like the *Sabras* or Jews born in Israel.'

'I like it she said,' standing back to admire the sculpture.

'I've noticed that Luke has become interested in Jewish things lately...first the hand and now this.' She looked at me inquiringly.

I smiled and instead of answering suggested we have coffee.

We talked about her burgeoning business until she asked. 'You haven't said whether you're happy being back in Melbourne?'

My fingers gripped the chair. She wasn't the first person to ask that question. My thoughts of Vienna were focussed around

Luke and she didn't know about my liaison with him. I wasn't sure how to answer her. I hesitated briefly.

'I'm dying to hear,' she said.

'Vienna was different this time. I found the people narrow minded and rude.'

'But the culture, the scenery?'

'I'll miss that, of course…and the cafés, but I prefer the freedom and ease of life in here in Melbourne.'

When she left, I thought about our conversation. Her direct manner had forced me to clarify my feelings, and I was grateful to her for that. At least I did not have to choose between Melbourne and Vienna. I enjoyed both.

Six months had passed, and though Luke and I continued to communicate regularly, I grew less hopeful that he would join me. The strain of waiting after years of longing to be together began to tell. I slept poorly and became ill with flu and later bronchitis.

At last he phoned with good news of the sale of the house. He had a definite starting date at the university and he would be in Australia within a few weeks. We would have three months together in Melbourne before he took up the position in Adelaide. Each day of waiting for Luke to arrive, I made a cross on the calendar. The last time I had counted days on the calendar was in my final term of senior school, when I could not wait to be free.

Sixty-Three

The aromas of baking and flowers pervaded the apartment. The bed in the guest room was made up, not that Luke would sleep there. He would use it if he sought seclusion.

When he walked through the glass security doors at the airport, I ran to greet him. In each other's arms, we ignored the crowd around us. He looked well and had gained weight. Gone was the bony gauntness. The beginnings of a stubbly beard, was the only noticeable difference in his appearance. As I unlocked the door to my apartment, he quipped, 'you can take the champagne out of the fridge, this is the start of a new life for us.' I joked that our first few days together were so romantic that they could have been crafted in Hollywood. But by Saturday the mood changed, when he asked me where the closest synagogues were. His recent emails were about his work and weekends spent hiking. There had been no mention of religion.

Now he was adamant. 'I've attended a service every Sabbath for months and I don't want to break the pattern here. You can stay home or come along if you like… but naturally I hope you'll join me.'

I did not reply, slightly peeved by the implied pressure in his comment.

He looked out of the window and smiled ruefully. 'What started with my guilt and crying for atonement has given me the hope of a new belief.'

'Am I hearing right … a new belief?'

'I think so.'

'What about your own religion?

He wiped his hand across the table dismissively. 'I'm through with that, it belongs to another time.'

'Are you telling me that you want to convert?'

'Well, I'm thinking about it.'

I didn't reply. What I'd thought was a passing interest, had become an essential part of his life.

He spread himself between the bedroom and the guestroom making place for his books and his lap top. While I was at work, he continued his research, read and went on daily long walks. Often he cooked a simple meal that was ready to eat when I returned. It was a workable arrangement.

I prepared our first Shabbat dinner and invited Anton. In my enthusiasm and hope for an enjoyable meal, I cooked too much. At a shop that sold silver ware for Jewish festivals, I bought a pair of candlesticks and tiny cups for wine. "Handmade in Israel", the woman said.

At sunset, I lit the candles. As I did not know the blessing in Hebrew, I said it in English. The ceremony of the woman of the house welcoming the Sabbath by lighting the candles was an ancient ritual and I was starting to be part of it. I had been to Ruth and Paul's and was aware that my attempt at preparing a Sabbath dinner was amateurish. I would have to learn some Hebrew and so would Luke, if the meal was to be authentic. I waited anxiously for Anton to arrive. How would he react to the Sabbath table and the prayers? Perhaps I ought to have warned him.

The dinner was ready and the three of us stood around the table, decked with candles, a decanter of ceremonial red wine and a *challah.* Luke read the translation of the prayers, and then following the tradition, broke the *challah* and passed the pieces around. Anton, who had been silent until then, held up his hand.

'Hey, what is all this... what's going on? And what's this book? It has Hebrew writing and the opposite page is in High German?'

'Careful with that. It's a *Siddur*, a prayer book that Mama's friend Ernst gave me.'

Anton paged through the book and replaced it.

'Please, you explain,' I said, nodding in Luke's direction.

'Let's finish our meal and then I'll tell you all about it.'

Anton shrugged and started to eat. Over coffee, Luke spoke at length. He told Anton about how his interest in Judaism had begun and that he was now attending synagogue regularly.

Anton screwed up his face in distaste. 'But that's weird! What you want to do that for? You're not even Jewish.'

'Anton!' I exclaimed.

Luke's cheeks flushed. 'I set myself a task to learn about the Jewish religion and ended up admiring it…. preferring it to my own.'

Anton was silent, his head bent. Wisely Luke shifted the conversation to sport and the two men watched a soccer game on television.

On Saturday morning, I accompanied Luke to synagogue. We chose the synagogue I had been to with Ruth. This time I remembered my prayer book. As I took my place in the gallery, I allowed the intoning of ancient prayers to drift past me. I was there to please Luke. The ancient chants and rituals connected me with my past, but I doubted that I would continue to attend regularly.

When Anton came for dinner the following Sabbath, he brought a yarmulke along, purchased in the city. He appeared to be prepared to join in with the Sabbath ritual. I steered away from gefilte fish and other typically Jewish dishes and cooked sauerbraten with potato dumplings, favourites of both my men. They ate with gusto and just managed a desert of fruit and icecream.

'Thanks Mutti, a delicious meal, as always,' Anton said as he sat back in the armchair.

'Perhaps you'd like to bring your friend, Jodi, along one Friday night.'

'Thanks Mutti … but we've broken up.'

'Oh, I'm sorry.'

Anton shrugged. 'It's better that way. She wasn't for me.' He sighed and sank deeper into the chair's folds. 'And anyway lots of things are changing in my life.'

'Oh.' I tried not to appear too inquisitive.

'I know it will disappoint you and dad but I can't see myself carrying on in either law or business once I've finished my course... it's not me... not what I want.'

I waited for him to continue.

'I think I'd like to work with people... help in some way... possibly psychology or social work, but I'm not sure yet. I'll wait until these studies are behind me and then...'

'You know, any time you want to talk about it, I'm here.'

Just then Luke chipped in with sport talk. I waited for a break in their conversation. I wanted to catch Anton's attention before the soccer game began on television. Perched on the side edge of Anton's armchair, I chose my words carefully.

'I'd like to ask if you would like to join us at synagogue one Saturday. It's your heritage. It's not your fault that you haven't learned about it. Neither your father nor I gave you boys the opportunity to find out about your background... and we should have. But now, thanks to Luke, I have learned a little more and you can too. It's up to you to decide.'

Anton stroked the side of his face and sipped his wine. 'I wouldn't mind coming along, seeing what it's like.'

'I know this is sudden but we're going to synagogue tomorrow. What about joining us?'

His answer was swifter than I expected. 'I suppose, I might as well come along... find out what all this is about.'

This would be my last visit to Synagogue for a while. And this time I was going for Anton. He arrived early and we left together. It felt strange and wonderful at once to have at least one of my boys with us. Anton was dressed in grey flannels and a sports coat and to my "mother's eyes", he looked handsome. I covered my anxiety with smiles and small talk. He crunched his knuckles, a childhood nervous habit. When we arrived, he was amused that Luke knew far more about synagogues and Judaism than I did. Luke pointed out the different parts of the building and described their function. He also outlined the order of the service so that Anton would be able to follow.

The two entered the prayer hall together. A novice and a gentile, I thought, as I climbed the stairs to the gallery. From there I looked down on them in their yarmulkes and borrowed prayer shawls. In the background the cantor's voice resonated.

After the service, Anton said nothing until we were in the car. 'It was like going to a foreign country with a foreign language.'

'It would sound foreign to you. It's all new. I felt the same the first time I heard Hebrew.'

'So, we belong to *that* tribe? It's hard to believe,' Anton quipped.

'But what did you think of it?' I asked anxiously.

'The synagogue is great. It's peaceful and the sound of the prayer was... different but stirring. It went on for much too long but I think I liked it... and it made me think of our family and its past. There's a lot to find out. I wish Gabe was here with us,' he said wistfully.

'Will you come to shul again?' Luke asked.

'Maybe... I'm not sure.'

We dropped Anton off and drove on. The tension that had accumulated during the morning dissipated. I took a deep breath. Anton's response was more positive than I could've hoped. It was a beginning and a salve to my guilt.

Instead of going back to the apartment, we stopped at the beach and inhaled the fresh, salty air. The bay was dotted with sailing boats on its gentle waves.

'Isn't it pretty here?'

I pointed to the café at the head of the pier. 'Let's go there.'

We entered the strange hat shaped building, protruding into the waves.

'I love it here, it's like being on a boat with the sea on all sides,' he said.

'Cafés were so important to us in Vienna. I guess we can enjoy them here too... but in a different way,' I said with a laugh.

He squeezed my hand.

As the following week drew to a close, I wrestled with my lack of desire to attend synagogue. Before the sun set on Friday afternoon, I made my decision. There was no point in attending the services to please Luke. When I was ready, I would return.

Sixty-Four

R ichard and I made the effort to remain friends and we met occasionally. Over lunch, he looked pale and strained. By the time our food was served he told me that he and Jennifer had split up and that she had left the company. He talked and I listened. Sadly he revealed that it had taken him some time to understand why he, an outsider, had been sent to manage the Australian arm of the company. Brake disc pads and linings for the Australasian market were manufactured almost entirely in the Melbourne factory, while the same products for sale in Europe were made in Germany. The split was an unusual one but it had been successful until recently. Apparently major problems in the Melbourne manufacturing process had been ignored previously, and now complaints from owners of 4WD's were pouring in and a countrywide recall of vehicles was imminent. He called himself the "bunny" and I could not help feeling for him.

Before we parted I told him that Anton had accompanied us to synagogue. He appeared pleased and began to ask me about Luke's new interest in Judaism. I felt uncomfortable discussing Luke and was relieved when our discussion was interrupted by a phone call.

Magda and Karl invited us to join them for a camping weekend at Wilson's Promontory. As Luke was eager to go, I put my reservations aside. We weren't prepared for the striking beauty at the campsite, the white beaches and towering granite studded cliffs. Luke and Karl were such experienced campers that the process of erecting the tent and settling in went smoothly. The pleasure on Luke's face as he surveyed the quartz beaches and rare rock formations compensated for my earlier reluctance.

After a brunch of eggs, sausage and fried bread we were ready to explore. Karl suggested a route that led to a lush rain forest and dense gully. We had reached the edge of a birch forest when piercing screams halted us. The screams continued unabated. The two men hurriedly pushed back the undergrowth and entered the forest. They had disappeared from sight, when their raucous laughter reverberated. Magda and I found them in a clearing watching a lyrebird, fan spread and in full parade.

'This is our culprit,' Karl said, struggling to stop laughing. 'They're incredible mimics of animal and human sounds.'

We returned to the camp as the sun slipped over the mountains. Too tired to talk, we ate a quick meal, followed by bed. I lay awake listening to the sounds of the night and placed my arm around Luke's sleeping body. I kissed his neck and bare shoulder. He was strong and healthy now.

🐎

During our first month and half together, we had established a pattern and balance of work and shared time that suited us both. Luke was well enough to stop taking his tablets and appeared content. He was nearing the end of writing his research paper and I promised to edit it for him.

He intended to leave for Adelaide in January of the New Year, two months away. We would have the Christmas holidays together and hopefully a visit from Gabe and Gina. We had not planned any further ahead.

One Sunday over lunch he put his knife and fork down and placed both hands on the table. 'There's something I must discuss with you.'

'I'm listening,' I said as I sipped the last of my wine.

'I want to talk about a religious issue.' Luke pulled at his beard that had grown quite long by then and was rather straggly

'I'm listening.'

'The rabbi is starting up a study group on Monday nights. I spoke to him about my… situation… and I was surprised, he agreed to me joining. I'd like to go but wanted to discuss it with you first.'

'I see…'

'I would've started Hebrew classes if I was staying here longer but I bought language cassettes in the meanwhile. I'll learn a little that way.'

'You don't need to discuss any of it with me first, you know my feelings. I don't mind you steeping yourself in religion if it makes you happy… but it's not for me.'

'I suppose I was hoping…'

'Actually, I've been thinking of doing more with my piano playing… joining a small orchestra.'

'That's an excellent idea,' he said and carried on eating. 'You haven't been using your talent… and you should.'

Sixty-Five

Luke called out to me. 'There's someone called George on the phone asking to speak to you. He's got a foreign accent.'

'It must be George Barrineau, the art dealer?' I rushed to the phone.

'Please sit down Madame. I have some very good news for you.'

'Come on tell me!'

'We sold your painting for one and three quarter million dollars, Madame.'

I don't know what I said next but I jumped and shrieked with joy. Luke grabbed me, lifted and twirled me around. Even after the dealer took his commission, I would be richer than I could imagine. We drank champagne with chocolate biscuits to symbolise the luxurious life to come. After my third glass and several biscuits, I lay back on the couch and saluted the copy of the Pissarro on the wall opposite. My head spun with a mixture of the champagne and shock. I closed my eyes and thought of my father and his selfless gift.

Too excited to sleep, I attempted to come to terms with my windfall. I could give up work and buy almost anything I wanted... but what did I want? I wanted that ephemeral something that everyone else wanted, *to be happy*. I told myself I was going to use the money to try to achieve that. I would give away a big chunk to charity and another lot to the boys. And then what?

I woke certain that I would not go back to work. I had not formed lasting bonds with my colleagues. The job had merely filled my time and provided me with a living. Any sense of belonging I had gained over the months was due to the café I visited each morning.

The next day, George transferred the amount, less his cut, into my bank account electronically. At least it was all achieved without any effort on my part. Determined to use the money well, I talked to a financial advisor at the bank. Within hours any of my money concerns were out of the way. He helped me to set up a trust for my sons, and donate substantial amounts to several charities. The remainder I invested.

Too restless to return to the apartment, I stopped the car at a park and walked. The routine of life had allowed too little time for introspection. Luke was due to leave for Adelaide in a few weeks, but after our longest period of togetherness, we were jogging along with no plans for our future.

Since Luke's depression, the passion in our relationship had waned. We were older now, but there was more to it. The romanticism of previously snatched time had increased our lust for each other. Lately, with the titillation of sex mostly out of the way, we had become friends. For the first time since we were childhood sweethearts, I questioned our future together. We had little in common other than our background. Luke's interest in Judaism had become a virtual obsession, and Geology, his previous interest, now took second place. I knew he was disappointed in me, that he had hoped his involvement in the religion would inspire me to provide him with a traditional Jewish home life. When I told him that I would be attending synagogue less often, he tried to mask his dissatisfaction. He made it clear that my being Jewish and yet not wanting to embrace my religion by prayer at the synagogue, frustrated him.

Once I had caught up with household chores, left undone for months, I had time on my hands. While Luke worked on his research or studied, I went to art exhibitions, midday concerts and Melbourne's museums.

The Holocaust museum was on my list. I had avoided similar museums in Europe through fear of being confronted with the awfulness I would find there. Now having read extensively about that period, I thought I knew what to expect at the Melbourne museum. But I was unprepared for my guide, Rosa, a survivor of Treblinka Concentration Camp. She had been a child in the camp and lived due to the care of loving adults who fed her part of their food rations. She was a cheerful woman in her eighties who proudly showed me the tattooed number on her arm.

She was at my side as I made my way through the exhibition, beginning with a description of the culturally rich and diverse world of European Jewry before the Second Wold War. There were displays of documents, mainly donated by Melbourne survivors, photographs and artefacts depicting the horrors of Nazism and the camps. The images were not new to me and yet my reaction of horror was as fresh and deep as if I had seen them for the first time. I read each article carefully and stopped before each photograph. The exhibition ended on a positive note with the celebration of life and the accounts of survivors who came to Melbourne and had raised their families here.

Rosa suggested I visit the Jewish Museum as well. 'It's a more general and current account of Jews in Melbourne's Jewish community. I think you'll enjoy it,' she said with one of her friendly smiles. I spent a day at the museum studying the exhibits and reading the background to Jewish immigration to Australia, and more particularly Melbourne. I found that in 1788 eight Jewish convicts were sent to the then Botany Bay, later to become Sydney. A hundred years later, the number of Jews had increased due to the Gold Rush in the state of Victoria. But the end of the Second Wold War brought the greatest influx of homeless Jews to Melbourne and Sydney. I was surprised that there were thirty synagogues in Melbourne now and that about 120,000 Jews lived in the cities of Australia.

I was about to leave, when I spotted a brochure asking for volunteers. I placed it in my handbag, as I did with many brochures. That evening I read the brochure. The idea of becoming a guide, appealed to me. If they agreed to train me, I would gladly give my time.

❧

We invited Ruth and Paul for Sunday brunch. I rose late and hastily tidied the apartment while Luke dressed in his dull beige pants and a conservative jumper. He now resembled the men of his age at the synagogue, I thought cynically.

It was a balmy day without even a breeze as we sat on the small balcony. I had told Ruth about Luke's interest in Judaism and when she asked him about it he smiled and nodded.'Yes, I've been studying the basics of Judaism, and Ella will tell you that I've almost become carried away with it.'

Ruth looked surprised 'I had no idea you were so involved...'

'He goes to synagogue every week and is attending the rabbi's study group,' I added.

Luke gave Ruth his rebellious look that I recognised from years earlier.

'It may sound crazy to you but I'm considering converting.'

I caught Ruth and Paul eying each other. After a few seconds Paul spoke. 'Conversion to Judaism is no simple matter. Perhaps talking to the rabbi would help to clarify a few things.'

I took a deep breath and looked away.

'I agree. Our young rabbi is very approachable. I'd discuss it with him.' Ruth added. 'I know him quite well and if you like... I'll try to set up a meeting for you.'

'That's a good idea... thanks. As soon as you can organise it.' Luke said.

I was relieved that neither Ruth nor Paul made light of Luke's intentions. Perhaps discussion with a rabbi would help him.

I brushed flecks of dust off Luke's dark suit and then kissed him as he left for his meeting with the rabbi. Before closing the door he checked his pocket for his *kippah* and car keys. He was serious about conversion, but I was almost sure that this rabbi or any other, would try to dissuade him. Wherever possible, prospective converts were steered away. There was an enormous amount he'd have to unlearn before embracing the study of Judaism. And then, after years of further study, he'd have to be circumcised. I was convinced he was toying with an idealised lifestyle, one he admired from a distance, but if he adopted it, it was likely to be nothing like the one he imagined.

I waited anxiously for his return. When I heard a key turn in the door I jumped up to greet him.

'So how did it go? What did the rabbi say?' My questions ran into one another.

'He's a very nice young man, quite modern in his thinking... for a rabbi.'

I detected disappointment in his voice.

'So?'

'He did his best to put me off, side track me. He told me what a difficult and lengthy process converting is. He warned me about joining a group of people who are despised by many and how much anti Semitism is still with us.'

'He's right, of course. Jews have been hated by different groups throughout history and it doesn't look as if it has stopped.'

His expression was downcast. 'I know all that!'

'You told him... about yourself?'

'Yes, I told him the truth about my background, naturally he was suspicious of my motives. He obviously thought guilt was driving me as it had many who were the offspring of Nazis. I tried to reassure him, to tell him that though I would feel shamed and guilty for the rest of my life, that I had it in perspective now. That I admired the Jews and their religion and that my aim was to become Jewish too. It would be the greatest honour for me.'

'And so?'

'We talked about the concept of "original sin" not existing in the Jewish religion. That instead Jews seek forgiveness from God and repent with prayer and their deeds.'

I nodded.

'I told him that I knew all about that, and that I wanted to break away from the Christian concept. The belief in Christ had no longer any meaning for me.'

'Uhuh.'

'He said he understood that I wanted to convert but a person's mind could play tricks, drive one in unusual directions. That before I was to begin with any studies for conversion, I should see a therapist and explore my guilt. After therapy I could see him again.'

'Well, he didn't turn you away. He wants you to be certain before you embark on a long and difficult path.'

Luke was pacing now. 'I can see his point... but... a therapist?'

'You hoped it would be simpler.'

'Oh yes,' he replied curtly. 'I'll have to think the whole thing through.'

He walked towards his room and I heard the door close.

A phone call from Gabe dashed my hopes that he and Gina would join us over the Christmas holidays. Gina's mother was ill and the couple were going to Switzerland to see her. Anton's disappointment was the worst part.

During the week that followed we were both preoccupied. I had not told anyone other than Luke about my sudden wealth and I was still wrestling to come to terms with it. Luke was struggling to absorb the rabbi's words.

The summer heat was scorching. I had never experienced such intense heat and collapsed under the air conditioner. On cooler days we had a picnic at the beach or in the Dandenongs under shady trees. Our time together was pleasant enough but the element of ordinariness had crept in. If I closed my eyes, I might as well have been with Richard.

Sleep did not come easily during those steamy nights. And once again I dreamt that I was in a shaky booth on the old Ferris wheel, looking down on the city of Vienna. The wheel spun frantically, the booth tipped me out to plummet into a void. I woke drenched and shaking.

One morning, while Luke was reading, I poured myself a strong cup of coffee and took it out on to the small balcony. The sun hadn't reached that side of the building and the canvass awning swelled and fell in the breeze. The unpleasant recurring dream was still with me. I knew it, the message reflected my uncertainty about my relationship with Luke. I was being thrown into an empty union and uncertain future. As much as I dreaded thinking about it, it was obvious, the vibrant, attractive man I had loved so intensely had nothing in common with the religion obsessed, bearded man he was now.

Soon he would leave for Adelaide. I was determined not to dodge the topic until the last moment. When I asked him when he intended to leave, he scowled. 'In a week or two.'

'What's bothering you?' I asked.

He stared at the carpet.

'Well?' I prompted.

'It's the rabbi. He wasn't unkind, just honest. Conversion is a massive undertaking.'

'Absolutely.'

'I've decided to keep going to synagogue and studying, but I have to think hard about taking that big step.'

I felt relieved, took his hand and kissed it. 'Yes, take your time, see how you feel in a few months. You could talk to another rabbi in Adelaide.'

'Good idea.' I took a deep thankful breath.

I stood and then silently paced the small room.

Luke eyed me. 'What's the matter with you?'

'I'm concerned about your move to Adelaide. I intended to join you there but now I'm not sure.'

'I want you to come...but I know, another move will be difficult for you...and I understand that.'

'You're right, I'm not keen on moving.'

'That's why I've been thinking of finding a place that's big enough... for you to visit or stay over.'

It was one of those moments when I knew with certainty that he did not want me to follow him to Adelaide, and that I did not want to go. An image of us playing together as children in Leopoldstadt flashed past. After our years of longing to be together, it was ridiculous.

He smiled wistfully. 'Things between us aren't the same... as they were. 'We're growing older, *Shatzi*.' he placed an arm around my shoulder.

Luke's romantic use of the word *Liebchen* belonged to the past as well.

'It's not only that we're getting older.'

He drummed his fingers on his thigh. 'Anyway, I'll have to book my flight and find a hotel or motel for a few weeks until I find a place to stay.'

'Oh, I thought you had already booked your ticket.'

'Not yet. I've been delaying it while I think it through.'

I felt my forehead crinkle. '*Think it through! Think what through!*'

He held his hand up to prevent my comment. 'I'm going to take a long walk,' he said, moving towards the door.

He didn't return until the evening and when he did, he went to bed.

After another sleepless night, I was determined to obtain an answer from him about his move to Adelaide. Over breakfast my question was direct. 'Well, are you taking up the position at the university or not?'

He sighed and stared out of the window.

'It's a major career move, I know, but I've had thoughts of scrapping the whole thing…returning to Vienna.'

'So, you're going back home, then?'

My chest was tight and I could hardly breathe. I had to move away from him and went out onto the balcony. I wiped away my tears. 'I think it's my turn for a walk.

It was breezy outdoors and I zipped up my parka. How could I help my frustration? After years of longing to be together, talking and dreaming about it, we were turning our backs on our togetherness.

Later, Luke cancelled his trip to Adelaide and apologised to the university. I didn't listen to his phone conversation but I imagined it was heated. He looked relieved.

'We'll still see each other, of course,' he said, taking my hand.

'Now and again…like before,' I replied.

He stroked his beard before speaking again. 'It's for the best. I'm flying back to Vienna tomorrow night.'

'Yes, it'll be better that way.'

We had a day to fill before his flight. He had not yet bought gifts for his family. We went to the shopping mall and we hunted for the perfect presents. I noticed a travel agency that was advertising cheap flights to the Middle East and Israel. As I scanned the poster advertising the Israeli trip, I felt as if a light had turned on inside me. I left Luke and inquired about the dates and times of their flights. My enthusiasm was sudden but it felt right. The trip would be my pilgrimage. Perhaps in Israel I would learn what being Jewish really meant. We left the mall with Luke's gifts and my handbag filled with brochures about travel to Israel.

We had lunch in one of our favourite cafés, both relaxed, at ease with our decision to part. That afternoon, Luke loaded his suitcase into the boot and we drove to the airport. After his last wave, I rushed outdoors and took a deep breath. The breezy night air was refreshingly cool. My single footstep clicked reassuringly on the cement paving.

Later I spread the brochures I'd collected on the carpet. Impulsively I decided to phone my boys. If I was going to Israel I would offer them the opportunity to join me during their end of year holidays. I phoned Gabe first. I woke him but he was good natured about it. When I suggested the trip, his voice faltered. He would've liked to join me, but he was running a summer school during the holidays. Quickly I dialled Anton's number. He was home and answered. His answer was immediate. 'I'd love to come, Mutti. When do we leave?'

By the end of the week, I had booked the tickets. We would leave in three days.

'We'll be going to Yad Vashem, the memorial to those who died in the Holocaust, and to the Western Wall, I told him. Don't forget to pack your *kippah*.'

Sixty-Six

We began our bus journey to Jerusalem from Ben Gurion International Airport. The long trip to Israel had been exhausting and I longed for sleep. However, I forced my eyes open so as not to miss a thing. On the sparsely populated land on the road to Jerusalem, skeletons of burnt out armoured vehicles littered the roadside, monuments to the convoys that had played such a vital role during Israel's War of Independence in 1948. As we crossed the harp shaped bridge, there before us, nestled in the Judean Hills, was the holy city of Jerusalem.

Anton grabbed my hand, searching for words. 'I couldn't have imagined anything like this, Mutti... it's...'

My heart was beating fast, my throat too tight to speak. I squeezed his hand instead.

'We're here', our guide said, as the tourist bus slotted in among the many others ferrying thousands of visitors from all over the world to this holy site.

There it was before us, the *Kotel*, the Western Wall, the holiest place in Judaism. My attention sharpened, the light seemed brighter and clearer as I took in the scene. Crowds had congregated before the ancient stone wall, the remains of the last temple, destroyed by the Romans in 70 AD. Amongst the throng were groups of pilgrims, young students, men in the black garb of the ultra - orthodox, and soldiers on leave, guns slung over their shoulders, snatching a few moments to pray at the wall. A young man was reading his *barmitzvah* portion from the *Torah*, guided by the rabbi and the elders of his family.

Anton placed his *kippah* on his head, touched my hand, and walked towards the men's section. Overcome with awe, I took a few deep breaths before joining the women. Slowly I approached the wall. As I placed my hand on the warm stone that so many had touched before me, I knew I was where I belonged – where the soul of all Jews belonged. I thought of Mama and all she had missed by excluding herself from her Jewishness, of my father's suffering and my grandparents' lives destroyed by the Holocaust. My tears were a blend of pain and joy at being there. Like the other women, I rolled my piece of paper with its message into a coil and placed it in a crack in the wall.

I looked across the dividing *mechitzah* to the men's division, and spotted Anton amongst the crowd. He seemed oblivious of the *barmitzvah* group or the circle of singing soldiers behind him. He placed his forehead against the wall and was wiping his eyes. As I had, he put his message in the crevice amongst the stones. I listened to the men reciting the afternoon prayers and overheard men reciting the *Kaddish*, the prayer for the souls of the departed.

Yitkadal veyit kadash shme raba... amen.

My tears spilled down my cheeks, as I said my own prayer... that my son would find his link with his Jewish past and present.

Lightning Source UK Ltd.
Milton Keynes UK
UKOW04f1432070716

277879UK00001B/35/P